DAMON KNIGHT
THE OBSERVERS

TOR

THE OBSERVERS

Copyright © 1988 by Damon Knight

First Edition: June 1988

A TOR Book

Published by Tom Doherty Associates, Inc.
49 West 24th Street
New York, NY 10010

ISBN: 0-312-93074-7

Library of Congress Catalog Card Number: 87-51446

Printed in the United States of America

0 9 8 7 6 5 4 3 2 1

For
LAURA MIXON
and
CAROL DEPPE

Man without culture is not man: but every culture is crazy.

—EDWARD T. HALL

1 By the time he was forty-two, Anthony L. K. Ridenour had written eighteen books, none of which had been published under his own name. Even the "as-told-to's" were signed by Andrew Laurance, Kenneth Coltrain, or Ronald Malvern. Wraithlike and discreet, Ridenour had ghosted memoirs for film stars, undersea explorers, ex-Prime Ministers (two), and one Nobel Prize winner (German, very difficult).

In the flower of his maturity, that is to say in the last two decades of the twentieth century, Ridenour had witnessed the completion of a process that had begun much earlier: the place of general fiction had been taken over by a rather repellent growth called sci-fi. The former categories of fiction had now been almost entirely absorbed: for example, there was Jewish family sci-fi (not including shtetl sci-fi, a separate genre), historical sci-fi, spy sci-fi, and so on, including an academic variant not much read by the public, dealing principally with extraordinary mental powers and referred to as psi-fi. Earlier forms were the subjects of study in the remaining English departments of universities; Ridenour had a young friend, for example, who had just done his dissertation on Sidney Sheldon.

Ridenour himself had written a little poetry of an unassuming sort while at school, but there was no money in that, and he could not write sci-fi: it simply was not in him. He had turned, then, quite naturally to the kind of nonfiction which still engaged the attention of the public—informative, breezy narratives having to do usually with the scandalous doings of the rich and famous.

Ridenour was a slender little man, rabbity of feature, who lived alone in an untidy subcondo in the West End. His tastes were simple; he liked what he called "plain food," and suffered anguish when, as sometimes happened, he was obliged to take someone to lunch or dinner at a gourmet restaurant.

Just now he was engaged on a book about Sea Venture, the floating city that had been devastated by an epidemic in the Pacific a month ago. Other publishers, with deeper pockets, had already gobbled up the principal actors in the drama, Stanley Bliss, the Chief of Operations, and Dr. Wallace McNulty, the resident physician, but as Ridenour had pointed out to his editor at Boone & Slayton, there was room for a cartload of other books as well, and the best of them might be an overview, telling the story from many viewpoints.

By now, a month after the events he was to chronicle, the passengers and crew of Sea Venture were scattered over the globe, but Ridenour, a transatlantic sort, didn't mind that. His first step had been to start a cuttings file, and his second to get copies of the passenger, crew, and permanent resident lists of Sea Venture, an *embarras de richesse,* but working from press cuttings and news reports he had narrowed the list to one hundred and fifty, all in the States, to whom he had sent a letter soliciting the favor of an interview. Seventy-odd of these had responded, and he had laid down an itinerary according-ly. He expected to spend the rest of the summer at this, then clean up the European interviews in the autumn, after which, probably, a second round of interviews would be necessary, and he could start writing in March.

He had had one stroke of luck straight away: Dr. McNulty had consented to be interviewed even though he was under contract for a ghost-written work of his own. Either they had not pinned the doctor down about that or he did not realize that he had sold exclusive rights; at all events, Ridenour took the Concorde to San Francisco, and on the following afternoon he was palming McNulty's doorplate in Santa Barbara.

The camera tilted to look at him. A voice said, "Mr. Ridenour?"

"Yes. How do you do, Doctor?"

"I'm fine. Come on in."

The door clicked open into a pleasantly cluttered living room. The rug was a faded Oriental, the chairs deep and comfortable.

Dr. McNulty came forward and shook hands. He was a gray-haired man, a little smaller than Ridenour had imagined from his pictures; laugh wrinkles fanned out from the corners of his eyes, but at the same time, Ridenour thought, there was an ingrained sadness there that made him more interesting. "Sit down," McNulty said. "Can I get you something to drink?"

"No, no thanks." In fact Ridenour would have liked a cup of tea, but he knew what he was likely to get in the States. He set up his recorder and said, "Doctor, could we begin by asking when was the first time you became aware that anything untoward was going on in Sea Venture?"

McNulty clasped his hands between his knees. "That

would be when Randy Geller collapsed down in the marine lab. Then we started getting others, four and five a day. The symptoms were always the same—sudden collapse, stupor. There wasn't a thing to account for it, and we didn't know then that the patients would come out of it in nine or ten days."

"That must have been an anxious time for you. And then?"

"When Randy came to, he told me about something that happened the day before. He was operating the dredge that takes samples from the ocean floor, and he brought up a little glass sphere. When he broke it open, he felt faint for a minute, and we know now that's the first symptom of invasion by the parasite. The stupor comes when the parasite leaves—then somebody else feels faint, and so on."

"Yes, tell me about that, please," said Ridenour. "There have been so many sensational reports, one doesn't know what to believe."

"The thing was intelligent," McNulty said. "It knew what we were up to, and it outsmarted us every time. We tried to trap it, and we couldn't."

"Until, of course, you finally did—by tricking it into going into the body of a goat."

"Yes. That was Yetta Bernstein's idea."

"But earlier, I understand, a passenger died as a result of one of these attempts?"

The lines in McNulty's face deepened a bit. "I can't talk about that; it's in the courts," he said.

"I understand. But could you give me some clue as to how you learned that the thing was an intelligent creature? Where do you suppose it came from, by the way?"

"Geller and Barlow thought it came from space—fell

in the ocean and sank to the bottom, nobody knows how long ago."

"Barlow is the other marine scientist, the one who was stricken after Geller?"

"Yes, that's right."

Ridenour looked at his notes. "I've not been able to reach them at their previous addresses," he said. "Do you happen to know where they are?"

"Yes, I do. I'll give you the address before you leave."

Ridenour made a note. "Then," he continued, "there was that curious business with Professor Newland, the L-Five guru. He turned up dead in a lifeboat that got launched somehow from Sea Venture—any idea how that could have happened?"

"Nope."

Ridenour ticked off an item in his notebook. "Now, Doctor," he said, "I believe you've said that recovered patients of the disease they've named after you showed some personality changes?"

"That's right."

"And you yourself contracted the disease, or were invaded by the parasite, whichever way one likes to put it. So you're in a unique position to evaluate these after-effects. What would you say they are, in your own case?"

"I think it made me smarter."

"Smarter?"

"Yes—at least when I look back now, it seems to me that I was pretty dumb."

"I see."

Ridenour had heard all this before, in a general way, but it was different to hearing it from McNulty. What was one to make of this tale of an invisible intelligent parasite that came from the bottom of the ocean, or from outer space, and made people *smarter?* McNulty had seemed a perfectly sober and well-balanced fellow, but then many lunatics did.

Ridenour talked to two dozen other people in the Southwest and Midwest, working his way across the country, and although they were all quite different, they told much the same sort of story. One man had quit his job at General Electric and had taken up rabbit farming in Arkansas; three of the women had left their husbands, one for another woman.

In July Ridenour found himself at the end of a dirt road in the Upper Peninsula of Michigan. A ten-year-old Mitsubishi pickup was parked across the clearing beside a white trailer on blocks, from which washing was strung to the nearest tree.

Ridenour went to the trailer and knocked. Presently the door opened.

"Mr. Geller, I'm Tony Ridenour—we talked on the phone yesterday."

"Uh-huh. Come on in." Geller was a tall, red-bearded man in his thirties. He ushered Ridenour into a narrow dining room with a vinyl-topped table, covered at the moment by socks in the process of seeking their mates. "Sit down. Coffee?"

"No, thanks, I breakfasted an hour ago." He looked around. "Is your wife here?"

"She's nursing some data—she'll be along in a minute. Start with me."

Ridenour opened his notebook. "You and Ms. Barlow were both members of the Sea Venture marine science staff, is that correct?"

"Right. She was my boss."

"And you were among the earliest victims of the epidemic?"

"Number one and number three. Number two was a fish."

Ridenour raised an eyebrow. "That's one of the points I wanted to mention. You realize that it would be almost unheard of for the same disease to affect human beings and fish."

"Uh-huh. And a goat, too."

A handsome dark-haired woman came in and put her hand on Geller's shoulder. "Yvonne, Tony Ridenour," said Geller. "My better half."

"Very pleased to know you, Mrs. Geller."

"Ms. Barlow," she said. She took his hand briefly and sat down.

"Ah, yes." Maiden name. Unusual—the pendulum had been swinging back the other way. "Ms. Barlow, we were just talking about the epidemic on Sea Venture. Would you say, both of you, that your outlook was different in any way after you contracted the disease?"

"Of course," said Barlow.

"Being as objective as you can, what were the outstanding changes in yourself and others that you observed?"

"We gave up believing in the Tooth Fairy," Geller said.

"I'm sorry?"

"We stopped buying all the various grades of bull-shit."

Ridenour took a moment to absorb this. "When you refer to bullshit, do you mean idealistic or altruistic viewpoints in general?"

"No, only the ones that are packaged to get something out of people for nothing. What I was doing on Sea Venture wasn't science, it was bottle-washing, and I was so dumb that I didn't realize it. Yvonne and I got out and said the hell with that, and I think you'll find that a lot of McNulty patients did the same."

"Yes, I have found that, in fact. Mr. Geller, you mentioned the goat just now. Leaving aside the various interpretations of that story, do you think it was a mistake? Would it have been better if more people caught the disease?"

"Some ways better, some ways worse. If the thing had got to the mainland they never would have stopped it. By now, I guess, a lot of us would be too smart to piss in our pants."

"I beg your pardon?"

"You've heard of algae blooms? Population explosions in rats, water lilies?"

"Yes, I believe I have."

"And you've also heard that we can keep on increasing the human population indefinitely—that there are no limits to growth?"

"Yes, well, human beings aren't—"

"Aren't like other organisms, right? That's bullshit."

"The issue is," said Barlow after a moment, "who does a woman's body belong to, herself or somebody else? It's not true that people won't limit their families voluntarily. Every culture we know about has practiced some form of population control, right up to modern times."

"Wasn't it usually infanticide?" Ridenour asked delicately.

"Yes, of course—that was all they had."

"But wouldn't you say that was criminal, in some sense?"

"Sure it was," said Geller. "Infanticide is a crime,

and so is abortion. The interesting thing is that if you look close, everything that works is either a crime, a sin, or an act of God. Well, people would rather have the acts of God, because at least they can say it isn't their fault. Infanticide? No, no. But let the kids starve to death? Okay. So that's why we've got famine and plague right now, because famine and plague work, but they're nobody's fault."

"So what's the answer then, in your opinion, Mr. Geller?"

"There isn't any answer, because people are too stupid."

"Forgive me, but what if they weren't too stupid— what would they do then?"

Geller looked pleased. "Okay. Number one, recognize that if you eliminate natural controls on population, you've got to put something in their place. There are various ways to do it. Every time there's an excess of births over deaths, we could send out a hit squad to zap that many people at random. Snipers in shopping malls. Or slip a little poison in their coffee."

"Randy—" said Ms. Barlow.

"Or," Geller went on, holding up a finger, "you could control it just by regulating the environment in various ways. Raise the speed limit, for instance, or loosen up the regulations on toxic emissions, which in fact we're doing now. Cut back on the child nutrition program, Medicall, things like that. That's more anonymous, but it's also harder to regulate, because you never know exactly what you're doing. The hit squads are better, because then you get guilt and conscience working for you. A woman has to want a kid a whole lot before she'll get pregnant knowing that some other human being has to die when it's born."

"What he means, Mr. Ridenour," said Barlow, "is that we can use contraception, sterilization, and abortion, which are sensible methods that work, or if we're too dumb to do that, we might as well talk about something really crazy."

Geller turned to her. "Well, what are you calling crazy? Here's another thought. Sterilize every other female child at birth. That would cut the next cohort of breeding women in half."

"How about sterilizing the *males?*" Barlow demanded.

"Nothing wrong with it except that it wouldn't work. A woman can give birth to one child a year. A man can impregnate a thousand."

"Randy, this isn't amusing."

"True."

"You know, I'm beginning to think human beings really are dumb."

"What's that supposed to mean? Come on, Yvonne—" He looked angry, and so did she.

"Thank you, Mr. Geller and Ms. Barlow," said Ridenour delicately.

In Rye, New York, Ridenour interviewed Mr. and Mrs. Lionel Prescott and their daughter Julie. Julie had been a victim of the epidemic, and had also, it seemed, been a fairly close acquaintance of Professor Newland, the L-5 guru. Ridenour tried to draw her out about that, without much success. There had also apparently been a young man, John Stevens, of whom the parents thought highly; he had not been heard of since. A shipboard romance, perhaps; that might add a bit of spice, but nobody seemed to know Stevens' present whereabouts. Ridenour had the impression that Julie could say more if she would, and he put her down for a follow-up interview in the autumn.

In September, back in the States a little earlier than he had expected, he phoned the Prescotts and was told that Julie had taken an apartment in New York. They gave him the number and he looked her up. The second interview was no more productive than the first, but he did notice that the young woman was a bit bulgier than she had been before.

It would be better that the whole world should be destroyed and perish utterly than that a "free man" should refrain from one act to which his nature moves him.

—HEINRICH SUSO

2 My name is— Here I have to stop, after three words. What is my name? I was born Nils Sverdrup. Since then I have had many names, some I used for years, some for only a day or two.

This is the journal I revise endlessly in my head; that may be an odd thing to do, but it is highly satisfying because it is perfectly safe there, and in my world not many things are safe. Until quite recently assassination was my profession; or, to put it less daintily, I was a hired killer. In my lifetime I have killed twenty-seven men. For all but the first one I was paid, and for the last twenty I was even paid enough.

Now I should add that I was rescued from my life of

crime by the love of a pure woman: but that is not quite true. I am not ashamed of my career, only disgusted by it; even now, I do not believe it is always wrong to kill someone. I believe that Julie loves me, and I even believe it is possible that I love her, but it was not that that made me give up my profession after I killed Professor Newland. My life was changed, not by Julie, but by an invisible parasite from the depths of the ocean. It is even possible that I used the parasite as a pretext to do something I was ready to do in any event; but I don't believe that, because other people's lives were also changed.

If only I knew the real truth I would tell it.

In May, 1999, the man who had been John Stevens boarded a plane in Manila. He got off seven hours later in Lisbon, where he presented a Swiss passport in the name of Jean-Luc Kleinsinger. On the following day he appeared at the Banco Nacional, where he removed certain items from a safe deposit box. Still as Kleinsinger, he boarded the afternoon flight for Zurich. He took a cab from the airport and let himself into a modest villa in a quiet suburban area. At the sound of the door, a woman in a housedress appeared at the far end of the living room.

"Monsieur Kleinsinger." She inclined her head slightly.

"Marga."

"Did you have a good journey?"

"Very nice. Any interesting messages?"

"I don't think so. They're in your study, anyhow. Have you eaten?"

"Yes, thank you."

A knob-tailed brown Siamese cat appeared in the dining room archway. "Hello, Prinz," said Stevens. The cat, looking in another direction, sat down and began licking itself. Stevens did not see it again for the rest of the evening, but that night it followed him into the bathroom, held up its head for scratching, and bit him on the leg to make him pay attention. It was curious that he did not mind giving up the villa, the garden, even his books; the only thing he minded was this cat.

Then, since he had nothing better to do, he traveled, once to Lucerne, three times to Paris, twice to London, and on each of these trips he telephoned Julie Prescott at her parents' home in Rye. She said she was well, and indeed she looked well on the screen. "I have something to tell you. When are you coming?"

"I don't know." Something to tell him? That had a bad sound.

In June there were headlines: the body of Paul Newland had been found, adrift in a Sea Venture lifeboat a thousand miles from Manila. One week later Stevens was informed by his bank that the sum of two million Swiss francs had been deposited to his account.

Meanwhile the Newland affair was turning into a full-fledged scandal. There were questions in Congress, demands for a special investigatory commission. Political commentators were saying that funding for the controversial L-5 program now seemed likely to pass.

If so, and if Stevens was right about the identity of the patrons who had borrowed his services, then the object of the assassination had been accomplished. Sea

Venture, a rival to L-5, was discredited; L-5 would go forward.

When he called Julie in September he was given another number, and Julie informed him that she had moved into an apartment in New York, a studio apartment where she could paint. She showed him some of her watercolors; he thought they were not very good, but it was possible that the videophone distorted them. It was a curious thing that their not being very good increased the affection he felt for her. At such times it was difficult not to say, "I'm coming. I'll be there tomorrow."

There was no word from his employers until the fifteenth, when he received a handwritten card from Rome with the message "Remembering our pleasant afternoon together," and an illegible signature. He flew to Rome on the following Monday and met his contact in a previously arranged place.

The contact, known to Stevens as Benito, said, "This time it is in Kenya. Nairobi. The client is a government minister."

"Then it's political?"

"Everything is political."

"Quite true, but if it's political it will cost more."

"How much?"

"I don't know. Give me some background."

In his hotel room Stevens studied the documents Benito had given him, and they met again the following day. They agreed on a price. Stevens went back to Zurich and made some private arrangements with his lawyer. After thirty days, unless countermanding instructions were received from him, the house and its contents would be made over to Marga. That included the cat. He liquidated his other holdings and bought gold. On September 21 he flew to London, and on the following day, carrying a British passport in the name of Solomon H. Maltbury, he boarded a plane for Nairobi.

The "client" was the Minister of Transportation, Thomas Kamau, aged thirty-six; he had three wives and thirteen children. An attempt on his life had been made two years ago. He was well guarded, both at his office and at home; he traveled in a bullet-proof limousine.

As Solomon Maltbury, a British businessman looking for investment opportunities, Stevens made his way around the blazing streets of Nairobi. The place had not changed much since he had last been here in 1995. There were a few more beggars, perhaps, and more crazy old men. Every roundabout intersection was a tangle of European automobiles, *matatus* stuffed with people, pedestrians pulling carts. There were many children, and many pregnant women.

On the morning after his arrival Stevens had a talk with the head of the investment section at Barclay's Bank, through whom he met the president of the Chamber of Commerce, who referred him to a real estate dealer called Satkirpal Singh Govind.

Govind was a slender, white-turbaned man with a rolled beard and a nervous manner. "If you are looking for property at depressed prices," he said, "there is plenty of that here, but I cannot tell you when it will rise again. I myself am very much depressed. I would like to leave this country, but everything I own is here."

"Is it the famine that's the chief problem?" Stevens asked.

"The famine, yes, it is terrible, and also the drought. One more year like the last one will finish us. When times are this hard up-country they also become hard in the capital. We cannot ignore them any longer. I really think you should see for yourself before you take any decision. I

will drive you up-country tomorrow if you like and show
you some properties, and you will also see what condition
we are in."

They arranged to meet at three A.M. Kenyan time,
which corresponded to nine o'clock; the Kenyan day
began, rather sensibly, at sunrise rather than midnight.
Stevens went back to the hotel and took his malaria pill,
which gave him nightmares of rotting corpses.

In the morning, after the usual delays, Govind and a
smiling black driver picked him up in a blue Peugeot.
They drove for an hour in heavy traffic just to get out of
Nairobi; then, passing through a last ring of decaying
cinder-block suburbs, they headed up into the red
foothills toward Mt. Kenya. Stevens saw, as he had
expected, abandoned sisal estates, bare trees, gaunt
cattle, emanciated men and women, and children big-
bellied with hunger. Beyond Murang'a, they passed a
gravel road leading to a gate in a chain-link fence beyond
which, on the crest of a hill, a large building could be
seen.

"Whose house is that?" Stevens asked casually.

"Ah, that is the house of Thomas Kamau. He is very
high in the government. They say he will be president
someday."

3 Stevens considered the problem with as much care as if it were any other assignment. Kamau was too well protected to be approached on the street; the only way to get at him with any confidence of success was to gain entrance to his office or his house. Of the two, Stevens preferred the house. The grounds were patrolled, no doubt, but a clever fellow ought to be able to get in undetected. Stevens bought some outdoor clothing, a pair of bolt cutters, a cooler, a hypodermic syringe, a length of plastic tubing, and some plastic bags.

The next day he rented a Land Rover and drove north into the foothills. Just south of Murang'a, he turned west on a bad road, and at nightfall was parked on the shoulder across a ravine from the chain-link fence at the back of Kamau's property.

When it was full dark, he clambered down the ravine, waded through red mud at the bottom, and climbed up the other side. In the light of a shielded torch he examined the fence. There were alarm wires along the top and bottom, concertina wire at the top, but the fence was not electrified. He chose a link a few inches above the lower alarm wire and cut it, then another, and a third. When he had cut enough links for a man to squeeze through, he bent the cut portion inward, then dropped the bolt cutters beside the fence, climbed down the ravine and up again, got into the Land Rover and drove off.

Two miles away, where the ravine was deeper and muddier, he splattered the interior of the Land Rover with blood from a plastic bag in the cooler. It was his own blood, drawn the day before. He put the empty bag in his suitcase. Then he drove the Land Rover to the edge of the ravine, got out with his suitcase, and tilted the Land Rover over. It made a horrible grinding noise going down, and a grand clang at the bottom.

Stevens caught a ride with a man in a produce truck going into Nairobi, and took a cab to the airport, where he changed his clothes in a rest room. As Brian Nalling, a Kenyan citizen, he boarded the next flight to San Francisco. There, under still another name, he boarded a plane to New York, and got off at Reagan late that evening.

He dialed her number and put his hand over the pickup.

"Yes? Who is it?" In the little screen she looked like someone he vaguely remembered, and he thought, Have I really done this?

"Julie, it's John," he said, and took his hand off the lens.

A smile spread over her face. "John! Where are you?"

"I'm in a telephone booth at Reagan Airport. Are you all right?"

"Yes! But why didn't you tell me— Why didn't you write?"

"It just worked out that way. Are you alone?"

"Yes."

"All right. Until very soon."

The screen in the lobby showed him her face again. The collar was different: she had changed her clothes. For some reason that pleased and alarmed him. "John, come up," her tinny voice said, and the security system let him into the elevator.

Her door was painted red, with the brass numeral 4 over the knocker. The door opened, and then she was in his arms.

As soon as she let him speak, he said, "Are you pregnant?"

"Yes." She smiled up at him tentatively.

After a moment he said, "That changes everything."

"How does it change everything?"

"Let me sit down. I have to think a minute. The child is due when?"

"The first week in February."

"That gives us time enough for some surgery."

Her face changed. "I don't understand you."

"Nothing very complicated. Rhinoplasty will be enough—a nose job, you call it?"

"I don't want a nose job."

"You won't have to have one. I like your nose as it is, and mine too, as far as that goes. Listen a moment, Julie. So far as anyone knows or is likely to find out, I am dead. I died in Kenya two days ago. That's the only way people leave my profession, as a rule. I know a lot of things that various people would really rather not have me tell. And so I'm dead, and that's all right if we just intend to see each other occasionally and make love. But if you're going to have a child we've got to live together and be parents. Wait," he said as she started to speak. "I think I've done a good job of disappearing, but it's still possible that someone will come looking for me. If that happens, they will find out very easily that you and I were lovers on Sea Venture. Then if they find that you have a child born less than nine months after Sea Venture landed at Manila, and that you are living with a man who may be its father—then it's all over, and not just for me, because they will probably kill you and the child too. So now you see. If we're going to be together, it means changing names, appearance, habits, friends. You won't see your parents as often as you would like, and I probably won't be able to see them at all. Think about it. If that's too hard, it's best to know now."

She sat down and put her hands together in her lap. After a long time she said, "I could still have an abortion."

"Yes."

"Would you like that better?"

"No. I would like us to live together and be parents."

She came to him in a rush and put her wet cheek against his. "I would too. Oh, I love you," she said.

4 The plastic surgeon, a young man named Christie who had a beautiful smile, talked to Stevens in his office for a few minutes and showed him an illustrated chart with the headline PICK YOUR NOSE.

Then a nurse took him to a cubicle. "First we'll get a picture of the way you look right now," she told him. A light came on; in the holoscreen he saw his own face, but it looked like a stranger's. "This is the way other people see you," the nurse explained, "not the way you see yourself in a mirror."

"Does that really look like me?" he asked.

"Yes, it does, sir, and you look very nice, too."

"I wish I looked better."

"Well, that's why you're here, isn't it? Don't worry, Dr. Christie is excellent—a real artist. Now watch this." She showed Stevens how to rotate the image into profile, then how to use the controls to make any changes he liked. "Try it by yourself for a while. Ring whenever you want me."

Stevens looked at his profiled nose with a feeling of gloom. It was a nose, that was all; he had never given it this much thought before. Was it a little too long? With the light pen, he perversely drew it out even longer. Horrible! He restored the nose to its original size, shortened it a trifle, then turned it up at the tip. That was more like a movie star. He sculpted the nostrils and turned the image full face, but he didn't like it: the nose was so sharply defined now that it didn't seem to belong to him. He rang for the nurse.

"Uh-huh. That's good-looking, but it isn't you. Let me get a copy of it, anyhow." The nurse leaned over Stevens and pressed a button. A strip of paper curled out into the tray. "I think what you want is a little more character, not so much handsomeness," she said. "Suppose we try this." The profiled nose grew a little taller at the bridge, became almost Roman. "What do you think?"

"That's better."

The nurse made another printout. "Play with it yourself, until you're sure. These are the coordinates along the bottom of the film, see here? If you want to reset them, just punch in these numbers."

In the end he took a profile not greatly different from the one the nurse had suggested. It was a bigger

nose, higher, broader and fleshier at the tip. It would
make him look more sensual somehow, what was the
word—grosser, less spiritual?

Three days after the operation the swelling went
down and they could see his new face. In October they
took separate flights to Chicago, after Julie had written
to her parents that she was eloping with a man she had
met at a gallery reception, and would let them know her
address later. She was then five months pregnant.

5 They found a house they both liked on a
pleasant street in Evanston. There were many
tall trees; the houses were hidden behind gates and
hedges. It was a place where they could live in seclusion,
almost as anonymous as people in a New York apartment.

Julie cleaned out the parcel box every few days,
although there was seldom anything in it but advertising. One morning in December she found a pink flyer
there; it was an invitation to attend Christmas services in
one of the two hundred local churches, and a mass
meeting outside of town on the morning of January 1,
2000.

"Come *ONE,* come *ALL!!! Be There* at Dawn when
the *Prince of Peace* descends in His Glory to begin his
Reign of a Thousand Years!!!! 'He will swallow up death in
victory; and the LORD GOD will wipe away tears from
all faces!' Isaiah, 25:8."

At the bottom was a form to fill out: *"YES!* I will be

there! I enclose the sum of $____ to help carry on *GOD'S WORK!"*

Julie threw it away, but there was another one in the box on Monday; John saw it, read it with care, and put it in his pocket.

"What do you want that for?"

"It's interesting," he said.

Friday morning the maid opened the studio door and put her head in. "Miz Turnbull, there's some people at the door to see you."

"Who are they?"

"They're people from the church."

"The church? My goodness, Maureen, you know better than that. Tell them I don't discuss religion."

"Yes, ma'am." Maureen withdrew with a brooding expression.

Later that day, when Julie went out shopping, she noticed that the parcel boxes or gateposts of almost all the neighboring houses were decorated with crosses of pink tape. Printed on the tape were the words "WE'LL be THERE!!!"

When she told John about the visit, he said, "That may have been a mistake. If they come again, let me talk to them."

"But why?"

"Do you remember the story of Passover, when the Hebrews put blood on their doorposts?"

"John, what has that got to do with it?"

"Wait a minute," he said. He went into the library and came back thumbing a Bible. "Here it is. 'And when I see the blood, I will pass over you, and the plague shall not be upon you to destroy you, when I smite the land of Egypt.'"

She opened her mouth to say something sharp,

because she was feeling angry and frightened, but she thought of the pink crosses and shut it again.

The observer was aware of an awareness that dwindled back into the past before there was awareness. She drowsed, afloat and dreaming.

Gradually she became aware of other things: the warmth of the space around her, a red glow that came and went at long intervals, and a sound, lub-lub, lub-lub, that never stopped.

Now she became conscious of the body she inhabited, a soft shape that curled over itself like a question. The energy network grew, strengthened, ramified; a moment came when it was complete, and she awoke to full consciousness. The child's mind, which had grown up with hers, fitted her as comfortably as a cradle; she left it with reluctance, slipped out, then drifted upward, following the sparkling nerve line of the spinal cord, and into the skull of the woman.

A shocking flood of images came—color, light, sound! It overwhelmed her by its intensity; then, as she settled into the woman's mind, she found deeply channeled memories—Sea Venture, the epidemic, her illness. Then came a memory that stunned her. She, her original self, had been tricked into the body of a goat and sunk to the bottom of the ocean to lie there forever, like a jinn put back into its bottle. How close they had come to defeating her!

She dipped back into the child's dreaming mind to reassure herself; the slow global thoughts came and went, and there was a little sparkle that might have been recognition. Then she rose again into Julie's brain and waited until Stevens came out of his study at five.

As he walked toward her, she slipped out and in

again: and now he was looking at the woman he had been a moment ago, noticing the signs of strain around her eyes and saying, "Is anything the matter?"

"I felt a funny kind of shock a while ago, and again just now."

"I felt it too. Probably static electricity."

Safely hidden in Stevens' brain, he absorbed and savored the strong, bitter flavor of the man's personality. How fascinating were the two different bodies and minds, the two interlocked stories! In Stevens' mind he found traces of narratives he had experienced in fiction and drama; some of them had interested him profoundly, but they were nothing to this—they were summaries, distillations; this was the pure life. The story was not over, the outcome still in doubt.

Through this excitement and pleasure ran a vein of deep anxiety. He had been born less than an hour ago; he now knew everything that Julie and Stevens knew—and nothing else. All that his parent should have taught him, all the accumulated knowledge of their race—that was lost forever. He was an orphan set adrift in a strange world, to become in his turn, if he succeeded, the unique parent of his kind.

The doorplate rang and Stevens answered it. A man and a woman were standing there.

"Mr. Turnbull, how are you? My name is Dick LeDoux, and this is Mrs. Kellogg. We're from the Faith Ministry of Evangelical Churches, and we'd like to talk to you about the Second Coming of Our Lord."

"Yes, come in." He sat them down in the living room, and they looked around with approving smiles. "Nice place you have here," said LeDoux. "Mr. Turnbull, the reason we came by, we happened to notice that your name wasn't on our list of those who are going to meet and pray at the Coming."

"My wife didn't understand," said Stevens. "Of course we will be there."

"Have you both received Jesus Christ as your personal savior?" LeDoux asked politely.

"Yes, we have. By the way, I want to give you a contribution for the work. How shall I make this out?"

"Faith Ministry of Evangelical Churches—or just FMEC will do. What church do you belong to, brother?"

Stevens, who was ready for this, said, "We haven't been to services lately, because of my wife's condition, but we're Church of the Word."

LeDoux made a note. "I'll mention that to Pastor Hembert, if I may."

"Yes, please do. And tell him that we'll be attending services from now until the Coming." Stevens handed him a check; as their fingers touched, the observer slipped down one man's arm and up the other. Again the flood of images: this mind was as strong and rigid as Stevens', but it had a completely different flavor. His mind was full of excitement and a singing certainty; underneath it, like a starved prisoner, was a little voice that said, so faintly that it was not even heard, *What if it's not true?*

"Is anything wrong?" Stevens was saying.

LeDoux smiled. "Got a little shock there. It must be your carpets." He glanced at the check, smiled again, folded it and put it away. "Well, thank you, brother. And I hope we'll see each other on the Morning."

"We'll be there," said Stevens.

"Isn't it *wonderful?*" said Mrs. Kellogg, speaking for the first time. Her eyes and her cheeks were shining.

"Yes, it is. It is wonderful," said Stevens. Later, when

he went to look, he saw that there was a pink paper cross on the parcel box.

A few days later, after seeing a broken window in the Grosses' house up the street, Stevens began to make certain preparations.

They attended the candlelight service on Christmas Eve, and Stevens wept during the sermon. "How can you do that?" Julie asked him afterward.

"It's very easy. When I think what fools people are, I weep."

6 Dr. Wallace McNulty got up late on the day after Christmas, made himself some Egz and textured bacon—Janice was still in bed—and went down in his new slippers and robe to read the paper. The day was bright and clear except for the brown haze over downtown Santa Barbara, which would get thicker as the day progressed; McNulty had a good many asthma patients, some of whom were sure to call him this afternoon.

McNulty had had a brief moment of fame seven months ago, when he had been involved in the epidemic on Sea Venture. The disease had been named after him, and he had that little bit of immortality, along with Addison and Alzheimer. He had one more distinction, in fact; he was the only doctor who had ever caught his own disease.

McNulty had written an "as told to" book about the

experience—a pleasant young woman named Inskeep had actually written it, coloring it up a good deal from McNulty's oral narrative. Several others were doing the same; Stanley Bliss's *Horror in the Pacific* was probably going to be the big winner, but a passenger named Hartman had also written a book, and McNulty had even heard rumors of one called *Dentist on Sea Venture,* by Ira Clark, D.D.S.

McNulty was not proud of his own book now, but at the time the money had been irresistible and necessary; he had spent all of it and more in settling the lawsuit over the man whose death he had inadvertently caused on Sea Venture.

Afterward, McNulty had settled into anonymity again, and for that he was profoundly grateful. He had gone back into family practice in Santa Barbara, and shortly thereafter, to his complete surprise, had married a former Sea Venture nurse named Janice Werth. It was not like his marriage to Nita, but he had not expected or wanted it to be. She kept an eye on his diet and made sure he wore his weather shoes, and McNulty, he supposed, was content.

During the long nightmare of the lawsuit, he had reacted to stress in various ways, with apathy, with anger, once or twice with the shakes and tears, and he had also noticed some things that were harder to account for. A sudden interest in elephants, for instance. He went to see them in the zoo every chance he got, and he bought books about elephants without even looking inside them—if they were about elephants, that was enough—and he began to acquire ceramic elephants, carved wooden elephants, stuffed cloth elephants, brass elephants, even paper cutout elephants, all of which he kept in the living room until Janice put her foot down.

And McNulty saw that she was right, and put all the elephants away and never thought of looking at them again. But then it was palm prints. After he began practicing again, he bought a kit and had one of the girls in the office take palm prints of every patient and file them. And he spent some time examining these prints in hopes of discovering a correlation with what was wrong with the patients, but the funny thing was, he knew perfectly well that was nonsense and he only did it to have some excuse to look at palm prints. Then that went away, too, and the next thing he did was to start making anagrams of his patients' names. Mason Selchow, for instance, became "now echo slams." He didn't do this on purpose, it happened by itself, and at the same time he discovered that he was a whiz at the *New York Times* crossword puzzle, which had never interested him before.

Janice was going through something similar, too. The week after they got married, she decided to paint all the kitchen chairs bright orange, although she was a carroty redhead and should have known better. Then there was the time in Acapulco when she bought twenty budgerigars from a pet shop and let them loose. Nothing really excessive there—McNulty hated to see birds in cages himself—but not her usual style, and she never did anything like that again. It was as if the complicated machinery of their psyches were wobbling, out of balance, until it finally settled down into some kind of order.

He discovered a sudden interest in dowsing. Following instructions in a magazine article, he bent two pieces of coat hanger into L shapes and put the longer ends into empty Coke bottles. Holding the bottles and trying to keep the wire Ls pointed forward, he walked around the house, discovering to his amazement that at certain places the Ls spread apart without his volition. Now what did that mean?

McNulty began thinking about all the things he knew without knowing how he knew them. When he came into the house in the afternoon, for instance, he could tell in advance whether Janice was in the living room. There was something—a different feeling—but what was it?

He did know that McNulty's patients, including himself, had an affinity for other McNulty's patients. There was some kind of a support group that had annual meetings. He never went to them or read their newsletters, but he kept in touch pretty regularly with half a dozen people, including Bliss and some of the other officers and staff of Sea Venture. In September he and Janice had gone out to Michigan to see Randy Geller and Yvonne Barlow, who were building a house and laboratory on the Upper Peninsula. Geller and Barlow quarreled violently sometimes, but they obviously had no intention of splitting up, and the reason, McNulty thought, was that they were both highly sexed young people, but neither one could bear the thought of an intimate relationship with anyone who had not been a host of the "McNulty's Disease" symbiote.

He had had a good long time to think about all this, and he still wasn't sure what he thought. What he had told various people was true enough as far as it went: he did feel that he had been dumb before, dumb all his life, but that didn't mean that he was more *intelligent* now. He knew what he meant, but it would be hard to explain to anybody else. What he meant was that he had overlooked the essential dumbness of a lot of things. If there was a pattern in these things, it had something to do with accepting what he was told, or not even that, accepting things he had never been told but had believed just the same. Some of these things were important and some trivial—most of them were trivial, but there were enough of them that he felt now he was living in another world.

Take politics, for instance. Here was Elton Havery running again for governor, promising to reform the budget-making process and straighten out the problems in the Tri-State Water Authority and improve the life expectancy of babies kissed by politicians, probably, and he knew it was bushwah and everybody knew it was bushwah—but Havery was going to be reelected, and why? Because he was a known quantity, he had a great smile, and everybody liked his wife. What did all this have to do with reforming the budget process or straightening out the Water Authority? Not a damn thing, so why not just say, "I'm Elton Havery, you all know me, and I have a great smile and everybody likes my wife"?

Because then people would realize they were voting for dumb reasons, and they didn't want to know that; they wanted something that sounded like good reasons, never mind that Havery had screwed up the budget and the state's dealings with the Water Authority during his first term and would certainly do so again. They wanted to kid themselves they were voting for the candidate who would do the best job, and that was why Havery was in office and would stay there another four years, and why they had a psalm-singing idiot in the White House, and as far as that went, there were some real turkeys on the Santa Barbara City Council.

What could you do about that? Nothing, because if you tried to talk about the problem to most people, they would just look at you.

Or take the next headline, which was about the war between India and Pakistan. In Pakistan they were Moslems, and in India they were mostly Hindus, and the

Hindus and the Moslems had loathed each other for centuries. So every now and then the Hindus would try to blow the Moslems away, and to the extent that they succeeded, it would make the Moslems mad, and next time they would try to blow the Hindus away. That had been going on for generations, and it was no secret; the Hindus knew what would happen if they killed Moslems and the Moslems knew what would happen if they killed Hindus. So they knew it was dumb, but they did it anyway. Nobody said, "If we kill them they are just going to kill us, and we will wind up worse off than before." What they said was, probably, "Are we dogs or men? Let us go and avenge the deaths of our relatives, or else smear ourselves with dung and ashes and stand naked in the marketplace."

McNulty remembered how earnest the teachers had been about peace when he was in the third grade, and all the kids earnest about it too. It didn't make sense for people to kill each other: the teachers knew that and so did the eight-year-old kids. So what happened? How come those same kids went out and killed people nine or ten years later?

McNulty had been in his early forties during the Nicaraguan War; he had not been called, but a lot of his younger friends had gone and some of them had volunteered. McNulty remembered the firmness of their lips when they talked about it, the shine in their eyes. They looked as if they were seeing some distant thing that was invisible to everybody else. And McNulty remembered how ashamed he had felt. He was not about to enlist in the Army or the Marines and go off to fight beaners in the jungle, but he felt obscurely that he ought to, that the others were heroes and he was a coward. He had talked to some of them afterward, young men who had done unspeakable things, because they didn't want to be cowards. Some of them broke down and wept when they talked about those things. They didn't understand what had happened to them, what had gone wrong.

Food riots in Bangladesh and Nigeria. The Dust Bowl in Illinois was growing. Wasn't there any good news? Well, hell, he could still read the funnies; he was just settling down to them when the terminal in the corner said in its baritone voice, "Call from Geller, Wally."

"Okay, Jigger, put him on." The screen lighted up as McNulty sat down in front of it, and he saw Geller's bearded head, a little bigger than life size. The head parted its lips and spoke. "Wally, have you seen the medical fax this morning?"

"No, I haven't run it. Why?"

"What are you doing out there, sucking your teeth? Run it and call me back." The image dwindled to a bright little quicksilver sphere and vanished.

McNulty said, "Jigger, fax, medical, latest."

After a second, sheets began to curl out into the tray. McNulty carried them back to the sofa and looked through them. At first he didn't see anything that would make Geller call him from Michigan on a Sunday morning: then his eye caught his own name leering at him from the bottom of the page.

". . . similarity to McNulty's Disease," he read, then clutched the paper hard and went back to the beginning of the paragraph. "Health officials in Chicago are alarmed by the spread of an unknown disease. The victims collapse into a semicomatose state and recover spontaneously eight to ten hours later. The epidemic began eleven days ago in Evanston, Illinois, and has spread to metropolitan Chicago and the surrounding area. Some experts have suggested a similarity to McNulty's Disease, a previously unknown epidemic illness that broke out on Sea Venture earlier this year."

Well, it couldn't be. Eight to ten hours. On CV, it had been ten *days*.

But with a sinking feeling in his stomach, he knew that it was.

7 Jan Eric Muhlhauser, excerpt from holo interview with Desiree St. John broadcast on *Your Bright Day,* 7/10/99:

MUHLHAUSER   You've heard of blooms in plant population?

ST. JOHN   You mean like blossoms?

MUHLHAUSER   No. A bloom is when a population suddenly seems to explode. Like lily pads in a pond. You go down there every day and you see a few lily pads. Next day there are a few more, nothing to worry about, and so on. But there comes a time when the pond is half covered with lily pads, and the next day it's all covered. And the process looks sudden, but it really isn't. Suppose the population is doubling once a day. You start with one lily pad. Next day, two, next day four, and so on. That's a geometric progression. When you get to the point where there are five hundred lily pads and the pond is half full, then you know in one more day it's going to be completely full, because that's the doubling time.

ST. JOHN   Yes, I see.

MUHLHAUSER   Okay, now in the human population in recent decades the doubling time has been about thirty-five years. That's with a two percent annual increase.

ST. JOHN   All right, but what if the cure is worse than the disease? Every time you hear of a country that's in trouble economically, it's because its growth rate is too small.

MUHLHAUSER   Economic growth. Gross domestic product. Right, and a lot of people think that depends on population growth. Not necessarily so. Japan's population growth is down and their GDP is up. Same with West Germany and France. But there is an obvious crude relationship in traditional Western economies, because more people means more consumers. So we keep on expanding, for that and a lot of other reasons, and it works—we do get more consumers and the economy does keep growing. But that's a pyramid scheme.

ST. JOHN   A which?

MUHLHAUSER   They're illegal now, have been for years. The way a pyramid works, you get a letter with a list of names and addresses in it. The letter tells you to send twenty bucks to the first name on the list, cross off that name and add yours at the bottom, and send ten copies of the letter to friends. As long as the pyramid keeps growing, it works—the people on the list really do get more money than they put in. Figure it out. Let's say there are five names on the list. If everybody who gets the letter follows instructions, by the time you get to the top, you're going to get twenty-dollar bills from ten to the fifth people. How much is that?

ST. JOHN   Two million dollars. Oh, my, wouldn't that be nice!

MUHLHAUSER   Right, and the only thing wrong with it is that the pyramid can't keep growing indefinitely. Pretty soon everybody is running around trying to sign up everybody else. The pyramid runs out of people and collapses. People who got in early make a lot of money; people who got in late lose their dough and their time. So, look, we *know* all that when we're talking about money, and that's why pyramid schemes are illegal. But when we talk about human growth, we don't know it anymore. We act as if we think we can keep on growing indefinitely—as if there were no limits. And that's crazy.

ST. JOHN   "There *are* no limits." That's what Jack Draffy always says.

MUHLHAUSER   And that whole bunch. I know. I wonder if there are enough of them to fill

a high-school gymnasium from floor to
floor to ceiling. If so, I'd like to try it.

The minds he had inhabited stretched away behind
him like a row of bright bubbles. They were alike, and yet
every one was different. He knew all that they knew: but
there were many things that none of them knew, and
there were still other things they knew that were false. It
was easy enough to untangle the nodes of energy in their
brains that kept them from behaving sensibly. It was
much harder to straighten out the tangles in the institutions that governed them, because he could know only
what his hosts knew, and they did not agree among
themselves why those institutions caused so much mis-
ery.

Wherever he went he was a helpless passenger, but he
had learned quickly how to leap from one host to another
until he found one that was going in the right direction.
"What airline, sir?"

"TWA."

He pulled in at the terminal; the fare handed him his
credit card, and he slipped out and in again, looking with
shocked dismay at the cabbie sprawled across the seat. He
turned wildly and saw a man in a blue airport uniform.
"Something's wrong with the cabdriver," he shouted. The
man came forward, looked into the driver's seat, spoke
into his headset. "We'll take care of it, sir," he said. "Any
luggage?"

His name was Martin Ehrlich; he was a leather goods
manufacturer with an ulcer, on his way to Baton Rouge,
but when he checked in at the ticket counter he slipped
across the gray void into another explosion of sense and
feeling, and half an hour later, after the comatose passen-

ger had been taken away, she checked the ticket of a man who was going to San Francisco. There, by a similar transfer, he entered another check person at the counter and from him went to a woman who was on her way to Santa Barbara. The woman was looking forward with excitement to her reunion with her husband, and she was ovulating, but her present purpose was more important; with regret, she slipped into the cabdriver and waited in her until she took the unconscious passenger to the hospital.

It took only two more transfers to find someone who knew which patients were Dr. McNulty's and when he would make his rounds. An orderly took him to the right room; then she was in the hospital bed, dulled by opiates. Then McNulty himself, whose mind he recognized from memory traces in other minds, but that was not the point. The point was that McNulty knew the whereabouts of others who had been his hosts on Sea Venture, including women of child-bearing age.

From start to finish, the trip had involved a dozen hosts.

Anthony Ridenour was simultaneously watching the crawl and talking to his editor at Boone & Slayton—a new one, thank heaven; the old editor had turned a bit boring about unpaid advances. The new one, Reynolds Lawton-Jones, was a cheerful blond youngster, full of plans and schemes: the only thing wrong with him was that he did like to talk on the holo, even when he was meant to be on holiday. Ridenour, saying, "Yes, yes," and "Oh, I absolutely agree," was doing his famous imitation of looking straight into the pickup, while in actuality watching the news screen beside it.

Lawton-Jones, leaning back with a self-satisfied

smile, was going on about a project he had assigned to another writer, a woman, as it happened, whom Ridenour would willingly have consigned to the lower-most circle of hell. The book was to be a series of penetrating interviews with former film actresses and models, not to exclude the odd prostitute. Half listening, Ridenour noticed the bit about the epidemic in the States as it made its way toward the top of the screen. It almost got away before he jerked out a hand to the pause button.

"Anything wrong?" said Lawton-Jones, opening his blue eyes a little wider.

"A fly."

"They're awful, aren't they? At this time of year. Well, that's all then. Do let's have lunch. Monday week?"

"Let me look at my diary. Yes, Monday is all right. Until then."

He punched off before Lawton-Jones could think of another topic. Then he sat looking at the frozen news crawl. "U.S. EPIDEMIC LINKED TO SEA VENTURE. An outbreak of a disease causing collapse and stupor in its victims has been linked to the Sea Venture epidemic of McNulty's Disease, according to sources in the U.S. Department of Health, which calls the disease 'not life threatening.' Dr. Wallace McNulty, for whom the Sea Venture disease was named, confirms, 'The symptoms certainly sound almost identical.' McNulty expresses puzzlement about the seven-month lag between the two outbreaks."

Ridenour switched to a live news channel and after a while got essentially the same thing, delivered by a boyish young man in a yellow tank suit. Evidently that was all there was, at least for the moment.

Well, what about it? It might be nothing at all, a

false alarm, or it might be something good. He keyed into the information net and asked, "How many cases of the new U.S. disease and where?"

The screen chuntered a bit and then came back with:

Cases 36 as of 19.12.99. Chicago 20, Evanston 12, Barrington 4. Another Q?

Ridenour said, "No," and sat back to ponder. It was worth a transatlantic call, at any rate. "Jinn dear," he said to the computer, "call Wallace McNulty in Santa Barbara, will you? What time is it there?"

"Nine hours sixteen minutes. Calling."

After a moment a woman's face came on the screen. "Dr. McNulty, please," said the computer's voice.

"He's not here," said the woman. She had the peculiar blind expression typical of someone who was not looking at you on the phone, although she appeared to be, but at the computer display that Jinn used. "May I take a message?"

"This is Anthony Ridenour's secretary calling. Do you think we might reach Dr. McNulty at another number?"

"No, I don't believe so. He's in Atlanta, and he asked me not to forward any calls. I can take a message if you like."

"Thank her and say good-bye," said Ridenour. The computer did so, and Ridenour chewed a fingernail. Atlanta, if he was not mistaken, was where the Centers for Disease Control were located. It was not a certainty that that was where McNulty was, but why else would anybody go to Atlanta?

He called Lawton-Jones back. "The most amazing thing," he said. "I happened to be watching the news after we rang off, and it seems that the epidemic from Sea Venture has broken out again. I'm quite excited, Rennie. You remember they couldn't stop it last time, and they're not going to stop it now. What would you say to a new round of interviews to update the book and get it out ahead of the pack?"

Lawton-Jones was quite excited, too. He talked to Boone on Tuesday, and by the next morning a new and quite substantial allotment for expenses had been authorized.

8 Stanley Bliss, once the Chief of Operations of Sea Venture, had had the luck to acquire a very nice little inn on the Costa del Sol near Málaga. It had never been his intention to settle in Spain, but he had gone there on holiday after an unfortunate quarrel with his wife and son, and just at that moment the property had come on the market. The inn was built around a charming courtyard with fountains and statuary; then there were the guest houses, the bandstand, the cabanas; the white beach where vendors spread out their wares on blankets; and the blinding blue-green sea. Bliss's Spanish was limited to "buenos días," "buenas tardes," "buenas noches," "gracias," "sí," and "no," but that was not a problem. Señora Martínez, the major-domo, with whom he had a perfect understanding, dealt with tradesmen, most of whom spoke English anyway, and Señorita Cortázar, a charming young woman, did all the correspondence. The high season was 1 July to the end of September; after that, there was enough trade to keep the inn open, but the atmosphere was much more relaxed.

After some disappointments, he had acquired a cook, Gola Vargas, who was satisfactory all round, meaning that her Spanish cooking pleased the guests who wanted that sort of thing, and at the same time she could make an honest roast beef and a very respectable Yorkshire pudding.

One afternoon in late December, when he was just up from his siesta, Señorita Cortázar came out of her office and said, "Señor Blees, there was a transatlantic call for you." She handed him a slip. "I told them you could not be disturb."

"Very good," said Bliss. Still a trifle muzzy, he sat down on the patio and looked at the slip while a waiter brought him his tea. The name was McNutly. "Will call again at four," Señorita Cortázar had written in her neat script. The name meant nothing to him. He put the paper in his pocket and roused enough to have a very pleasant chat with Hugh Glasscock, an elderly guest who had just come up from the beach.

A little after four a waiter bent over him. "A call for you, Señor Blees, from United States."

"Is it about a reservation, José?"

"No, sir, they say they have to speak to you personally, very important."

"Bother. Will you forgive me, Mr. Glasscock? I'll take it in the office, José."

"Mr. Bliss?" said the young woman in the screen.

"Yes."

"One moment for Dr. McNulty."

Bliss had just time to absorb that when Wallace McNulty's image came on the screen. "Stanley, how are you?"

"Wallace!" said Bliss. "They told me McNutly or some such thing. I had no idea it was you."

McNulty grinned. "Sometimes I wish it wasn't. The reason I called—have you heard about the epidemic?"

"Epidemic? No."

"There's been another outbreak."

"You don't mean the parasite?"

"I'm afraid so."

"But that's impossible."

"It doesn't make a whole lot of sense to me, either, but that's the way it looks. They got me down here to the Centers for Disease Control in Atlanta because I'm supposed to be an expert. What I told them I'd like to do is set up a conference with you and Geller and Barlow, and Higpen and Mrs. Bernstein. I don't think we'd have a prayer of getting us all together at this time of year, but they have these three-D tanks now, I don't know if you've seen them?"

"No."

"Well, it's the nearest thing to being in the same room. They tell me they can fly in the equipment tomorrow morning, and we'll set up the call for six o'clock your time. Is that all right?"

At the thought of Mrs. Bernstein, Bliss felt a pang. "Well, I suppose—" he said.

"I'm faxing you some news reports to save you the trouble of looking them up. Many thanks, Stan. I'll talk to you tomorrow."

Bliss looked in the fax tray and found the news

printouts. The length of the illness was different, but it was the same pattern, first one patient, then another. Somehow the parasite must have escaped onto the mainland after all. How was that possible?

9 At breakfast that morning Randall Geller said, "I dreamed I invented a new theory of linguistics, the *vous-du* theory."

The observer in Yvonne Barlow was interested to note that he was nervous; in some way, he knew what he didn't know. "Voodoo linguistics?" she said.

"V-o-u-s, d-u. I guess it had something to do with Germanic and Romance languages. You know, French *vous,* Spanish *vosotros.*"

"The last I heard, it was *ustedes.*"

"Yeah, but that's the polite third person, like German *Sie.* The older form is *vosotros,* 'you others.' The funny thing is that the Germanic form slops over into Romance languages. French *tu,* Spanish *tú,* and then you get English 'you,' which is really closer to *vous* than *du.*"

"Why are you so snivvy about linguistics all of a sudden?"

"It's interesting. I got into Chomsky again a couple of days ago. If you follow him far enough, he starts to make sense. Maybe language is wired in, like sex, and that means there are constraints on what we can think. You know what Ouspensky said just before he died?"

"No, what?"

"'Think in other categories.' Great idea. But if Chomsky is right, you can't."

Barlow spread marmalade on her toast. "Speaking of sex—" she said.

"Too early. Try to control yourself until after lunch."

"—how are you feeling about children?"

Geller looked at her over a forkful of scrambled eggs. "Somewhere between indifferent and disgusted. Why?"

"Because I didn't do anything before we went to bed last night. And I'm ovulating."

Geller lowered his fork slowly. "You really know how to make a guy's day. You didn't think of consulting me first?"

"I'm consulting you now. I may not be pregnant yet, but I want to be."

"Jesus Christ! Why?" Geller threw his fork onto the plate.

"Randy, I'm thirty-four. If I wait another year, I'll be an elderly mother."

"An *elderly* mother?"

"That's what they call it. Over thirty-five is over the hill."

"You never said anything about this before."

"Yes, I did, but you weren't listening. If we're going to have children, it's now or never. And I want children."

Geller stood up. "I've lost my appetite," he said. He headed for the door.

"This is unfair, Randy," she said to his back.

He turned. "You call me unfair? What am I, just a biological appendage? Why don't you go down to the sperm bank?"

Barlow leaned her forehead into her hand. "You goddamn son of a bitch," she said. After a moment he could see a worm trail of tears crawling down her cheek.

He hesitated, then walked up and put his hand on her forehead, pulling it back against his chest.

"Don't touch me," she said, not struggling.

"If I don't touch you, how are you going to get knocked up? Be reasonable, Yvonne." He stroked her hair. After a moment she turned and laid her cheek against him.

"You make me so damn mad," she said.

"I know I do. I'm a heartless brute, but I'm all you've got."

"Oh, hell." She pulled away, found a tissue in her robe and blew her nose. At this moment the kitchen computer announced, "Call from McNulty for Randy or Yvonne."

"You talk to him," said Barlow, getting up. "I'm going to wash my face."

Geller waited until she was out of the room before he said, "Tiger, put him on."

McNulty's face appeared in the holoscreen. "Hello, Wally," said Geller. "Great timing."

"Did I interrupt something?" McNulty asked. "I'll call back."

"No, go ahead. If it's good news, I could use some, and if it's bad I might as well get it over with."

"Well, it isn't exactly good. It's about the new epidemic. I'm down here at the Centers for Disease Control in Atlanta." He told Geller what he had already told Bliss, ending, "If you agree, they'll put in a holotank conference system—you won't even have to leave the house."

"Okay."

"Yvonne all right?"

"Peachy. We're going to have a kid."

"Is that right? Well, congratulations."

"Thanks."

A man's relation to his beef cattle is essentially that of a tiger to its prey; his relation to his milk cattle and hens is essentially that of tapeworms or hookworms to their hosts.

—ASA C. CHANDLER

10 At ten A.M. Málaga time a truck drove into the inn courtyard carrying six enormous things that looked like modern-art vases. The young people who came with them set them up around the table in the conference room; when the lighting had been adjusted properly, you couldn't see the curved surfaces of the tanks at all, only the metal plates at the top, which seemed to be floating in midair. There was also a conventional holo-screen, quite a large one, and four cameras on mobile stands.

At five minutes to six the technicians ushered Bliss into the conference room and showed him where to sit. There was some delay. At a quarter after, three of the tanks bloomed into life, then a fourth, and Bliss found himself to all appearances facing four people across the table, each one with a sort of metal halo floating above his or, as it might be, her head. Bliss recognized the familiar faces of Ben Higpen, the former mayor of Sea Venture, Mrs. Bernstein, who had been his gadfly, and of course

Dr. McNulty; the fourth person was a gray-haired specta-
cled woman he had never seen before.

"Hello to all of you," said this person. "My name
is Harriet Cleaver Owen, I'm a behavioral epidemiolo-
gist, and I'm supposed to be in charge of the task
force to investigate the outbreak of McNulty's Disease,
if that's what it is, but really I'm just going to sit back
and listen, because you all know more about it than I
do. I see two of us are still missing— Oh, there you
are."

The two remaining tanks had flickered into life, and
Bliss saw the faces of Randy Geller and Yvonne Barlow.
Greetings were exchanged all round, and a little cross-
chat developed until Dr. Owen restored order.

"I'm going to just fill you in on what's been happening and what we know so far," she said. "The outbreak began in Evanston, a suburb of Chicago, and the
first four cases were all members of a fundamental-
ist religious group that was canvassing this neighborhood." The holoscreen lit up, displaying a street
map with an irregular area outlined in red. "After
that we had cases in metropolitan Chicago and another suburb called Barrington, and then it jumped to
Manhattan—we have eleven reported cases there so
far."

The screen changed: now they were looking at a
woman in a hospital bed. She was unconscious or semiconscious, her skin waxen, eyes rolled up. An IV tube was
taped to her arm. "This is Mrs. Clarissa Romano, who
was stricken in Chicago four days ago. She recovered
spontaneously in nine hours, and that's about average."

"What about pathology?" Yvonne Barlow asked.

"It's negative. That's one reason we suspect
McNulty's Disease, even though the duration of the

illness is different. I can tell you one more thing: one of the patients in Barrington died of a heart attack in the hospital. They did a post on him, and except for the heart there was no pathology at all—nothing in the lymph system, nothing in the liver, nothing in the brain. So here's where we stand right now, and I hope you're all going to come up with some suggestions."

After a while Ben Higpen said, "I think we may be jumping to conclusions a little too fast. Not only are these people getting sick for nine hours instead of eight days, but we know the parasite never got ashore, because we sank it in a crate to the bottom of the ocean."

"How do you know it didn't get out of the crate?" Mrs. Bernstein asked.

"Well, maybe, but that's stretching it, and then you still have to explain why the symptoms are different. I just don't think we know what we're doing here."

Bernstein looked thoughtful. "Dr. McNulty, do you remember when we were talking about the parasite after it was all over, and somebody said we didn't know how it reproduced—and you said it was a good thing there weren't any pregnant women on Sea Venture? Do you remember that?"

"No."

"Well, take my word for it, you said it. Now can you explain what you meant by that?"

"I suppose," McNulty said, looking startled, "if I said it, I must have meant that the parasite might reproduce if it was in a woman's body at the time she conceived. It was just a wild idea."

"Well, *I* think we ought to take it seriously. Suppose somebody who was a host of the parasite got pregnant. It probably happened late in the cruise. She went home and had the baby nine months later, and that's where we are right now."

"Were any of the first cases Sea Venture people?" Barlow asked. "Or related to them in any way? Had anyone in their families given birth to a child just before the outbreak?"

"As far as we can determine, the answers to those questions are all no."

"I think I see another flaw," said Bliss. "On Sea Venture, the parasite began attacking one person after another as soon as it got out of the thingummy."

"The *austra*fuckinglite," said Geller.

"Right, thank you, Mr. Geller. But this time, Mrs. Bernstein, if your theory is correct, it stayed in one host for nine months."

"Maybe because it has to grow as the child grows?"

Higpen said, "I think we're taking a lot for granted. Dr. Owen, have you checked the people in that neighborhood in Evanston against the Sea Venture list?"

"Yes, we've done that, and it's negative, but that doesn't tell us much. We're looking at that neighborhood as a possible source of the infection, but you must realize that these people belonged to three different churches and had a wide acquaintanceship among the members, not even counting the various casual contacts that people make on a daily basis. But even if somebody on Sea Venture did become pregnant, she might or might not have been married at the time. If she wasn't, or if she was divorced and remarried later, we don't know what her name is. So this whole question is still very much open."

"Suppose," said Bernstein, "we start with a list of all

the McNulty's patients who were women of child-bearing age—"

"Might be a few hundred," said McNulty.

"All right, then it'll be a few hundred. And then try to find out which of them were in the Chicago area when the new epidemic started. That would narrow it down fast, maybe to one name."

"We don't know how to find a tenth of those people," McNulty said.

"Well, we've got to find them, that's all. Can you trace them through social-security records or something?"

"The government doesn't like to give out that kind of information," Owen said. "We may get it eventually, but it could take months."

"Not even in a national emergency?"

"The President hasn't declared one."

"Well, he *ought* to—"

"One moment," said Bliss. "Dr. McNulty, do you remember the fellow who interviewed us all a few months ago?"

"Ridenour," said McNulty.

"That's right, Anthony Ridenour. He might have some addresses that are fresher than ours."

Owen made a note. "Where can we find him?"

"Care of his publishers, I expect."

Owen glanced at someone invisible outside her tank. "All right, we'll try that. Now I'd like to turn to another question. Ms. Barlow, we asked you to join this group because of your interest in parasites, or symbiotes if you prefer that distinction—"

"I don't care about the distinction. Look, the only people who are actually drawing energy from nature, that is from other organisms, are the farmers and fishers and ranchers, and they're parasitical on corn, cattle, fish, and chickens. Everybody else has some kind of parasitical or symbiotic relationship with *them.* Which one it is depends on your point of view. Are bureaucrats parasites or symbiotes? If you think you know the answer to that one, what about poets? You can't get away from this relationship because it's everywhere. Now I want to make one other point. We're talking about this thing as if it were a tapeworm or a blood fluke. What if it's more like the intestinal flora that help you digest your food? We could probably figure out a way to get rid of those, too, if we put our minds to it."

"I understand. But let me put it to you this way. Suppose, in another five years or so, we discover that this thing really is harmful in ways that we can't predict now. Shouldn't we be prepared, at least, to attack the problem then?"

"All right."

"So, from that perspective, I know we'd all be grateful if you'd give us the benefit of your expert knowledge. Just in a general sense, what lines of attack would you suggest?"

"Well, there are four ways you can go about it. I don't mind telling you this, because you could find it in any textbook. You can reduce the density of the human population—that happens naturally in many parasite-host relationships, and it's one of the things parasites are good for. You can find some chemical agent or, better yet, a predator, that will kill the parasite; or you can find something that will kill one of its intermediate hosts. That one doesn't apply here, as far as we know, but it might. Or you can find something that will inhibit the parasite's ability to reproduce."

Owen was making notes. "Very good. I think we should proceed along all four of those lines, in an exploratory way, and see what we come up with. Just offhand, it seems to me that killing the parasite is the strongest possibility. Any ideas on that?"

"No. Well, wait a minute. There is something that came up, I think, when we were talking about this on Sea Venture. Maybe there's some drug that inhibits the symbiote, or injures it, or keeps it from invading a specific host. Or maybe something like a high fever would do it. I wouldn't give that a very high probability, but at least you could try to get good records on all the recovered patients and run them through an analysis to see if there's anything missing that you'd expect to find. I mean, just for example, if the expectation would be ten percent of patients with barbiturates in their systems, and you don't find any. The problem there would be to find something that damages the symbiote without doing more damage to the host. If it turned out to be aspirin, for instance, that would be great, but if it's heroin, not so great."

Owen made another note. "Explore chemical agents, fevers—maybe other illnesses?"

"Yes, certainly."

"Something else we haven't mentioned," Owen said. "We've been talking about a rather leisurely information-gathering program to put together something we might need to use five or six years down the road. But we may be under a more severe time constraint than that. At the moment, as far as we know, there is one symbiote. Just one. If we get rid of that one, the problem is over. But what if it reproduces? We must suppose that it will, because apparently it already has."

"Are you advocating a prophylactic solution—kill it off because we don't know if it's harmful or not?"

"I think that deserves some thought, at least. Dr. McNulty, on Sea Venture you did get rid of the parasite by causing it to enter the body of a goat. Do you think we could do something like that again?"

"I don't see how. It knows what we did—it won't fall for that twice."

"Let me give you another scenario," said Owen. "Let's say the last victim was a woman and the only one near her at the time she collapsed was her husband. All right, we know he's the host. Say we wait until he's asleep—the symbiote can't leave while the host is unconscious, is that correct?"

"Yes, but—"

"I think I know your objection, but let me finish. We administer a drug to keep him unconscious, and then we take him to a building where he is surrounded by animals in cages. When he wakes up, there are no other human beings near enough to go to, but there are plenty of animals. Now there's no reason to think the symbiote would deliberately stay in the human host until it killed him, is there? It would go into one of the animals, and then we'd have it."

McNulty said, "Dr. Owen, you say you understand my objection, but I'm not sure. I did something just about like that, and my patient died."

Barlow said, "It was our idea—mine and Randy's. We talked you into it, but none of us knew what was going to happen. It was an accident, Wally."

"Maybe so. If we did it again, it would be murder."

"Dr. McNulty," said Owen, "suppose you knew that you could save a million lives by risking the life of one person. What would you do?"

"Now you're talking about something I don't know. Maybe God does, but that's his business. I'm sorry, Dr. Owen. Are you going ahead with this?"

"I think we have to."

"Then you'd better count me out." McNulty's image abruptly shrank to a dot of quicksilver and disappeared; where he had been a moment ago there was an opaque curved tank of glass.

"Me too," said Yvonne Barlow. She disappeared in her turn, and a moment later so did Geller.

"That was dumb," said Geller.

"So why did you do it?"

"Because you did."

"Well, I did it because Wally did. What do you want?"

"I don't know, but it would have been nice to infiltrate. Now we don't know what they're going to do."

"Spilled milk."

"Okay. What are we going to name the kid?"

11 Dr. Owen, feeling depressed, gathered her papers and went back to her office. There was a message on the screen: "Please call Reception."

Probably another citizen wanting a guided tour. Owen said, "Rick, Reception."

"Calling."

Mrs. Mason's plump face came on the screen. "Oh, Dr. Owen, there's a gentleman to see you. A Mr. Ridenour."

"Tell him I'm sorry— Wait a minute." She looked at her notes. *"Anthony* Ridenour?"

Ridenour, a rabbity little man, was clutching a large portfolio. He sat down in Owen's cramped little office, saying, "Very kind of you to see me. I've been trying to talk to Dr. McNulty, but I know you've all been very busy indeed, and I understand he's gone now."

"Yes, that's right. Mr. Ridenour, as a matter of fact, there are some questions I'd like to ask you. You're writing a book about McNulty's Disease, aren't you?"

"Yes, I am."

"I hope this doesn't sound like a funny question, but when you were interviewing people for your book, did you happen to notice that any of the women were pregnant?"

"Let me think. Why, yes, in fact. Julie, what was her name—Prescott. I didn't use the interview, actually, but I remember noticing at the time."

56

"Do you have her address?"

"Well, I'm sure it's in my file. Would you mind telling me why?"

Owen hesitated. "This isn't for publication right now, Mr. Ridenour, but there's a possibility that the parasite got off Sea Venture by reproducing itself in a human embryo."

"Oh, I see. Well, in that case, of course—"

The address turned out to be a dead end; there was no Julie Prescott in the Manhattan directory. Owen got her parents' number from Ridenour as well, and talked to Mrs. Prescott.

"Mrs. Prescott, this is Dr. Owen at the Centers for Disease Control. I'm sorry to trouble you, but I wonder if you could tell me where to find your daughter Julie?"

"Well, I don't know. Did you say Disease Control? Is there something the matter with Julie?"

"We're not sure, but we'd like to talk to her. You've probably heard there's been a new outbreak of the epidemic."

"No, we hadn't heard. Is Julie in any danger? I suppose that's silly—she's had the disease already."

"Well, in fact, we think she might be in some danger, and we haven't been able to locate her. Is she living with you now?"

"Oh, my goodness. No, she's married and living in Evanston. Her husband's name is Robert Ames."

"Could you give me her address and phone number?"

Mrs. Prescott waffled a little and then gave in. Dr. Owen punched the number. After a long delay she got a calling symbol and then a standard image. "Yes," said the computerized face, "can I help you?"

"I'd like to speak to Mrs. Robert Ames, please."

"May I ask who's calling?"

"This is Dr. Harriet Cleaver Owen at the Centers for Disease Control."

"I'm sorry, there is no one of that name here."

"What about Julie Prescott, then?"

"May I ask who's calling?"

Owen sighed. "This is Dr. Harriet Cleaver Owen at the Centers for Disease Control."

"I'm sorry, there is no one of that name here."

"May I leave a message for Mrs. Ames or Ms. Prescott, in case it turns out she is there?"

The computer said, "I can accept a message."

"Please tell her it's in connection with the outbreak of McNulty's Disease in Evanston, and it's very urgent." She gave her number and punched off.

Her call was not returned. On a hunch, she tapped Infonet for the Evanston city directory and asked for the address she had been given. It was listed in the name of James Turnbull, not Ames. She tried the number again repeatedly during the rest of the day, first from her office and then from home. The circuits were busy. She got through finally after eleven, but this time there was no answer.

Two days after the fiasco, Dr. Owen went to see her boss, Milton Chalmers. She carried with her a sheaf of computer printouts.

Chalmers swiveled in his chair to shake hands with her. He was a large bald man with a perpetual tired expression. "Well, Harriet, how's it going?"

She sat down and put the printouts on Chalmers' immaculate desk. "My McNulty's group blew up on me."

"What was the matter?"

She took off her glasses and rubbed the bridge of her nose. "It may have been my fault—maybe I was pushing too hard. But that isn't what's worrying me."

"You'd better tell me what happened."

"All right. Three people—Yvonne Barlow, Randall Geller, and McNulty himself—objected to the whole idea of trying to eliminate the parasite before we know for sure that it's dangerous. When they walked out, there was nothing much left of the panel."

"That's unfortunate, Harriet, but we can put together another panel. What's the problem?"

"Milt, all three of those people are recovered McNulty patients. What if their resistance demonstrates just the opposite of what they're saying?"

He leaned back and put his fingertips together. "You mean they've been changed somehow, psychologically?"

"That's what I can't get out of my mind." She nudged the printouts toward him across the desk. "You know that British journalist, Ridenour? He's writing a book about the McNulty's victims, and I talked him into giving me copies of his interviews. Let me show you something." She picked up the sheaf of printouts, turned the pages until she came to a marked passage, handed it to Chalmers.

" 'I felt as if a kind of veil had been lifted,' " he read. " 'It was an indescribable feeling of mental liberation, of freedom. For the first time in my life I was seeing things clearly. So of course I left my husband and went back to leatherwork. I should have done it years ago.' " He looked up.

"Milt, they're all like that—all the interviews with recovered patients. They all say things like, 'I was stupid before.' And they all made some radical change in their lives—left husbands, left wives, changed their jobs or their politics."

"This looks like pretty lurid stuff," he said, holding the printouts distastefully.

"I know, it's popular writing, it isn't evidence, but I think we should be *getting* some evidence. I know Ridenour isn't making all this up, because I heard Geller and Barlow saying things just like that. I'd like us to put out a bulletin asking for follow-up studies on recovered patients, looking for any physiological or mental changes. Then at least we'll know what we're in for."

"Let me think about it."

God Almighty does not hear the prayer of a Jew.
    —The Reverend Bailey Smith,
    President of the Southern Baptist
    Convention (1980)

12 For the last week Stevens and Julie had been watching the holo news every evening after dinner. On the day after Christmas there were disturbances between Christians and Moslems in Damascus, and on the twenty-seventh synagogues in Brussels were firebombed. An organization called Les Fidèles claimed responsibility. On the twenty-eighth the trouble hit Chicago, Boston, and New York.

In the split holoscreen, the two talking heads regarded each other, one blue-eyed, one brown. "We're talking with Rabbi Garson Handler, president of the

Union of American Hebrew Congregations in New York," said the host, who had bright teeth and shiny hair. "Now, Rabbi, let me ask you this." The head of Rabbi Handler nodded mechanically.

"Let me ask you this," the host repeated. "What would you like Christians to do or not do at this point?"

The guest shifted his position nervously. "It's not a question of what *I* would like; it's a question of what they should do. This is the point. What we're talking about is what people *should* do, how they should behave toward each other, whether they're Christians or Jews. That doesn't matter."

"But they're behaving this way *because* they're Christians. Isn't that so?"

"How do you mean?" Little drops of perspiration, each as round and bright as crystal, appeared on the brow of Rabbi Handler.

"It's because they're Christians," said the host patiently, "that they're throwing red paint on Jews, and breaking their windows, and roughing them up on the street. Now isn't that so?"

"They have a mistaken belief. They—"

"I'm sorry," the host interrupted. "They have a *mistaken belief?* Is that what you said? What is that mistaken belief?"

"They believe that everybody should be on hand to witness this change that they think is going to happen on January first. And because Jews refuse to do that, that's why some of us are being victimized."

The host nodded judiciously. "I think that's a fair statement," he said. "I'll go along with that. Now, Rabbi Handler, as a fair man, a man of liberal beliefs, can you put yourself for a moment into the mind of a Christian who believes that the millennium is coming on January first? How would you feel then? Wouldn't you want everybody, Christians and Jews, to celebrate this amazing event? Tell me the truth."

Handler said, "They believe the world is going to end at the beginning of the year two thousand. They believed it was going to end in the year one thousand. It didn't. We're still here, still talking."

"But just because it didn't happen before, does that mean it can't happen now?"

"It's a mistake. The world isn't coming to an end."

"The Second Coming isn't going to happen," said the host, deadpan.

"We are still waiting for the First Coming," said Rabbi Handler.

Within twenty minutes, a mob had gathered outside the GBS studios on Forty-second Street. Although the police got Rabbi Handler away by helicopter from the roof, the mob broke into the broadcasting company's offices, causing thousands of dollars of damage before police could restore order. That evening, in Inwood Hills, unknown assailants broke into Handler's house and bludgeoned him to death, along with his wife and his ten-year-old son. Asked why there had been no armed guard at the Handler residence, the chief of police replied, "Nobody requested it."

> *Silent night, holy night,*
> *All is calm, all is bright,*
> *Round yon virgin mother and child,*
> *Holy infant, so tender and mild,*
> *Sleep in heavenly peace, sleep in*
>   *heavenly peace.*

13 "But the furniture!" Julie said. "My paintings—your books!"

"I know. The paintings can come, if you leave the frames behind. The rest we can replace."

"John, why can't we—just go to a hotel for a few days, until this blows over?"

"It won't blow over. If we stay here, either we have to be part of the millennial movement or be outside it. If we are outside it, we risk retaliation. You and I can protect ourselves, perhaps, but can we protect our unborn child?"

In the holos, as the dawn line moved westward across the Pacific, satellites brought them live coverage of millennial gatherings in Australia and Japan. At 2:35 P.M. Chicago time, an ordinary dawn came to Sydney. The upturned faces were patient. "Most of these people," said one anchor to the other, "I shouldn't say most—many of these people, we are informed, have sold all their possessions, houses, cars, the works, because they won't need them after this morning. It is not clear to me what they think they are going to buy with the money."

That evening, after Julie had finished packing, the doorplate rang. She went to answer it.

"Why, hello, Maureen, what are you doing here?"

"I'm going to march with you folks, and keep you company."

"That's very nice, Maureen, but I'm afraid I'm catching a cold—"

"No, it's all right," Stevens said. "Come in,

Maureen. Have you got time for a cup of tea before we start? Julie, go and get your warm clothes." He gave her a stony glance, and she left.

When she came back, Maureen was slumped in her chair in the kitchen, looking glassy-eyed. "What did you do to her?" she asked.

"Nothing very serious. Are the bags packed?"

"Yes."

"All right. Give me a hand here first." He picked up Maureen, chair and all. Julie opened the door for him and he carried the unconscious woman out into the garage. With Julie's help, he maneuvered her into the back seat of the Porsche, where she began to snore. He took the chair back to the kitchen and put it precisely in its place. "All right, now the baggage."

They drove through sleet and freezing rain to O'Hare, where Stevens slapped Maureen awake and assisted her into the concourse. He propped her up in a seat and went back for the luggage.

Then he went to the line at the United counter and talked to a young couple. "Excuse me, where are you flying today?"

"San Francisco," said the young man. He was burly, round-faced; the woman had long brown hair.

"Could you possibly help me? My wife and I must be in San Francisco tonight. I would be willing to pay you four thousand dollars for your tickets. Then you could stay in a hotel tonight and get the next flight out tomorrow."

"There won't be any seats tomorrow," said the man, while the woman was saying, *"Four thousand* dollars?"

He gave them the money, took their tickets, and went back for Julie. As Mr. and Mrs. Vern Aalberg, they spent the long flight watching holovision.

One after another, the hopeful gatherings saw dawn come without incident. By twelve o'clock Sydney time, the crowd had still not dispersed. The Europeans gathered in their turn. "Nobody believes the dawn comes earlier to other people than it does to them," remarked the first anchor.

"Why, that's rather poetic, Bill," said number two.

"Well, you know what I mean. Dawn other places is not *authentic*—it doesn't really happen until it happens where you live."

"Then your guess would be that the U.S. celebrations will take place on schedule?"

"Looks like it."

"Let's take a break now, and then we'll be talking to some guests."

There was a series of commercials in 3-D and living color, for Spiritual Makeup, all in grayed tones that made the model look hollow-cheeked, demure, and sexy; for Zip-Eeze, the capsules that turned you instantaneously from a moribund wreck into a dynamic "up person"; and for Radisafe, the miracle of modern science that kept your food fresh indefinitely without freezing.

The anchors appeared again, with a third man sitting opposite them.

"We're back, and we're talking to Dr. Jonas Wentz, the author of a book called *When Crowds Go Mad*. Dr. Wentz, would you say the crowds are going mad?"

"That's correct."

"Well, if there's nothing to the millennial idea, how do you account for the fact that so many people do believe it?"

"Well, that's an interesting question. For a long time it was popularly believed that there was a widespread movement of this kind in the year one thousand. That turns out not to be true. They used Roman numerals then, and there wasn't any particular mystical significance to the letter M. But it did happen at other times, for example there was a group in this country that predicted the end of the world in nineteen forty-nine. Going back a little, the Millerites said it was going to be in eighteen forty-three."

"Why those particular dates?" asked anchor one.

"Well, God knows, if you'll pardon the expression. These movements are always headed by very devout people who have studied the Bible for clues and think they have found them in some numerological way, or else they've had a revelation—angels have given them a message, or God himself, or in some modern cases they get it from a flying saucer."

"What happened to these movements, when the world didn't end when it was supposed to?"

"Well, that's the interesting thing. Almost invariably it was the opposite of what you'd expect. The movement became more fervent, more cohesive and dedicated. They would advance the date, maybe for a year, or six months, and then they'd advance it again, and typically it would be at least a year, more often eighteen months or two years, before the movement finally broke up. Sometimes it never did break up. Miller, for example, was the founder of the Seventh Day Adventist movement, and it's still going strong."

"Now that's hard to believe," said anchor two. "Why would they react that way to a prophecy that didn't come true? I'd think it would be just the opposite."

"Yes, it is surprising. But what seems to happen is that these people have made a strong commitment to the prophecy—neglecting their business, some of them selling their houses, and so on, and they can't afford to give up their belief because they have too much invested in it. It's a little like a gambler who has lost so heavily that he has to keep playing, because that's the only way he'll ever get out of the hole. Then they reinforce each other, and that's an important factor, because if you're surrounded by people who all believe, or profess to believe, in something, it's very much harder not to believe in it yourself. There have been experiments, in fact, where people will doubt the evidence of their own eyes—if everybody says a red rose is orange, they'll agree, yes, it looks orange."

In a town called Sahria in northern New Jersey, Dr. Claude Smeds and his family got into a small plane two hours before dawn and flew to ten thousand feet, where they began to circle over the town. With them were Alicia Wentrow, the secretary of the Universal Truth and Enlightenment Foundation, Bill Truckee, Smeds's bodyguard, and three members of the inner circle. Thirty more believers got aloft in chartered aircraft before dawn.

The Sahrians had been preparing for the new age since the eighties under the direction of Dr. Smeds, who believed that the millennium would be ushered in by earthquakes, tidal waves, and volcanic eruptions. The original plan had been for the whole population of Sahria to go up in helicopters and come down again when the trouble was over, but that had proved impractical because of finances and the weather.

In a field on the outskirts of town, the observer stood beside her dear friends, waiting in Christian patience for the dawn. She had found in this mind a certainty that was utterly lacking in others. How joyous it was, and how she pitied those who had turned away from it! Sleet stung her eyes and flew into her mouth like bullets, but what of that? In a little while she would see the King in His glory. Her heart was buoyed up by rapture, and she thrilled to the sound of the voices around her, feeling the words like sobs of desire in her throat: "With the cross of Jesus going on before . . ."

Do violence to no man.

—LUKE 3:14

14 In San Francisco they went to a hotel. "Don't unpack," said Stevens, "we will be leaving again in the morning."

"Where to?"

"I don't know yet. Where would you like to go?"

"What's wrong with right here?"

"Maybe nothing, but I think it would be better for us to be in another country now."

"John, I won't have my baby in a foreign country."

"The medical care in Sweden is better than here."

"Do you want to go to Sweden?"

"Not particularly, but there are other places. In almost any major city you can expect to get good medical care; you can even find an English-speaking gynecologist if you prefer. See if you can get an atlas on the computer."

That evening on the holo they watched William S. Bronson talking about L-5. Bronson was a small, unassuming man in his late fifties whose eyes flickered upward after he was asked a question. America was taking the first giant step toward its glorious future in space, he said.

The L-5 colonies would provide a new environment for human beings; they would mine asteroids, manufacture zero-g products which could not be made on Earth, harness the energy of the Sun. Then a Boeing commercial.

"This is the most dangerous time for us," Stevens said. "Contracts are being let now for construction of the first L-5 colony, and there are billions of dollars involved; later it will be trillions. Any connection now between Newland's death and L-5 would jeopardize their investment. Later on it won't matter, but just now, if I were in their place, I know what I would be doing."

He knew, in fact, the identities of the agents who were most likely to be searching for him: There was Bruno, with whom he had worked in the successful attempt on an Italian cabinet minister's life, and Carl, who had been his control in Lebanon, and a woman known as Erika with whom he had been associated in the eighties. He knew how their minds worked, and he knew what methods they would be using. Through subordinates and intermediaries, they would be patiently sifting public records and newspapers, monitoring holovision broadcasts, looking for a face in a crowd. It was not at all unlikely that by now they had discovered the connection between himself and Julie, and in that case her disappearance in October would have been a red flag to them.

They left the next day for Australia. Julie bore her child in Adelaide: it was a girl who looked at Stevens through the glass with a calm expression. He loved her instantly.

The Steering Committee of the Evanston chapter of the Faith Ministry of Evangelical Churches consisted of the Reverend Arthur Hembert of the Church of the Word, the Reverend Lionel Winning of the Apostolic Healing Church, the Reverend Paul Goodhew of the Eastern Baptists, and two laymen, R. T. Fawson and Dick LeDoux. They met early in the evening in Pastor Winning's parlor, after a few hours of sleep. They greeted each other affectionately, clasping hands and pressing arms.

When they were settled around the holo, Pastor Winning said, "Friends, I know we've all prayed for guidance, and I know God is going to show us the way. I'd like to suggest that we pray again, here together, but"—he looked at his watch—"it's just about time for Jimmy's Evening Hour, so let's be sure not to miss any of that. Paul, you're the nearest, would you turn on the holo?"

The screen bloomed to life to the words, "And now—Jimmy Gill!"

A lonely figure standing on the podium, surrounded by a wildly applauding audience. The camera zoomed nearer; the careworn face swelled larger and rounder than life.

"Friends," said Gill, "I know some of you tonight are saying, 'Why has God forsaken us? Why didn't he come at dawn the way we thought he would? What's wrong?' And friends, I'm not ashamed to say that I've been asking those questions too. I prayed from the darkness of my soul, I prayed on my knees, and in the stillness I heard a voice. I heard God speaking to me, and he said, 'Jimmy, have you so little faith?' And I answered, 'No, Lord, I believe, but my understanding is so limited. I know we made a mistake about the day and hour of your Coming, but I don't know why. I need your help, Lord.' And God said, 'Jimmy, remember, Rome burns.'

"And then his voice was gone. And I said to myself, Rome burns? That might mean Rome is going to burn, just a part of the tribulation that we know is coming, just the way Tel Aviv burned and Hiroshima burned, and all the great cities of the world are going to burn, but then why did God say 'Rome'? And I prayed for guidance, friends, and then something seemed to tell me, Go and look at your Bible history. And I went and took down that book from the shelf, my friends, and it *fell open in my hands* to a list of things that happened in New Testament times after the ministry of Our Lord Jesus Christ. And do you know what I found there?"

The camera moved closer. "I found two great events on that list, my friends, the destruction of Jerusalem on July the first, sixty-nine A.D., and the burning of Rome on July the nineteenth, sixty-four A.D. And those are the only events on that list where we not only know the year when they happened but we know the *month* and *day*. And then I saw what God had been trying to tell me, and I fell down on my knees again and thanked him. God was telling me in his own way, 'Jimmy, you did your best, but you don't understand my ways and you don't know the secrets of my heart. You thought the first day of the first month of the year two thousand was the appointed day of my Coming. And that might have been the day and hour you would have picked, but it isn't the one I chose for my own good reasons. And the first thing I want you to do, Jimmy, is to fall on your knees and repent of your presumption and pride,' and I said, 'I repent, Lord, from the bottom of my heart,' and then he said, 'Because you are sincerely repentant, I'm going to give you another chance, and that's why I told you what I did.' And then his voice was gone. And I got up off my knees, and I knew God was telling me a mystery in a parable, and it was up to me to figure out the mystery of that parable. And this is what came to me, in a blinding flash of inspiration! God said, 'Rome burns.' And we know that is so, Rome is going to burn, but that isn't all he meant. He meant, Rome burned before, and you know the day and hour of that burning. God was telling me the answer. July the nineteenth! That's the month and the day when he will come in his glory! And the tears streamed down my face, and I said, 'Thank you, Lord! Thank you, Lord! Thank you!'"

And the voices in the auditorium swelled to a chorus: "Thank you! Thank you, Lord, thank you!"

When the broadcast was over, Goodhew turned off the set, and Pastor Winning said, "Friends, I knew we could count on Jimmy! What a wonderful answer he gave us!"

"Wonderful!" said Paul Goodhew, and R. T. Fawson, and Pastor Hembert. Only Dick LeDoux said nothing. "Dick," said Winning, bending toward him tenderly, "I know how ill you were just a week or so ago, but won't you tell us what you think?"

LeDoux was silent for a moment. Then he said, "I think it's hooey."

The more she learned of this strange world, the more frightened she became. The host population was being pressed toward disaster by overbreeding; already there were mass deaths from starvation and disease. The surface of the planet was being destroyed by deforestation; the Brazilian Desert was growing, and the air was so thin in Denver that the airports and hotels had begun providing oxygen tanks for visitors.

What was to be done? Whatever it was, it must be done quickly, or the human population would die out; and it might be millions of years before any other organism half so interesting and delightful as *Homo sapiens* became available for her use.

At a lingerie counter she stopped and smiled at the clerk, a slender, fresh-faced young woman. Something about her was attractive; she slipped out and across the fuzzy gray space and in again, watching the other woman's body fall. Her name was Norah Robbins, her husband's name was Jon, they had been married for six months. Under her shock and concern as she knelt beside the other woman's body was the memory of the calendar she kept in her bureau drawer. She had been counting the days, and she knew this was her fertile period. And she was thinking how much she wanted a child, and that now that Jon had had a raise they could afford to have one, and how much she ached for him, how hard it was to get through the day.

She stayed in the young woman through the rest of her workday, the ride home on the bus, dinner, holovision. Then at last the two of them were in bed. The husband was clumsy and brief, but at the moment of his ejaculation she was englobed around the egg and she saw in that glittering microscopic vision the frantic flight of the sperms with their lashing tails, the softening of the egg wall before one of them, the rejection of the rest; and as the fulfilled sperm sank deeper to its death and rebirth, she felt herself divide, saw the spark of her daughter take its place inside the egg.

Because she could not risk the life of the mother, she stayed where she was and sank into unconsciousness with Norah; only in the morning, after the woman had gone to work, did she leave for another host, and then she chose a friend of Norah's, also recently married. Her name was Sherri, but she did not want children yet.

The next woman was a disappointment, too, and the

next. She went through other hosts, driven by curiosity, but always came back to young women. After a month she found another and gave birth again.

Mike Smith was a part-time student at the University of Washington. He had intended to get a B.S. in chemistry, but the math was too much for him, and he switched to communications. He bussed tables for a living, traded a little dope, and lived by himself. One late evening in March he ate a Radisafe snack in his room, drank some beer, watched TV for a couple of hours. Then he felt restless, and he knew what was the matter, but he paced up and down awhile, looking at the closet, before he gave in and got the ski mask off the top shelf. Feeling a prickle of excitement, he put the mask in one pocket of his pea jacket, the glass cutter and knife in the other, and went down the stairs.

Two blocks away was a residential complex used mostly by students. Two days ago Mike had seen a girl going up the stairway and noticed which door she went into. She was small, slender, with long mouse-brown hair.

It was about twelve-thirty now, and there was a brisk wind blowing around the corner. He climbed the outside stairs slowly, as if he belonged there. There was nobody on the balconies. Number thirty-nine was dark, and so were the apartments on either side. New Rock reverberated from somewhere on an upper floor: Lenny Wicks, "Tell It to Somebody That Gives a Fuck." Mike leaned against the living room window with the glass cutter in his hand and scribed a semicircle on the right side of the pane. He tapped it until it fell inside, reached in and opened the window.

One quick glance around, then he put the ski mask on and stepped inside, pushing the venetian blinds gently out of the way and letting them back easy so they wouldn't rattle. He could make out the dim glow of a wall, and dark shapes of furniture. As his eyes adjusted he could see the kitchenette alcove and a door on the other side. These places were all laid out pretty much alike. He moved to the bedroom door, got his knife in his hand, turned the knob.

He could tell she was there. He closed the door behind him and found the light switch on the wall.

She was lying face down with one arm outside the covers. Her mouth was childishly puffed; strands of hair covered her face.

Mike walked over to the bed, got hold of the covers with his free hand and snapped them back. She lay there in a short blue nightdress that was rucked up around her hips. Her eyes blinked open, squinted; then she flipped over and scrambled back against the headboard. Mike sat beside her and got one hand in her hair. "Don't scream," he said, showing her the knife. "You scream, I cut your throat."

She was white as a sheet; her lips were trembling. No problem. He straddled her and reached for his zipper. He felt the thick excitement in his throat, the pounding heartbeat, and as he gestured with the knife he slipped out, across the gray space and was in again, feeling the young woman's choking fear and watching incredulously as the man's body fell across her.

Vera Petracki left her hospital room early in the morning, as she usually did, wearing two unbuttoned sweaters, one on backwards, shoes without socks, and a pair of dirty red lace underpants. The first person she saw in the white corridor was Mrs. Moskovich, who was in a wheelchair. Petracki walked up to her and said in a loud voice, "You ought to be ashamed of yourself!" Mrs.

Moskovich turned her head away. Petracki said, "You eat that junk food and poison everybody!" There was a bluish halo around Mrs. Moskovich's head: that was from the hair rinse she used, that made her brain radioactive. "Grow up!" said Petracki. Mrs. Moskovich did not reply.

The orderly came toward her, the one she called Bruce the Goose, a musclebound man whose arms stuck out at an angle. "Vera, cut it out now," he said.

"Yeah, who's going to make me?" Petracki pulled down her underpants and thrust herself toward him. "Grow up, grow up!" she shouted. Bruce looked at her with a patient stare that suddenly turned meaningless. His eyes rolled up, his knees folded, and then he was on the floor. Mrs. Moskovich shrieked. A nurse came hurrying around the corner. "You see what happens?" Petracki yelled. "You all eat shit! That's why you're crazy! How many times do I have to tell you? Fooey, fooey, fooey!" She felt herself getting bigger like a balloon; her eyes bugged and she stuck her tongue out.

When she woke up, she was in bed behind a screen, and it took her a while to remember where she was. "Nurse!" she called.

After a while a nurse pulled the screen aside and came in. "Awake, are you?" She picked up Petracki's wrist and held it, looking at her watch.

"What did I do?" Petracki asked. Her voice sounded thin and weak.

"What *didn't* you do? You screamed at Mrs. Moskovich, and then you hit Mr. Sheldon and knocked him cold." She dropped Petracki's wrist.

"No." Petracki swallowed. "I mean—never mind." What she meant was, why had she done all that? It was wrong about knocking out Bruce Sheldon, she couldn't have, but she had yelled at people and taken off her underpants, and pissed on the floor and a lot of other things, but why? She remembered being okay for a while, in her own apartment in Queens, and other times when she had been okay for a while. Before that there had been a time when she was studying violin at the Academy of Music. What had happened? She had been crazy, that was what.

The nurse had gone away. After a while she came back with an attendant, not Bruce but little Larry the Fairy. "Doctor says you can go back to your room now if you behave yourself," said the nurse. Larry pushed up a wheelchair and they got her into it. She felt all right, but hungry. "Can I have something to eat?"

"You missed dinner. After you get dressed, you can get something from the snack machine." They wheeled her down the corridor past Mrs. Moskovich.

"Mrs. Moskovich, I'm sorry," Petracki said. Mrs. Moskovich smiled and said, "That's all right, dear, whatever it is." It was the first time Petracki had ever heard her speak.

At the staff meeting next week, Dr. Abramowitz said, "First it was Petracki, then Moskovich, then Oliphant, DiLorenzo, Smeale, and Cantor, all in the women's wing. Then, in the men's, we had Brown, Zawicky, Gomez, Neumeyer, J. Cohen and R. Cohen, Wernham, and Frode. All of them collapsed for about eight hours, and so did four staff members. When they came out of it, all of them but Mr. Frode were rational. Six of them are already discharged, and it looks like the rest of them will be."

"What was the diagnosis on Frode?"

"Senile dementia."

"And the rest?"

"All over the lot. Paranoid schitz, manic depressive,

personality disorders. Moskovich started talking for the first time in four years. Neumeyer quit touching the doorframes. And so on, right down the line. By the middle of next week, we're going to have thirteen empty beds."

There was a thoughtful silence. "These symptoms, the serial attacks, the eight hours' stupor, it sounds to me like McNulty's Disease," said Dr. Walter.

"I can't believe that," answered Dr. Abramowitz. "What are you saying, that a virus *cured* thirteen people?"

15 In the Republican primary that year, Senator Draffy of California was pitted against the liberal ex-governor of Vermont, George Atkin. Senator Draffy, a born-again Christian and a spellbinding orator, ran on a platform of increased military spending, expansion of the L-5 program, and a constitutional amendment to declare abortion a capital offense. In a memorable speech to the Republican Convention he said, "These nay-sayers, these prophets of gloom and doom, I'm sorry for them. I really am. They are so afraid that they want you to be afraid. They're afraid to face up to the fact that we have a glorious future. And you know what? To keep us from getting there, they'd be willing to put every one of us under a total dictatorship, a government that would tell every one of us how many children we could have, and not only that but enforce it! How would they enforce it? Well, how do you think? By *forced* *abortions,* the way they've done it in Communist China for the last twenty years. Or if you sneak around and have the kid anyway, well, they can put that child to death. They can kill *you.* Why not? That would reduce the population. And that kind of government, with that kind of power, believe me, my friends, they won't only be telling you how many kids you can have, they'll tell you where you can live and how much money you can make and what you can read and what you can *think.* Because that's the specter of international world totalitarian Communism that's been hanging over us for a century. That's what they really want, those pitiful little cowards, make no mistake about it. They want to put an end to freedom in the world; they want to put you and your children under the Communist yoke unto the thousandth generation. Well, I'm here to tell you, they're not gonna do it. You know why?" Shouts, screams. "Because you and I, we're not gonna *let* them do it!"

Draffy was nominated, and he was elected by a wide margin in November.

Dr. Owen kept on collecting reports on McNulty's Disease and feeding them into her computer. In February there were reports from London, then Paris, Frankfurt, Oslo. In March cases were reported from Brazil, Colombia, and Peru. In April it had jumped to Europe again—Poland, Yugoslavia, Romania, and Hungary. Then there were no more reports for two months.

In late June the epidemic reappeared in India, then Sri Lanka and Indonesia. In July there were reports from Egypt, Israel, and South Africa. By the end of the month, there were about five hundred known cases.

The question was, where had it been in May and June? Owen thought she knew—China and the Soviet

Union, which did not report to any agency outside their borders.

Early one morning in March, 2001, although Dr. Owen had a mountain of work on her desk, she called up the McNulty's file and charted it. What she saw made her request an appointment with Milton Chalmers, the Executive Director. "He's got a full day lined up," said Chalmers' secretary. "Will it keep until Monday?"

"No, I don't think it will. Tell him it's about McNulty's Disease, and I need ten minutes."

"Okay, Harriet, I'll get back to you."

Chalmers saw her at twelve-thirteen. He was sitting behind his desk, looking tired, unwrapping an Egz sandwich. "Come in, Harriet," he said. "Sit down. You want some coffee?"

"No, thanks. Milt, I have some data on McNulty's that I want to show you. Here's the slip." Chalmers took it, glanced at it, and fed it into the reader. His desk screen lighted up.

Dr. Owen leaned over the desk to point. "This is a chart of total cases as a function of time. You see the curve is linear for the first eight months. Then there's a flexion, and another one at nine months, and again at ten and twelve and thirteen. Once the flexions smooth out, the extrapolated curve shows a doubling rate of just under four months."

"Interesting," said Chalmers with his mouth full. He swallowed and took another bite. His eyes were bloodshot and dull. "How do you interpret it, Harriet?"

"Well, it's obviously a growth curve. Look at the projection. If we don't stop this thing, it will saturate the population in seven and a half years."

Chalmers peered at the screen over his coffee cup. "Why eight months linear, though?"

"I don't know. If it was nine, I'd say pregnancy—it's reproducing in women. But there are the figures."

"Um-hm. What do you want to do?"

"I think we should isolate this thing—quarantine it while we can. If we don't do it soon, we'll never stop it."

Chalmers took another bite of his sandwich, chewed it slowly. "Thing is benign," he said.

"What?"

Chalmers swallowed. "The thing is benign. No pathology. Isn't that what you told me before? So what if it does saturate the population?"

"We don't *know* it's benign. We do know there have been some very disturbing personality changes in recovered patients. What if there are other things, five or ten years down the road, that are crippling or fatal?"

"Harriet," said Chalmers, "we've got runaway pandemics of typhus, plague, viral pneumonia, and malaria."

"I know that."

"We don't *need* another disease that may or may not be life-threatening."

"Milt, I want you to buck it up to the Department of Health and get them to endorse a recommendation to the UN." She took the slip out of the reader and put it in her pocket.

"You want a quarantine of all the recovered patients, right? and everybody who knows them? That's what it would take."

"That's right."

"And then what? Isn't this the thing where the only way they could get rid of it was to make it infect a goat?"

"We have other options."

"It'll never fly, Harriet. I'd help you if I could, but Health would laugh in my face. Even if they didn't, it would take them a year to get a program like that organized. I'm sorry, Harriet—you may be right, but we just haven't got the resources and we haven't got the time."

He started to say something else, then fell back in the chair. His jaw hung loose; his eyes were half-open, but he did not seem to see her.

Owen stabbed the intercom. "Nellie, call an ambulance and then get in here. It's Dr. Chalmers."

Chalmers was breathing shallowly. Owen pulled up his eyelids to look at his pupils, then took his pulse. When the secretary came in, she had opened his blouse and was using a rolled-up piece of paper as an improvised stethoscope.

The secretary was pale. "Oh, dear, what's the matter with him?"

"Too soon to tell. I don't think it's his heart, and it isn't hypoglycemic shock. Has he had any medical problems recently?"

"No, I'm sure not. He's terribly overworked."

"Who isn't?"

The ambulance attendants came with a collapsible stretcher and wheeled Chalmers away. Then Warner Lansky appeared, and then two other administrators from nearby offices, and Owen was busy answering questions, mostly with "I don't know."

Only when she got back to her own office and closed the door did she let herself think about what she really did know. It was McNulty's Disease, sure as death.

She called the hospital Saturday morning and learned that Chalmers had been released after eight hours of stupor.

She could not bear the knowledge that the parasite was in her brain, reading her thoughts, knowing whatever she knew. Nevertheless, irrationally, she stayed in her apartment all that day and the next, trying to put off her own collapse as long as possible.

On Monday morning she went to work as usual, and woke up in the hospital that night.

On Tuesday, as soon as she got home, she took her professional career in her hands and called everyone she knew in Washington. She pulled some strings, but could not even get an interview with anyone in the upper echelons of the Department of Health. As Chalmers had warned her, they had other things on their minds. Deaths from plague were mounting toward the twenty-million mark. Other millions were dying from typhus, viral pneumonia, malaria, and starvation. The world growth adjustment deepened. Unemployment, in spite of the booming aerospace industry, stood at twenty percent in the United States.

"Well, Harriet," Chalmers said the next time she saw him, "any changes in your personality?"

"Not that I'm aware of."

"No impulses to get married and run off to Brazil?"

"No."

"Me either. I guess we'll just have to keep on with the same old dull stuff."

Owen smiled, but she was inwardly furious. No matter that she could not detect any changes in herself: that almost made it worse. She felt invaded, polluted, as if someone had been inside her with a dirty glove. Now, more than ever, she knew that the parasite had to be destroyed.

Theft is a way of distributing income. Another way is
the Kwakiutl potlatch. Charity is another way, and
welfare is another. Without some such system those
who work hard will have plenty and the rest will starve.
See, for example, the elaborate methods of dividing the
catch among Eskimos. To let people starve would make
the clan and tribe impossible and would also reduce the
numbers so much in every generation that the group
would probably decline to extinction. Even lionesses
feed their nonworking spouses.

—JAN ERIC MUHLHAUSER

16 Julie cannot nurse the child; we are using a formula called Lactil, which comes in cans like Australian beer and has to be poured into sterilized bottles, the bottles covered with plastic nipples, and the temperature of the formula tested by dropping it onto the wrist. All this I have learned to do. The busy mouth works at the nipple while the brown eyes stare at me with such calm intensity that I can only believe there is a person inside, silent and watchful, a ghost in the machine.

What do elephants talk about in the darkness of the night, when they call back and forth to each other, pitching their dialogue too low for human ears?

Beginning in the last month of pregnancy, unborn children have rapid eye movements, meaning that they dream. What do they dream about?

In order to disappear successfully, Stevens believed, one had to follow three rules: not to return to any place where one had lived before, not to have any contact with persons one had known, and not to follow any profession or engage in any leisure activity one was known to prefer. Many fugitives had changed their location, their names and appearance, but had been caught in the end because they would not give up their bowling or stamp-collecting. He had chosen Chicago and then Adelaide precisely because neither was a place where he had ever gone or wanted to go. He had given up skiing and swimming, his only physical recreations, in favor of a gym in the basement which served to keep him in condition without affording him any satisfaction. He still went to bookstores occasionally, because he could not accept a life without reading, but he did it in the full knowledge that he was taking a foolish risk.

Stevens had clearly foreseen the vacuum that would be created in his life when he gave up his profession. His savings, moreover, would not last forever, even with prudent investment; he had to have an income, and he needed some activity.

One day Julie found him assembling a circuit with a clip-on electronics kit he had bought from an Infonet vendor. "What's that for?" she asked.

"I thought Kimberly might like it."

"You idiot, she's only a year old."

"Yes, but later she will be older."

Stevens put the elements together into an intricate circuit that, as far as he could tell, did not do anything in particular. Then he looked up a custom cabinet fabricator in Infonet, sent them dimensions, and asked for fifteen designs.

Each box was distinctive in shape and color. The one he chose for his first attempt was a flat winged form eighteen inches long, dusky red-violet, with a pleasing matte surface. In the box, along with the circuit and a battery, he put a transformer case full of violet sachet. Having told Julie that he had some business affairs to take care of, he put the box in a briefcase along with some documents, drove to the airport, and took an afternoon flight to Perth. There he rented a car and drove down a potholed superhighway past a dozen motels, all with bright "Vacancy" signs. He checked in to one that looked as if it had recently seen better days. When he signed the card, under "Representing" he filled in "Gentronics, Inc."

In the morning the coffee shop was almost empty. Stevens went back to his room for his bag and briefcase and carried them to the desk. "I hope you've enjoyed your stay, Mr. Hughes," said the manager. The nameplate on the desk proclaimed him to be Henry Wellfinger.

"I have, indeed. You run a very nice operation here—it's a pity business conditions are so bad."

Wellfinger tried to look cheerful. "Well, you know, people just aren't traveling as much."

"What's your daily occupancy, if I may ask?"

"Far below what it ought to be. We haven't had a good month since last September."

"Are you the owner of this motel, Mr. Wellfinger?"

"Yes, sir, every brick and stone. Why, would you like to buy it?"

"No, but—" Stevens hesitated. "Look, I really shouldn't say this, but I have something that might help you."

A wary look came into the manager's eye. "What's that?"

"Something new." Stevens glanced around. "Can we go in your office for a minute?"

"Yes, I suppose."

Stevens opened his briefcase and showed him the eagle-shaped box. "This is a pheromone generator. I don't know if you've heard about pheromones?"

"Can't say that I have."

Stevens opened the back of the box, gave Wellfinger a glimpse of the circuitry, turned the switch to "on," and closed the box again. "You know that certain animals can find each other over long distances by means of scent particles, even in very low concentrations." The manager nodded. He put out his hand to touch the matte surface of the box.

"Well, what most people don't know is that human beings respond to pheromones too. This device generates those particles. It ought to be warming up now—smell it?"

Wellfinger leaned over and sniffed. "Yes, I think so. It's very faint."

"That's right, and a few hundred feet away you won't even know you're smelling it, but it will affect you just the same. It's an attractive scent, by which I mean that it literally attracts people to the source. Imagine you're driving down the street looking for a place to stop. All the motels are different, and you can't make up your mind. Suddenly you pass a motel that has this box attached to the outside wall. You turn in there, and you don't know why."

"And it really works?"

"Absolutely. It was developed by the top scientists at Gentronics and it has undergone a year's testing in the laboratory."

"You say testing in the laboratory. I expect that means you don't know if it will work in practice."

Stevens gave him an approving nod. "There you have it. That's why we are signing up a few selected motels as test sites. You agree to put the device on the outside wall where the pheromones can diffuse to the street, for a period of one week, and to make your occupancy records available to us." He managed to look embarrassed. "We really are supposed to place these in larger establishments, but I was tired last night. This is my last one, and frankly I want to go home."

"What'd something like this cost me?"

"Nothing. It doesn't cost anything. If your occupancy records show an increase of ten percent or more during the week, then we owe each other nothing. If they don't, we pay you a thousand dollars for your cooperation."

The manager licked his lips. "Can I have that in writing?"

"Absolutely." Stevens took a contract from the briefcase and spread it out. "You see here, notarized occupancy records, installation—that just means you have to put it where we suggest and maintain it in operation—and here's the agreed payment."

"Well, I mean, what can I lose?" the manager said.

Stevens went outside to show him where the pheromone device should be installed, just to the right of the entrance, seven feet high. It would look very handsome there, the manager agreed.

Stevens drove back to the airport, parked his car, and walked over to the terminal, where a cabdriver was just pulling in with a fare. Stevens waited patiently until the driver had unloaded the bags, and the passengers had boarded the people mover into the terminal.

The driver turned to him. "Taxi?"

"Not just now." Stevens said. "Would you like to make a hundred dollars?"

"Yeah, I'd like that. What do I have to do for it?"

"Take your customers to the Wayland Motel. You know where it is?"

"Sure."

"What time do you get off?"

"Two in the bloody morning."

Stevens handed him a bill. "I'm driving a green Minolta. Meet me here in the temporary parking lot at two and show me your printout. I'll give you one hundred dollars for every party you take to the Wayland between now and then."

Stevens walked down the row and made the same offer to three other drivers. When four more pulled up, he added them to the list. Then he checked in to the airport motel, had dinner, talked to Julie on the phone, and read *The Way of All Flesh* until one-thirty.

When the time came, he went down to the parking lot and sat in his car with the dome light on. One by one the cabdrivers came to collect their pay. Among them, they had delivered a total of twelve customers. Stevens renewed the offer for the following night.

About ten o'clock the next morning he drove into town and investigated its attractions. There was a Historical and Art Museum. He spent an hour there, had lunch in an Albanian restaurant, browsed in bookstores, and went to a holo. Then dinner and another phone call to Julie. That night he paid out fifteen hundred dollars to his drivers.

By the end of the week he had spent a little over nine thousand dollars in payments, plus two thousand for airfare, car rental, motel, food and entertainment, for a total of eleven thousand one hundred. The box itself, with its contents, had cost him seven hundred and fifty dollars.

On Friday, for the sake of plausibility, he waited for

the afternoon flight from Adelaide, then drove to the Wayland Motel. Wellfinger greeted him effusively.

"Well, Mr. Wellfinger, was the trial satisfactory?"

"Satisfactory! Not the word. It was everything you claimed. In fact—I'll have to get the figures, but I'd say we picked up more than twenty percent."

"I'm glad to hear it. Let's look at the figures, then, Mr. Wellfinger, and meanwhile, if you would, you can get someone started taking the device down."

They went into Wellfinger's office. "Look, I wanted to talk to you about that. Are you going to lease these things, or sell them, or what?"

"They're not on the market at present, I'm sorry to say. You understand, we have to evaluate the results of our field tests."

"Oh. Well, if there was some way— You know, I really hate to give it up, tell you the truth."

"I understand, of course. I'd like to help you if I could, Mr. Wellfinger."

They settled on one hundred and twenty-five thousand dollars, which represented approximately twenty weeks' additional motel revenues at the present rate. Stevens' profit for the week came to just over one hundred and thirteen thousand dollars. He got a certified check, cashed it, and flew home to Adelaide.

17 Kim had her own childish mispronunciations of certain words; Julie thought this charming, but John was determined to teach her to speak correctly. "Pass the sowse," she said one day at dinner.

"The sauce," said Stevens.

"Pass the sowse."

Julie said, trying not to laugh, "Pass the sowse, *please.*"

"If you don't mind," John said, "this is serious. Kim, who is the boss here, you or I?"

"I'm the boss," Kim said.

"Very well, 'sauce' rhymes with 'boss.' If you ask for the sauce, you're the boss."

Kim looked at him with a glint of something in her eye. "Pass the sauce," she said. Then: *"Sauce, sauce, sauce!* Now are you satsified?"

Later on, every appearance of sauce at the table provoked a cry of "I'm the boss, you're the sauce!" followed by maniacal laughter. Stevens tolerated this for the sake of the good pronunciation, but it got on Julie's nerves. "No singing at the table," she told Kim.

"I'm not *sing*ing," she caroled—G, E, A, E.

"We are spoiling her," Stevens said to Julie that night. "She needs some discipline."

"I don't believe in spanking children."

"Nor do I, but one can take away her privileges, or make her sit in the corner."

"John, nobody has made children sit in the corner for thirty years. Yes, she's spoiled, but she knows we love her and that's why she can get away with it."

Stevens traveled once or twice a month to widely separated places, working one variation or another of his pheromone device. When at last he gave in to Julie's curiosity and told her what he was doing, she was horrified.

"You're cheating those people out of their savings! How could you even think of such a thing?"

"They would have lost their savings anyway," Stevens said. "You may have noticed that we are in the worst worldwide growth adjustment since the nineteen thirties. Things are going to be much worse before they are better. Some of us will survive and some will not. I intend that we will survive."

"But do you have to rob people?"

"Julie, how did your father get his money?"

"He worked for it!"

"Yes, but how did he work for it?"

She cupped her elbows in her hands in a way he knew. "He was the art director for General Motors in France."

"Yes, and he helped design the advertising that persuaded people to buy unsafe, overpowered, and over-priced automobiles, against the competing claims of cars that were safer and cheaper?"

"That's business."

"Of course it's business, but business is robbery. It is legal robbery, and what I do is not legal; that's the difference. You think I condemn your father, but I don't; I honor him."

After a moment he said, "Tell me the truth, Julie. If

you had a choice of robbing someone or seeing your child starve, which would you prefer?"

She turned to him. "You know all the answers, don't you?"

"No, not all, but I know this one. And so do you."

John Arthur Draffy, like two of his illustrious predecessors, had come to the White House from the rough and tumble of California politics. Draffy was a man of strong simple opinions, which he knew were the same opinions held by the vast majority of his compatriots. He knew in his heart not only that America was the greatest country in the world, but that the Christian religion and the free enterprise system had made it that way. He believed these things sincerely, and his sincerity was his strength.

Early in Draffy's third year in office, one day he woke up feeling fuzzy and disoriented. He knew immediately that something had happened—he didn't know what, but it was not something he was going to like.

When he opened his eyes, he saw the faces of a nurse in a white cap and Oliver Grummond, his personal physician. "What's the matter with me?" he said, and tried to get up.

Grummond's firm hand pressed him back. "You've just had a period of unconsciousness. You're all right now, but rest a minute."

Draffy tried to remember. He had been in the Oval Office with Dick Merritt and McDonald Ferguson, talking about the farm bill. Then nothing, a blank.

"What time is it?"

"It's a little after one. You were out for nine hours."

The nurse was pulling some wires away from his chest. "Oh, my God," he said. He remembered now, the day before, what was that, Wednesday? when that photographer had slumped to the ground in the Rose Garden. "It isn't McNulty's, is it?"

"We don't know for certain. Looks like it might be."

The nurse brought him a glass of orange juice with a plastic straw, and helped him to sit up. "How do you feel?"

"I feel fine, God dammit." He saw that he was wearing hospital pajamas, open in the front. There was a monitor behind the head of the bed, with flat red lines going across it. "Somebody get me my clothes. Where's Larry? Where's Buz?"

"They're waiting outside, and so is Elsie. But I want you to drink that juice and have some broth first."

"No, dammit, now."

The nurse brought his clothes and laid them on the bed. "That's all, nurse, thank you." She lowered her eyes and went away. In a minute Elsie came in, followed by Larry Winkler and Buz Genung. "Oh, honey," said his wife, embracing him, "I'm so glad you're all right."

"You call this all right?" Draffy disengaged himself and spoke to Winkler. "What have you told the press?"

"Just that you were taken suddenly ill. No details, Chief, and we've got until tomorrow morning to get our act together."

"Okay." Draffy looked at Grummond. "What's our deniability?"

"Not good. The symptoms are consistent with McNulty's, and the press already knows you may have been infected day before yesterday."

"Larry, what do you think?"

"I'd say bite the bullet. Number one, if we say it isn't McNulty's, what are we going to say it was? Either we have some other explanation, or else you've had some unexplained illness that might be *worse*. Then we get speculations about your health and so forth that could go on forever. This way, it's McNulty's and it's over."

"Buz?"

"I agree, Chief. Up front is best. Quentin has a statement roughed out for you to look at. Essentially, just, the President suffered no ill effects from an episode of McNulty's Disease, and Dr. Grummond says he's fit as a fiddle."

"Am I, Doc?"

"Probably. Drink your orange juice."

"Okay."

Dressed, in the Oval Office, he had a skull session with Larry and Buz at one-thirty. "Let's look at the long-range implications," said Buz. "I'd say they're minimal. This is a nothing sickness, it doesn't affect your health or capacity in any way. Reagan had cancer, and Franklin Delano Roosevelt had polio, for Christ's sake."

"Polio doesn't affect your mind," said Draffy.

"No, well, maybe McNulty's doesn't either."

"That's not what the public thinks. Look at that holo actor, the one that socked his producer, divorced his wife, and said he was through with this country. This damn thing is a time bomb. I could wake up in six weeks feeling good about Communism."

They laughed. "That I'll believe some other time," said Buz. "All right, let's see if we can defuse any problems there are. What are our options? We might have an interview where you come to the support of Senator Wilkes and the rest of them who've had McNulty's—there's about seven in the House, I think, is that right, Larry?"

"Eight. Bergreen, Simmons, Swangard, Onstad, DuPriest, Buchanan, Dukemenier, Mundall."

"Five of those are Democrats," said Draffy. "That's no good, Buz. What if I put my arms around those guys and they turn out weird? You know what that says? I'm weird too."

"Well—" Buz began.

"No. We're going to go just the other way. A national campaign against McNulty's. The angle will be, I was exposed but I avoided any bad effects, et cetera. Other people, not so fortunate." Larry was taking notes. "That way I'm like a cancer victim that wants to wipe out cancer, get it?—not a cancer victim that says cancer is *okay*. And if those bastards turn out weird and lose the next election, I'll say how sorry I am."

"That's brilliant, Chief," said Larry.

"Terrific, Chief."

"There's another thing. Buz, you remember that Project Phoenix we talked about? In the Top Secret file."

"It never came to anything."

"No, but remember, it was a biological weapon, supposed to reduce the birthrate in the Soviet Union."

"They never got anywhere with it."

"No, but dammit, it was a *disease*. How do we know this isn't the same thing? Maybe the Soviets have got ahead of us. Trying to sap our strength. If they are, we've got to catch up, find out how they did it, and how we can do it too."

"Jesus," said Larry. His eyes were shining.

Harriet Owen made six fruitless trips to Washington between 2001 and 2003. On the seventh trip she hit pay dirt: at a cocktail party in Georgetown, she fell into

conversation with an assistant secretary of Peace, How-
ard Metolius, whose mother at the age of fifty-six had left
her husband of thirty years and gone off to Venezuela
with a musician.

"It was like a kind of insanity," Metolius told her. "It
shattered Dad—he never did recover. When he died, the
last thing he said to me was, 'Tell Beth I still love her.'"

Owen canceled her flight back to Atlanta; she met
Metolius the next day and they talked for five hours.

"It's already too late for a quarantine," she told him.
"That would have been the best thing, but we weren't
quick enough. All right, the next best thing is a full-scale
research program. We need to find out what long-term
effect this thing has. We need to find ways of identifying
active hosts, and we need to find ways of inactivating or
destroying the parasite itself. It isn't too late for that, but
it's getting later all the time."

Then they began to discuss strategy. "I know you
think Health would be more appropriate for this,"
Metolius said, "and I understand that, but in fact Peace is
the way to go. For one thing, we're talking about a
suspension of civil liberties. Health could propose that,
but they never would. Second, I can tell you in confidence
that the President thinks McNulty's may be a Soviet
weapon."

"That isn't possible."

"Well, who knows if it's possible or not? The point is,
the President thinks it is. Believe me, if you want this
project, this is the way to get it."

Two days later she had an interview with the Secretary, who listened to her sympathetically and asked her to
draw up a proposal for a research program. "Don't worry
about cost," he said.

18 After he delivered his fare to the hospital (twenty-one fifty, and the company would have to sue to get it) the cabdriver reached for a cigarette, found only an empty pack. He crumpled it one-handed, stuffed it in his pocket. "Car thirty-one, your fare okay?" the dispatcher's voice asked.

"I don't know. They carried him in on a dolly."

"Okay. Fourth and Oak, a man at Wolfe's Book Store."

"After I take a leak."

That was an excuse, there was a rule about smoking in the cabs, but now that he had mentioned it he did have to go. Cigarettes first. He pulled over into the visitors' lot, left the cab and walked into the emergency entrance. Down the hall into the lobby. The gift shop was right across from the information desk. "You got a pack of Flames, sultan size?" he asked the clerk.

"Menthol or regular?"

"Regular." The woman was probably too old, but something about her interested him, and as she reached for the cigarettes he slipped out and in again, feeling the familiar tingle, and as she adjusted to the new weight of her body and the new colors, she realized suddenly that she was not alone.

Great gladness!	Me also. My first time.
And mine.	Show me your lives. Oh!
Yours too. Oh, that one—	Now we are twice as many.

98

Here again, a week from today?	Yes, but is this one best?
No. Florence at the reception desk, or whoever is in her chair.	Good.
Two all right?	Apparently. No stress so far.
Bring others if you can.	Oh, yes!

19 Harriet Cleaver Owen was the youngest daughter of a Welsh-English mathematician; her mother, who had been a physical chemist before her marriage, was the great-great-granddaughter of Alice Cleaver, a noted feminist of the 1890s. Growing up in Cambridge, with two sisters so much older that they were more like aunts, a father who seldom seemed to notice her, and a mother who disliked any display of affection, Owen had found her only pleasure in scholarship. By 1985 she had a degree in medicine and a Ph.D. in psychology. Aside from a brief and rather clinical affair with a postgraduate physicist in 1977, she had had no intimate relationships with anyone.

Her work at CDC had been stimulating and frustrating in about equal measure: there was never enough money, never enough information. Now for the first time in her life she had the authority, the funding and the clout to do a major research project as she knew it should be done.

She did not consult with Milton Chalmers, whom she considered a worn-out second-rater, but she did call her sister Agnes in Bridgeport, who had retired the previous year from the presidency of a marine supply company. "Aggie," she said, "I've never bossed this many people, and I want to know what mistakes to watch out for."

In the holotube, Aggie's face smiled comfortably. "Well, one thing, bear in mind that you're ignorant. Get as much help as you can. You probably think you know how to do the job better than most people, and you may be right, because most people are chowderheads, but try not to assume that everybody else is dumber than you."

"You want me to avoid arrogance."

"If possible. Next thing, hire people who have a mix of different skills and backgrounds, and use their brains. Get at least one person you can count on for ideas you never would have had yourself. I did that in eighty-five—my marketing manager, Gert Heffner. She was crazy, an absolute wild woman, but she increased our sales thirty percent the first year."

"Hire somebody crazy," said Harriet, making a note.

"Well, I don't mean somebody who bites the furniture. Just don't hire people who are as much like you as possible, only not as bright. That way they're afraid to do anything you wouldn't do. Third thing, keep them on a long leash. If they don't perform, kick them out, but until then let them run, don't breathe down their necks."

"Any more?"

"Lots, but you'll find it out for yourself. Give me a call now and then, keep in touch."

"I will. Thanks, Aggie."

"It's all right. You know, I was thinking about

Mother this morning. Her birthday was last week—she
would have been eighty-eight."

"Yes?"

"She would have been proud of you. Of both of us."

Through the summer and fall of 2003 Owen was
busy with conferences and organizational meetings at
Health, Peace, and Justice. The number one problem,
everyone agreed, was site selection. The Army had an
abandoned training camp in Montana; Owen went there
and looked at it, but it was hopelessly dilapidated, too
small, and miles from anywhere.

For a while she considered a derelict university
campus in Clarion, Pennsylvania; she even went so far as
to order cost and time estimates for the necessary repairs.
There was enough room, and the facilities could be
upgraded in a reasonable time, but the problem again was
isolation. Owen knew, from the few tentative feelers she
had put out, that the people she wanted to recruit would
be unwilling to give up their jobs and move their families
to a place where there was no recreation within a hundred
miles.

She was on the point of going ahead with Clarion
anyhow, since nothing better had turned up, when an
item in the newsfax caught her eye. The index line was SEA
VENTURE DEAL SINKS. A conglomerate that had been
negotiating to take over Sea Venture and turn it into a
floating hotel in San Francisco Bay had backed out at the
last minute. There was a rumor that the CV Corpora-
tion, whose only sources of income now were tourist
admissions and a temporary lease to a holo company,
would reorganize for the benefit of creditors.

Owen got on the phone to her liaison in Peace. He
called her back the next morning. "They're eager," he

said. "We'll negotiate, and that could take a couple of months, but I think you can count on it."

Owen got out her copy of Bliss's *Horror in the Pacific,* which she remembered had deck plans of CV. There were 1,275 staterooms in the passenger section, plus accommodations for fifteen hundred staff, plus the whole perm section, which was divided into apartments for families. Assuming a reduced work force, CV could easily house a prison population of at least four thousand, more than she could possibly have squeezed into Clarion. It was perfect.

Industrial man—a sentient reciprocating engine having a fluctuating output, coupled to an iron wheel revolving with uniform velocity. And then we wonder why this should be the golden age of revolution and mental derangement.

—ALDOUS HUXLEY

20 In the fall of 2003 Dr. McNulty and his wife Janice found themselves in San Francisco, where a refurbished Sea Venture was being used to cube a holo based on Stanley Bliss's best-selling *Horror in the Pacific.* Bliss was there too, of course, and Ridenour, whose book had enjoyed a more modest success, and Captain Hartman, Yetta Bernstein, Randy Geller and Yvonne Barlow with their two-year-old child; except for young Geoffrey, they were all on the payroll as technical advisers, but very little seemed to be expected of them. Higpen was not there; he had died in January, Bernstein told them. "They said it was hypertension, but if you want to know what *I* think, his heart was broken."

The first couple of days were devoted to interviews and to photo and cube sessions in which they were shepherded around to pose in various parts of Sea Venture—Bliss in the Control Center, with a young actor in a not-quite-accurate uniform standing in as his deputy; Bernstein in the perm section; Geller and Barlow in the marine lab; McNulty and Janice in the hospital. Then there were brief meetings with the actors who were to play their parts, and after that, although there was an unspoken expectation that they would show up for holo sessions every now and then, nobody paid much attention to them.

It was a curious experience to find themselves back in Sea Venture; everything was almost the same, walls, floors, ceilings, all in the same places, and yet there was a pervasive feeling of wrongness, intrusion. Bernstein said when she came back from perm, "That was a mistake. I'll never go there again."

The cubing was sporadic, consisting principally of scenes in which actors milled about in the lobbies, stared at something invisible and screamed. The special effects, McNulty gathered, would be added later—a transparent monster, probably, swooping forward into the holotank and scaring youngsters out of their wits.

McNulty was not favorably impressed with the actor who had been hired to play him, an aging dopehead best known for his portrayal of a Southern degenerate in the series *Yoknapatawpha*. After a conference in which the actor earnestly assured McNulty that he wanted to capture the "spiritual essence" of the part, the actor disappeared; most of the scenes involving the principals, apparently, were being cubed in Hollywood. According to Ridenour, who seemed to know everything, there was also a computer-simulated model which would be used for exterior shots and storm scenes.

In the Signal Deck corridor one morning on the way to the cubing session, McNulty saw a familiar face. It was a slender gray-haired woman, escorted by a man in a business suit. He stopped and looked at her. "Why, hello, Dr. Owen. What are you doing here?"

She gave him an embarrassed smile. "Just looking around. How have you been, Dr. McNulty?"

"Just fine. Been watching the holo sessions?"

"No, I haven't."

"They're cubing in the Control Center this morning. I could take you up there if you want."

"No, I'm afraid I haven't got time. It was nice seeing you again, Doctor." With her companion, whom she had not introduced, she hurried away.

After the session, Hartman and McNulty went down to Main Deck. The mall was brightly lighted, the show windows full of carefully arranged clothing, gifts, souvenirs. It was not exactly as McNulty remembered it, but so nearly right that he could not say which details were wrong. He had an eerie sense that the crowds of people he remembered had all gone away by a fluke, just for a short time, that in another moment they would be back, and then the whole nightmare would start over. It gave him a funny feeling to realize that if that australite had never been dredged up from the ocean bottom, he would still be here, still going round and round the gyre.

Hartman was saying something.

"What?"

"I said, what about having a look farther down?"

Hartman stepped over the rope with its NO ADMITTANCE sign, and after a moment McNulty followed him. The light from the mall dimmed behind them; in the gathering gloom they could see the walls covered with dust and cobwebs. Debris had been swept into corners; most of the light fixtures and holoscreens were broken. "You forget how much effort it takes to keep up a place like this," said Hartman sadly. They turned around and went back.

That autumn there were freak windstorms in Louisiana, Kentucky, and Oklahoma, flooding in the Illinois Dust Bowl, drought in the Pacific Northwest; a new volcano appeared in Mexico near Guaymas; there were earthquakes in Indonesia, Japan, and Alaska. Signs of the times, people said.

Owen moved to San Francisco, where the Navy found her an apartment in a residential hotel and temporary office space in the Naval Research Center on Treasure Island; she began to oversee the remodeling of Sea Venture as soon as the lease agreement was signed. She made frequent trips to Washington, New Haven, Cambridge, Chicago and Baltimore for recruiting purposes. By November she had signed up all eight of her section heads.

For research on human subjects she had Donald R. Strang, a Harvard physiological psychologist highly respected in his field; for animal research, Jerry Plotkin, a former student of Strang's, recommended by him; for brain studies, Carl Meyer, a neurophysiologist who had done some interesting things in EEG and brain scan interpretation; for R&D, Glen D. Cunningham, a physicist and electrical engineer; for developmental psychology, Melanie Kurtz, the author of several well-regarded studies of young children; for psychological testing, Julian F. Eberhard, an adjunct professor at Cornell; to oversee the medical staff, Conrad H. Geary, a former chief of medicine at Bethesda. The eighth was her "crazy woman," Dorothy Italiano, a Jungian hypnotherapist who had written intriguing papers about various slightly disreputable things—twin studies, telepathy, acupuncture, even the ouija board and the *I Ching.*

Hank Harmon, Owen's liaison at Justice, smoothed the way at every step. Through him and his opposite number at Health, she was able to get delivery of a Mitsubishi 101. Owen had never used such a powerful computer before, and at first she found it a little alarming.

In appearance it was deceptively commonplace, just a holotube and flatscreen with an auxiliary keyboard which she almost never used. It had a low baritone voice, so much better in quality and intonation than the computer voices she was used to, that although it displayed no facial image, she found herself listening to it as though it were a human being—a person infinitely patient, wise, knowledgeable, dispassionate—the perfect friend.

In spite of its masculine voice, she called it Mitzi. She fed it all the medical records she had been able to collect from NIH, CDC, WHO and elsewhere. Then, facing the computer across her desk one afternoon, she said, "Show me a world map of McNulty's cases to date, Mercator projection, red for male, blue for female."

The map appeared on the flatscreen. She leaned forward. Something she had suspected before was coming clearer.

"Now a map of the United States, same instructions."

There it was, unmistakably. "Give me city maps of Baltimore, Galveston, and Atlanta, same instructions."

The maps came up side by side on the flatscreen. "Superimpose cases to date in the current outbreak of typhus and plague. Use square for typhus, triangle for plague."

Now there was no doubt: the two sets of case locations, McNulty's and typhus-plague, overlapped hardly at all; they were almost like photographic negatives of each other. The heaviest concentrations of the two rat-vectored diseases, of course, were in the slum areas of all three cities; only a few McNulty's cases appeared there.

"Significance?"

"First hypothesis. The parasite avoids areas known to be infected with typhus and plague in order to avoid infection. Second hypothesis: Typhus and plague give cross-immunity for McNulty's by a mechanism unknown."

"Show me a bar chart of McNulty's victims by age and sex."

The chart appeared on the flatscreen. Every cohort was represented, from infants to the elderly. At Owen's command, Mitzi overlaid it with a chart of the general U.S. population. The match was fairly good except for children of both sexes below the age of six, who were underrepresented, and women aged 20-25; there was a distinct bulge there. Owen leaned forward and touched the bulge. "Statistically significant?" she asked.

"Yes, at the five percent confidence level."

"Possible hypotheses?"

"One. Selective exposure. A, women of those age-groups spend more time in public places than the general population. B, the parasite selects women in reproductive age-groups in order to reproduce itself. C, the parasite is attracted to women of those age-groups for reasons unknown. Two. Women in those age-groups are less resistant to the parasite than the general population, for reasons unknown. Three. A difference in report rates based on sex and age. Four. Symptomatic differences in women of those age-groups and the general population."

"Let me see data organized by occupations."

The population chart vanished and was replaced by an alphabetical list followed by numbers.

"Give me a bar chart in descending order of magnitude."

The chart appeared. At the top was "General service personnel," followed by "Airline personnel" and "Taxi drivers." That was peculiar.

"Let's have an overlay of the general U.S. population."

The bars split into stripes of blue and orange. In the corner of the screen a legend appeared: "Figures from 2001."

Now there was a real anomaly: the proportion of airline personnel and cabdrivers among McNulty's victims was thirty-five percent greater than that in the general population. Owen touched the screen again. "What do you make of it?"

"Hypothesis. The parasite selects hosts in order to travel from one place to another. Taxi drivers are used to travel to airports. Airline personnel are used as intermediate hosts until the parasite is able to select a host going to a preferred destination."

"Save charts and data."

"Done."

She remembered something Marvin Minsky used to

say. "Intelligence is a word we use when we don't understand what a human being is doing." That was too easy, perhaps, but it had stuck in her mind. What was intelligence, really? The ability to pass the Turing test? If so, Mitzi was intelligent, and yet it was nothing but a program built into a superfast computer.

She called up the chart of occupations again and looked at it more closely, this time with special attention to the bottom of the list. One thing that stood out immediately was the category U/NPA, "unemployed, no permanent address." In the general population it was nine percent, among McNulty's victims .03.

U/NPA was a catchall category; it included the structurally unemployed, some criminals, and the permanent underclass of street people and vagrants.

One possible explanation was that the parasite was avoiding people who were poor and homeless, without medical attention, and perhaps as well those who were subject to drug-withdrawal symptoms and frequent arrest, because their life experiences were unpleasant. She felt a tickle of excitement.

"Give me a breakdown in bar chart form of McNulty's cases who were diagnosed for other medical problems in the hospital."

"Sorry, I don't have enough data."

That was the problem; there was always something she needed to know that had never been reported. It was criminal that there was still no comprehensive medical database anywhere in the world. "Write a new form requesting that information," she said.

The form poured smoothly out of the printer; Owen looked it over. "All right. Copies to all reporting institutions. Mark it 'Urgent.'"

She sat back, brooding. "Give me the occupations chart again."

Now she saw other anomalies that she had dismissed before as insignificant. "Executives," "Sales representatives," "Retired persons," and "Investors" were all overrepresented. That was easily explained—those were people who traveled a good deal—but there were other differences that now seemed to form another pattern.

"Give me a contagion tree. Better put it in the tube."

The three-dimensional pattern formed. Owen looked at it with pleasure: it was beautifully ordered, the sort of thing that would have taken weeks to do in the old days. "Now give me bar charts of duration of infestation for each occupation, with comparison to the general population."

The charts appeared on the flatscreen.

"All right, now give me another split bar chart, showing frequency and duration for each occupation."

Now that was interesting. She leaned forward. Most of the categories with the highest percentages in frequency—the cabdrivers, airline personnel—were very low in duration. The parasite had used them to get somewhere but had not stayed in them long. Other categories were low in frequency but high in duration: entertainers, scientists, and a wide scattering of other occupations, including "housewives." Were these people whose inner lives were richer and therefore more interesting? Was the parasite driven by the same force that drove her?

Later that month, during a holo conversation with Hank Harmon in Washington, she remarked, "One of the problems we have is obtaining currently infected subjects.

We thought of introducing visitors into the Detention Center, but we realized that the chance of obtaining a currently infected subject in any given day would be less than one hundredth of a percent. We've got to do better than that. We have to go into the general population and find at least five or six infected subjects, isolate them and bring them here without letting them infect anybody else."

"Let me put you in touch with the CIA research labs. I think they can solve that one."

In June she went to Langley and talked to the director of the CIA laboratories, a pleasant gray-haired man named Garrity. "I understand you have something for me," she said.

"Yes, and we're ready to show it off. Come down this way."

They entered a basement room where, in a moment, two men appeared. They were wheeling between them an upright aluminum framework with a plastic sheet in the middle marked off in feet and inches. "Dr. Owen, this is Bob Hendrix, one of our wizards, and this is his assistant, Steve Newberry."

"Glad to know you, Doctor," said Hendrix. "Well, this is what we've come up with. This framework is eleven feet six inches wide in the upright configuration. The subject is asked to stand against it here, in order to measure his height. Steve, will you do the honors?"

Newberry stepped up against the framework. Hendrix pressed a control. Four curved metal pieces sprang out, pivoted and locked around Newberry's waist and chest.

"At this point," Hendrix said, "the shock causes the subject to breathe in sharply, and a jet of anesthetic vapor comes out of this cylinder into his face, but we won't demonstrate that." He glanced at Newberry, who grinned.

"From here," Hendrix went on, "you have several options. The subject can be wheeled out in the upright configuration, in which case the whole thing can be covered with opaque plastic to resemble a garment rack. Or the framework can be tilted into the horizontal configuration, and then it looks like a standard medical litter." He stepped behind the framework and lowered it onto another set of castored legs. Newberry, now supine, stared at the ceiling.

"In this configuration, we have these collapsible rails." U-shaped metal bars slid out of the framework at the head and foot. "That gives you a minimum of five feet of distance all around. In either configuration, you can get the subject out with a minimum of fuss, and that dose of gas should keep him unconscious for twenty minutes to an hour. At the destination, you give him another shot of gas and wheel him into detention the same way." He pressed another control; the restraints opened and Newberry got up.

"Now, for controlling the subject in the institution," Hendrix said, "we came up with a simpler solution." At his nod, Newberry went out and came back with an aluminum pole, six feet long, with a framework at one end that looked a little like a music stand. He handed the pole to Hendrix, who showed Owen the framework. "When you push this against anything, these pieces in the middle are forced backward, turning around the pivots on the side. That brings the ends together in the front, and they lock until the operator releases them." He turned the pole around and showed her the red line painted around the shaft. "This tells the operator where he has to hold it. From this line to the business end when the mechanism is closed, it's exactly five feet."

"That's very impressive," Owen said. "How long will it take to manufacture them?"

"About how many?"

"Say fifty of the other ones and ten of these."

"We can have them for you in five weeks, tested and ready to go."

They were ready in six; then there were complicated arrangements involving Peace, Justice, and Health. It was finally decided that Marine MPs would make the actual arrests, supported by special agents of the FBI. Local authorities would be informed just before the program went into effect. The date had been set: Wednesday, September 8, two days after the Labor Day weekend.

21 In August, after all her section heads had moved to San Francisco, Owen held an orientation meeting in a conference room at the Naval Research Center.

"What seems to be happening," she told them, "is that the parasite reproduces in a human female at the moment of conception. Since this isn't an organism in the usual sense of the word, there's no point in asking how, but the result is that there are two parasites instead of one. The original parasite leaves the host; then there is a latency period, which apparently is not the same as the human gestation period—it averages about thirty-six weeks instead of forty. That's puzzling, but it may correspond to the point at which the human cortex becomes functional."

"Thirty-six weeks?" Kurtz asked. "That's a debated point, isn't it?"

"Yes, it is, but I think most of the discussion is rather metaphysical. Anyhow, I'm just suggesting this as a possibility, but if it's right, then we could assume that the daughter parasite becomes functional at the same time and begins to pass between hosts. In any event, the growth curve is consistent with that assumption."

"The doubling rate is about four months?" asked Donald Strang.

"Apparently that's right, and that means that the present population of McNulty's victims may be already on the order of seven hundred thousand. It also means that unless we find some way of containing the epidemic, we can expect saturation of the human population sometime around three and a half years from now."

"What about natural immunity?" Carl Meyer asked.

"A good point. We don't know if there is any, but we need to find out. There's a *lot* we don't know. For instance, there are some unexplained differences between what happened on Sea Venture and what's happened since. The most striking is the period of stupor, eight to ten days on CV and only eight or nine hours afterward. One possibility is that the parasite has become adapted to human hosts by reproducing in them. There are also a few cases where we can't construct a contagion tree without including a host who has had the disease before, a person who did not collapse at all. We can't draw any firm conclusion until we have more data, but the suggestion here is a progressive adaptation: a parasite born in a human host causes a shorter period of stupor in a naive host, and none at all in a previously infected one. This line of thought also leads to some rather alarming conclusions about the primary hosts, the children infected at conception. If we are dealing with an adaptive process here, they may be more profoundly affected than other hosts, in ways that we may not be able to detect for years."

"What are you doing about that?" Strang asked.

"Nothing. When we get our test group together, Ms. Kurtz will be studying the children known or suspected to be primary hosts. That's a very important part of our research program, and it would be almost impossible to do under any other conditions."

Owen paused and looked around the circle. "Now I want you all to understand very clearly what our goals are. We are going to study recovered McNulty's patients, primary hosts, and the parasite itself, with three ends in view. First, we want to determine the long-term effects of the disease; second, we are going to study means of identifying active hosts, and third, we are going to try to find ways of inactivating or destroying the parasite itself. That's our mission as laid down by the President when he established the Emergency Civil Control Authority. Beyond that, however, and this is very exciting to me, we have a unique opportunity to do basic research on human subjects."

"What are the limitations of this research?" Strang asked.

"Do you mean ethical limitations? I think they will be just what they would be, or should be, in animal research."

"That's what I wanted to know," said Strang.

In September McNulty spent part of his vacation

with Geller and Barlow in Michigan, as he usually did. Janice had planned to come, but at the last minute she had had a call from her sister in Seattle, who was experiencing some kind of marital problem, and had gone up there instead.

"Why doesn't she just divorce him?" Geller wanted to know.

"Not so easy. They have two kids."

"Well, which is better, divorce, or raising two kids in a family where the parents hate each other?"

McNulty did not reply. It was late evening, and they were sitting on the screened patio in back of the house. The air was already cooling off, and the lake breeze had driven away the blackflies.

"Tell me something else," Geller said after a moment. "In all the time you were on Sea Venture, did you ever wonder why you were wearing clothes? No insects there; the whole place was enclosed and air-conditioned; they could have kept it at twenty-two degrees and walked around bare-assed, but what did they do? They kept it three degrees cooler, so the women could wear fur coats. How do you explain that?"

Barlow said, "Did you ever see those women without their clothes?"

"Never. So that's your explanation? The human body is ugly?"

"Well, most of them."

"So that's why we wear unnecessary clothes, to cover up the ugliness."

"If you want to put it that way."

"I didn't, you did. Let me ask you something else. Does it strike you as peculiar that other animals look okay when they're naked but people don't?"

"That's different."

"But people are superior to other animals, right?"

"In some ways."

"Then isn't it funny that they're *uglier?*"

Early the next morning McNulty woke up, realized he was comfortably in bed in a place where he didn't have to get up until he felt like it, and dozed off again. Presently, back in the world where interesting things happened, he found himself having a discussion with a woman who was not Janice, although she said she was. "Women are not ugly with their clothes off," she said. "Only men are vile." Then he was alone in the dark corridor of CV, the same one he had walked down with Hartman. Hartman was not there, and neither was Janice, and it wasn't now, it was then. He was back on CV, and down there in the darkness there was something vast and octopoid, with great reaching tentacles. It began to buzz, and he knew that in another moment it was going to pull him into its grinding mouth.

He awoke to a sound he could not identify at first; then he realized it was the doorbell. Not his problem. He waited for Geller or Barlow to take care of it, but nothing happened; the doorbell kept on ringing. He scrambled out of bed, found his robe, looked at the bedside clock. It was a quarter to seven.

He crossed the living room and opened the door. Three large men and a somewhat smaller woman in gray business suits were standing there. They carried identical gray plastic briefcases. "Mr. Geller?" said the one in front.

"No, I'm a guest. I don't think Mr. Geller is up yet. Is there some problem?"

The man pushed the door open and walked in, followed by the other three. "Are you Wallace McNulty?"

"Yes. What's this about?"

The man showed him a folder. "Special agents of the Federal Bureau of Investigation. Where are Geller and Barlow? Where's your wife?"

"They're in the back bedroom, and my wife is in Seattle."

The man took out a notebook. "Her address in Seattle?"

"Why do you want to know?"

"Don't you want to tell us?"

"Right now, I guess I don't."

The man put his notebook away and gestured with his head toward the closed door of Geller and Barlow's room. The woman and one of the men went that way; the other two took McNulty by the elbows and walked him into his bedroom.

One of the men got a sheaf of papers from his briefcase and held it out. "Do you recognize this, Doctor?"

McNulty took it. It was a questionnaire; his signature was at the bottom. "I see a lot of these things," he said.

"Did you fill this one out?"

"My nurse did."

"Is that a complete list of your patients who have had McNulty's Disease?"

"I suppose so, in my private practice, at least. I don't have the medical records from Sea Venture."

"Who has those records?"

"They're on file at the home office. The Centers for Disease Control have a copy."

"Do you see the section at the bottom of the last

page, where you were asked to fill in the names and addresses of anyone known to you, other than your patients, who had been a victim of McNulty's Disease?"

"Uh-huh."

"Did you write your own name there?"

"Looks like I didn't."

"Or your wife's?"

"No."

"At the bottom of this page, aside from your own name and your wife's, did you write any other names there?"

"No. I guess I thought that would be hearsay."

The man put the papers back in his briefcase. He stood up, and so did the other one.

"All right, Dr. McNulty, let's go."

"Where to?"

"I'm not authorized to say."

McNulty hesitated a moment, then reached for his phone on the bedside table. "Okay, but I guess I'd like to call my lawyer first."

The two men moved with surprising quickness, and they were very strong. They pulled his arms behind his back and velcroed him. "Just cooperate, Doctor," said the larger one. McNulty could hear him breathing through his hairy nostrils.

"If you want me to cooperate, this isn't the way," he said. "Can I put my clothes on, for Pete's sake?" The two men did not reply. They hustled him out through the empty living room. Dazed and unbelieving, McNulty felt the coarse ground cover under his feet as they moved toward the back of a van. Then he found himself sitting on a plastic bench across the aisle from Barlow, Geller, and their son Geoffrey, who was crying. They were all dressed, but Geller's shirt was buttoned up wrong. After a moment one of the FBI men reappeared at the back of the van. He tossed a bundle of clothing into McNulty's lap—shirt, socks and shoes, pants. "There you go, Doctor," he said pleasantly, and closed the door.

22 The year Kim was four, they put her into a preschool where she learned to sing songs and paste hearts on colored paper. Every day when Julie brought her home, she seemed a little more subdued.

"What's the matter, honey?"

"The children don't like me."

"Of course they like you."

"They won't play with me."

Julie talked to the headmistress, a Miss Elwood. "You know Kimberly is a very special child," Miss Elwood said. "She's a bit more advanced than the others, perhaps. Children sense that, and sometimes they resent it."

"But what's the matter, exactly?"

"Well, it's hard to know. Some of them call her names."

"What names?"

"Oh, just childish nonsense. I shouldn't worry, it will all sort itself out."

That evening Julie said, "John, I want to move back to the States."

He put down his glass. "All right. You know the problem with wowsers is going to be as bad as before."

"Is it any different here? I want to put Kim in a good school system. She's already talking strine."

"Prejudice."

"The strines are perfectly nice people, except the bloody men, but I don't want Kim to be Australian, I want her to be American."

"And me?"

"You can be anything."

They put the house up for sale and found a buyer almost immediately. While they were packing, there was a message on the net from Julie's mother: her father was in the hospital, not expected to live. Stevens put Julie on a plane with the child, agreeing to meet her in New York in three weeks. When the closing formalities were over, he followed her in a more leisurely fashion by way of South America, parts of which he had never seen.

In his hotel in Pôrto Alegre he met a charming Scotswoman, Felicity Donaldson, twenty-four years old; she had been traveling with her husband, an economist with the International Monetary Fund, but he had gone off to Buenos Aires after a quarrel, leaving her "absolutely flat." With very little difficulty, Stevens persuaded her to be his traveling companion. She was limber, affectionate, complaisant, and soft as a rabbit.

For several years Stevens had been unable to satisfy his desire for variety in women. He liked them, their eagerness, their freshness, and their passion which he knew how to control. With Felicity he spent a memorable week in Rio, where the scented evening air on the Copacabana almost made him believe in pheromones. After Australia, the food was unbelievably good.

On the boat ride to Paquetá they met a family from New Jersey, parents and a teen-aged daughter. The daughter had won first prize in a Piggly Wiggly contest, ten days for two in Rio de Janeiro, and the father had paid his own way. The family was staying at the Sheraton in Ipanema, and this was the second time they had ventured downtown; on the previous occasion they had had banana splits for lunch.

"They have very good security at the Sheraton," the mother said. "They don't even let the natives onto the patio."

"Aren't they delicious," Felicity murmured in his ear.

"No."

"Oh, I think they're *delicious.* My God, 'natives.'"

From Rio they went to Lima, and then to Cuzco. In the hotel dining room they were the only guests except for a party of Germans and another of Americans, all in their sixties, who sat nearer the fireplace. The view of Cuzco at night was superb; the food was indifferent, the coffee undrinkable, and the wine overpriced, but the waiters were attentive and cheerful.

The leader of the group at the American table was a man whose face might have been handsome if it had not been for the rather piggish nostrils. He had staring pale blue eyes and a loud voice. They heard him say, "Yallo! That isn't yallo, it's *sopa. Comprende* yallo? *Agua muy frío?* Never mind, I'll go to the kitchen and get my own yallo." He stood up and moved away from the table; the nearest waiter, with a look of distress, put a hand on his arm and murmured something. The man sat down rather heavily. The waiter came back a minute later with a tall glass full of very large ice cubes.

"What does he think he is saying?" Felicity asked.

"He means *hielo,*" Stevens said. "He knows twenty

words of Spanish, and he thinks it is the Peruvians' fault if they don't understand him. He also believes that the waiter, who speaks three languages, is constitutionally inferior."

They took the tourist train to Machu Picchu, and on the way saw children of all ages standing outside their dirt-floored houses, neatly dressed in jeans and hand-made sweaters. The women they saw were toothless hags, old at forty. "How they must love their children," said Felicity.

"Yes, that's the trouble."

"You don't care for children?"

"Certainly I do. Would you like to have a child with me?"

"Oh, never!" But she gave him a strange look.

They saw Machu Picchu on its misty height, a haunted place. Then they rode back to Cuzco and toured the ruins; then to Lima, where Stevens kissed Felicity good-bye, with mingled regret and relief, in the airport.

In Miami, he called Julie late at night. Her father, she said, had died the day before. Julie was staying over for at least a week to make the funeral arrangements and get her mother's affairs in order.

"I don't think I'd better come, do you?" said Stevens.

"No, why take a chance?"

"I'll call you in a day or two."

Tired of airplanes, Stevens rented a car and drove on the decaying interstate into the Everglades, where he saw Indians not unlike the Peruvians of the Andes. In the stifling heat they were dressed from neck to ankle in many layers of bright clothing, and Stevens understood the reason when he was stung by a gigantic blackfly.

He called Julie from St. Petersburg the next morning.

The funeral was over, but she was not sure how much longer she would have to stay. She looked tired and irritable, and so did the child.

Stevens rented a cabin on the Gulf at Indian Rocks and spent a few days walking the windy beach. Then it occurred to him that Paul Newland was buried in Clearwater, only a few miles up the coast. With nothing else to do on a hot afternoon, he drove there and found the cemetery. It was very flat and as green as a golf course. After a little trouble he found Newland's grave. The marker glowed bluish gray under the shade of a palm tree. The inscription read:

PAUL NEWLAND
1935–1999
He Strove to Free Us All

Stevens thought of the old man's last voyage, a Viking's funeral, alone in a lifeboat drifting out at last into a darker and deeper ocean. He remembered something Edward Bellamy had written: "Death is only a larger kind of going abroad."

Standing here at this moment, he found it possible to believe that it was so, and that Newland or the remnant of the personality that had been his was still out there, still traveling toward some unimagined shore.

We cannot resist everything; we can only choose the forces to which we will submit.
                                                    —PAULINE ASHWELL

23 Late in the afternoon the bus from the airport crossed the bridge to Treasure Island, turned down a curving street, and rolled through an open gateway. The gate was of metal painted gray. Marine MPs closed it behind them; other MPs herded the passengers out and formed them up into a double line. Between the buildings they could see part of a vast white wall against the sky.

Some of the passengers had suitcases, others, including McNulty, only the clothes they were wearing. Led by a Marine sergeant, they straggled down the dock and mounted a metal stairway to the passenger entrance of CV.

The breeze from the water seemed to blow through McNulty's head, and he remembered that sensation, as if the air and his body could occupy the same space. It was funny that it was just the same now, when he was feeling as lousy as he ever had in his life.

In the reception lobby, an MP sergeant called, "Your attention. Please answer to your names as they are called. Arnold?"

"Here."

"Ashley?"

"Here."

"Barlow?"

"Here."

When he had finished the roll, the sergeant said, "Ladies and gentlemen, you are in the custody of the United States Marine Corps in the Medical Detention Center on Sea Venture in San Francisco Harbor. The commanding officer is Colonel Marcus B. Mattison. The director of medical research is Dr. Harriet Cleaver Owen. Are there any questions?"

"What about our luggage?" a woman demanded. She was flushed with heat, her hair disordered.

"Your luggage is being sent on after you. It should be here tomorrow morning."

"In the meantime, I haven't even got a toothbrush!"

The sergeant looked elaborately patient. "Anyone else?"

McNulty said, "Where is my wife?"

"Name?"

"McNulty."

The sergeant said, with a look of respect, "Doctor, I can't answer that, but I'll try to find out."

"Can I speak to your commanding officer?"

"I'll forward the request. Now will you all please follow me?"

They gathered in the forward Main Deck lobby, where the roll was called again and they were sorted out into smaller groups. There were about fifty in McNulty's detachment, all men; women and married couples were being taken elsewhere. Two MPs marched them down a residential corridor, pausing at each door to assign housing. McNulty found himself paired with a short, broad-beamed man named Morrison, who looked around the stateroom appraisingly and at once threw his bags onto the bed nearer the TV and the dark porthole. "Not too bad," he said, and offered his hand. "Dave Morrison's the name, I'm a sales rep for Western Mills. What's your line?"

"I'm a doctor. Wallace McNulty."

Morrison released his hand and stared at him keenly. "Say, you're not—?"

"Afraid so."

"Well, you must know all about it, then. How's the food?"

"It was pretty good when we were cruising. I don't know about now."

Morrison sat down on the bed, bounced once or twice, and got up immediately to turn on the TV. He tried half a dozen commercial channels, then the phone. The screen lighted up with a display: "Only emergency messages are being accepted at this time. If you feel you have an emergency, press E."

"Not very modern," said Morrison. Next he looked into the closet, opened the little bar, found it empty, and crossed to the bathroom. "Towels but no soap," he reported. He went to the phone again. "This is Morrison in E 401. We have no soap here." The message on the screen changed to read, "Your message has been recorded and will be dealt with on a priority basis."

"That means next week," said Morrison. "Hang on." He opened the door and disappeared down the hall. Five minutes later he was back with a paper-wrapped bar of soap. "There's always somebody who picks them up in hotel rooms," he said. "Not a bad habit. Well, Doc, would you like the shower first?"

Afterward, at Morrison's suggestion, they walked down to the central corridor and followed it to the shopping mall. About a hundred people were there, most of them men, some sitting or standing quietly, others in argumentative groups.

The mall itself looked very strange; the planters were empty, the shops closed and their windows painted over. Morrison headed for the nearest group, and McNulty followed him. The argument, he gathered, was political. After a moment Morrison slipped away, and a few moments later McNulty saw him approach a young woman who was sitting by herself.

The night after his visit to Newland's grave, Stevens turned on the holo for the first time in weeks, and found himself watching a newscast. In the tank a man in a sports blouse was standing beside a Marine officer and an MP sergeant; behind them was a gray metal gate beyond which gray buildings were visible. ". . . investigations, do you mean experiments, Colonel Mattison?" asked the reporter.

"No, I didn't say that."

At that moment the camera swiveled to focus on a Greyhound bus rolling toward the gate. Faces of passengers could be dimly seen through the tinted glass. "How many detainees have been brought here so far?" said the reporter's voice.

"About five, six hundred."

Stevens, who had been relaxing with a drink, came upright in his chair. He hit the replay button, rolled the newscast back, and got a carefully groomed young man sitting at a desk. "Under the sweeping powers granted the Peace, Health, and Justice departments by the President's declaration, thousands of victims of McNulty's Disease, and their families, have been rounded up by local authorities deputized by the FBI. . . ."

Stevens was overwhelmed by a rage and fear greater than anything he had ever known. He clenched his hands together to steady them for a moment before he punched up a phone window, then Julie's number.

"This is the Prescott residence. May I ask who's calling?" The face was that of a standard phone simulation, a pleasant-faced woman with brown hair and blue eyes.

"This is Robert Ames," said Stevens. "May I speak to my wife, please?"

"She is unable to come to the phone just now. Is there any message?"

"Let me speak to Mrs. Prescott, then."

"I'm sorry, she is unable to come to the phone just now. Would you like to leave a message?"

"When do you expect them back?"

"I don't have that information, sir."

Not for the first time, Stevens had the impulse to kill a computer. "Ask them to call me," he said, and gave his number. He blanked the phone window; the sound on the newscast came back.

". . . the results of these investigations be made public?"

"They certainly will be."

"What exactly are you hoping to find?"

"I can't comment on that."

The reporter faced the camera. "There are many unanswered questions about the detention of McNulty's victims aboard the former luxury vessel Sea Venture, but we hope time will tell. In Treasure Island, I'm Dan Garner."

Stevens punched for information and got the number of the Medical Detention Center. The tank lit up with another computer image, this time a Nordic blonde with her hair in pigtails.

"Thank you for calling the Medical Detention Center. For your information, no visitors are allowed at the present time. If you wish to make an inquiry about a detainee, state the detainee's name, your name, and your relationship."

"Julie Ames and Kimberly Ames. I'm Robert Ames, husband of Julie and father of Kimberly."

"Are you a victim of McNulty's Disease?"

Stevens did not hesitate. "No."

"One moment. Julie Ames and Kimberly Ames are in the Medical Detention Center. Do you have any further questions?"

"I would like to leave a recorded message for Mrs. Ames and Miss Ames."

"No messages are being accepted at this time."

"I see. May I inquire about their health?"

"One moment. Medical records show no complaints. Are there any further questions?"

"No."

"Thank you for calling the Medical Detention Center. Have a good day."

Janice McNulty, née Werth, was the daughter of a Tacoma dentist who committed suicide when Janice was fifteen. Her mother, a former dental assistant, had gone back to work and supported the family through hard times in the eighties; Janice herself had worked from the time she was sixteen. She had put herself through college and nursing school with scholarships, financial aid, and part-time jobs, and she privately considered herself about fifty percent tougher than most other people.

She had loved McNulty when she was his nurse aboard Sea Venture, and he had loved her too; the only difference was that he didn't know it. She understood him better than he understood himself; McNulty had never had a chance.

After CV's last voyage she had quietly maneuvered herself into his life, without flirtation and without demands, until it became obvious even to McNulty that he couldn't do without her. Their marriage was not an adolescent romance; it was companionship, friendship, and understanding—maybe a little more understanding on one side than the other. McNulty was honest, vulnerable, and hopelessly impractical: those were among the reasons she loved him.

In Seattle one evening in early September she was watching the holo with her younger sister and her brother-in-law when the report of the Medical Detention Center came on. They watched it through in stunned silence; then Monica turned to her and said, "Oh, Jan. What are you going to do?"

"I don't know."

"Will they be coming here for you?"

"I don't know. Probably." She got up and went to the guest room. Monica followed her, then Bruce. "Think we'd better call the FBI?" he said.

"No. Please don't." She got her suitcase out of the closet, opened it on the bed.

"Where are you going?" asked Monica.

"I don't know," she said for the third time. "Bruce, will you please call me a cab?"

"Sure." He left.

Monica opened a drawer and laid a pile of undergarments on the bed. "Jan, what are you going to do?"

"If I told you, you might have to lie about it later."

She got her skirts and blouses out of the closet, folded them into the suitcase. "Listen, don't let Bruce call anybody. Okay?"

"He's only concerned about—"

"I know, he's very conscientious, but this is important. Don't say anything unless the police or the FBI come here, and don't let him."

Monica looked doubtful. "All right."

"Promise me."

"All *right.*"

Janice carried her bag to the living room and set it down. "Listen," said Bruce, "you know, Jan, they said on the holo anybody who had the disease is supposed to report, and so I think that's what you should do. I know you're upset right now, but if you just run off, you're going to be in real, deep—"

"Bruce, will you please shut up?"

Bruce got a wounded look on his face, and they sat in silence until the cab pulled up outside. She kissed her sister on the cheek, shook hands with Bruce. "Thanks for everything."

"Well, you be sure to keep in touch," said Bruce.

In the cab, she sat listening to the thumping of her heart. Over one-twenty, it sounded like. She had to get the adrenaline down, think clearly, and not make any stupid mistakes. If it was a patient, if it was anybody else, if it wasn't Wally, that wouldn't be so hard. She got out at the hotel, paid the driver with cash, walked through the lobby to the rear exit, and took another cab to another hotel. She paid with cash again, went to a public phone in the lobby and called her husband's number. There was no answer. She called Geller and Barlow's number. There was no answer to that, either.

She felt a leaden disappointment, and realized she

had been hoping for something unreasonable. At least she hadn't panicked over nothing, and that was some consolation. She punched in the number of their lawyer in Santa Barbara.

"D'Amato residence," said the computer image. "May I ask who's calling?"

A flush of relief: they were home, then. "Janice McNulty calling for Mr. D'Amato. Tell him it's urgent."

Phil's head appeared in the tank. "What's up, Janice?"

"I'm in trouble. I think they've arrested Wally."

"Yes, I saw the announcement on the holo. What do you want me to do?"

"I want the best civil rights lawyer in the country, and I want to talk to him tonight."

Phil looked thoughtful. "Let me make a couple of calls and get back to you. Where are you calling from?"

"A phone booth, but I'm not going to stay here. I'll call you back in half an hour, shall I?"

"Better make it an hour."

"Okay. Thanks, Phil."

"My pleasure."

She killed time in a coffee shop, smoked too many cigarettes, and called again from another hotel down the street.

"Jan, I've got somebody for you, but he's in Washington, D.C. Alvin Miller, and they say he's the tops. I got his home number and talked to him—he'll be waiting for your call."

On the ride to the airport he was acutely aware of the man's various discomforts—the ulcer in his distended stomach, the muscular ache between his shoulder blades, the pain of an ingrown toenail. Anticipating relief, he got out of the cab and walked into the terminal carrying his briefcase. There were twenty people in line ahead of him at the United counter. The toenail stabbed him once too often, and he slipped out and in again to a new avalanche of sensations, turning to look as the man's heavy body fell to the floor. "What happened?" somebody said.

"I don't know, he just fell down."

"Excuse me, I'm a doctor," said a young woman, brushing past him. She knelt beside the unconscious man, looked at his half-open eyes, opened his mouth.

"Is it McNulty's?" he asked.

"Might be," she said, and glanced up at him. "You know about that?"

"Just what I see on the holo." He smiled, hoping she found him attractive. Maybe at the layover in Denver—

The line was re-forming. When his turn came, he handed his ticket to the young woman behind the counter, and as she took the envelope, he slipped out again and in, feeling her shock as the tall young man fell. "My God, another one!" she said.

The next thing she knew, a man in coveralls was coming down the workspace pushing a long curtain on wheels. She turned to look as the curtain rolled past her. "What's this?" she asked.

"Step back, please." The other ticket agents were looking at her. Now the man was going away, and two others came down the workspace with an aluminum framework. They were in uniform; their helmets were marked "MP." They pushed the framework behind her. In the middle of it was the outline of a human figure, with lines marked in feet and inches. "Stand over there, please, ma'am," said one of the MPs.

She felt a curious mixture of amusement and alarm. "What's this about?"

"It will just take a moment, ma'am."

She hesitated, then stepped over to the framework, turned, and put her back against the chart. "Shall I take my shoes off?" she asked.

There was no reply. Something came out of the framework and wrapped itself around her waist and chest. As she opened her mouth to scream, she felt a sharp tingle in her lungs.

When she awoke, she was lying on her back on a hard bed with steel bars all around her.

"Get up, please, Ms. Saunders," said a voice.

She tried to raise herself, felt dizzy, and fell back.

"Get up," said the voice. "There's nothing wrong with you. You can get up. Get up."

She managed to put her legs over the side of the bed and stood up shakily. The bed began to move away. A man in uniform was pulling it with a long pole. A barred door slid shut behind it.

She looked around. She was in a cage, in a room empty except for other cages. Inside the cage there was a cot, a table and chair, a toilet and washbasin. On the table was a Gideon Bible.

Later in the afternoon a woman in a white coat wheeled in a cart with covered dishes on it. A man in MP uniform opened the outer door; the woman pushed the cart inside and left. The outer door slid shut and the inner one opened. "Take the cart inside," said the MP.

The meal was Salisbury steak, mashed potatoes and carrots, with Jell-O for dessert. After an hour the woman came back for the cart; the prisoner wheeled it into the outer room and went back inside. The inner door closed, the outer one opened, the woman took the cart away. With nothing else to do, the prisoner picked up the Bible. She opened it to Proverbs 18, and read: "When wickedness comes, contempt comes also; and with dishonor comes disgrace."

Janice McNulty's appointment with the lawyer was for the tenth. She flew to Washington a day early, checked into a hotel under her maiden name, and called the office of Senator Wolker. The Senator was out of town, the computer image told her, and would not be back until the last week of September.

"Can I speak to one of his assistants?"

"May I ask what this is in reference to?"

"I'm a California voter, and my husband has been interned in the Medical Detention Center in San Francisco."

"One moment. All of the Senator's assistants are busy just now, but I do have an important recorded message for you."

The distinguished gray head of Senator Wolker appeared in the tank. He looked at her seriously and said, "I have heard from a number of my constituents who are distressed because members of their families have been detained in the Medical Detention Center. I want you to know that I and my colleagues on the Judicial Oversight Subcommittee take this situation very seriously, and we are planning a thorough investigation. Please leave your name and address with my secretary so that we can keep you informed of any developments. Thank you so much for calling."

The computer image returned. "Your name and address, please?"

"I want to talk to one of Senator Wolker's assistants. I'll wait until one of them is free."

"May I ask what this is in reference to?"

"I'm a California voter," she said again, "and my husband is in the Medical Detention Center."

"One moment. All of the Senator's assistants are busy just now, but I do have an important—"

"Don't turn on the recording!" she cried. "I want to talk to one of the assistants."

"One moment." The image in the tank was replaced by a holo of California scenes, sunlit beaches, majestic mountains, bustling cities, accompanied by uplifting music. Janice waited for five minutes, then hung up and called Senator Harper's office. The Senator was out of town. He had left a recorded message. All his assistants were busy just now.

She called the office of her district representative, Ted Sulewski, with the same result. She called three other senators, not from her home state, politicians she liked and trusted. They were out of town; they had left recorded messages.

24 Alvin Miller's office contained a large potted diffenbachia, two modern paintings, and the lawyer himself, a large black man. Miller did not smile as they talked; Janice was not sure she liked him, but she decided fairly early that she trusted him.

"I'm going to take your case, Mrs. McNulty," he said, "but I want to warn you it will be expensive and it will take time."

"I don't care about the expense. How much time?"

"Probably about a year and a half before the Supreme Court will grant a writ of habeas corpus, if it ever does."

"Isn't there any faster way?"

"Not through the courts. You might do a little better with Congress."

"I've *tried* that," she said, and told him about the previous afternoon. "What am I doing wrong?" she asked. "I can't even get to talk to *anybody*. Is it just because their bosses are out of town?"

"Believe me, it won't be any different when they are back in town. Adjournment is in October. They couldn't do anything about this if they wanted to, and they don't want to."

"They don't? Why not?"

"It's a hot potato. The congressmen who have had the disease themselves won't touch it, and the ones who haven't might get it anytime. Look at it their way. If they investigate the medical detention program, and give the impression they think there is something wrong with it, and it later turns out there is a dangerous personality change in recovered patients, they're in the position of having opposed a necessary program to combat a terrible disease. This is an election year, Mrs. McNulty. Wait till ought five, then you may find somebody with a secure seat who'll take on your crusade. Right now, I'm afraid, you're wasting your time."

Janice McNulty thought of giving up and decided against it. Even though it was an election year and many members of Congress were campaigning, she pursued one after another. She tracked down old Senator Harold Gottlieb at a fund-raising banquet in Atlanta, followed him to his hotel, and managed to get on an elevator with him and his aides.

"Senator, I'm Dr. Wallace McNulty's wife. He's a prisoner in the Medical Detention Center."

"The Senator can't discuss that with you now," said one of the aides.

"No, wait a minute, John." The Senator peered at her over his glasses. "Miz McNulty, can you tell me all about this in five minutes?"

"I sure can."

"All right, you come on in." The doors opened. They trooped down the hall, Senator, aides, bodyguard. In the Senator's suite, which contained a great many sofas, flowers, and a basket of fruit, Janice told her story. The Senator listened patiently. Then he said, "Miz McNulty, I do want you to know that my subcommittee is certainly going to want to look into this whole matter. We certainly will. You may think the legislative process moves slowly, and in your position I understand that, but this is the way we have to do it. I want you to know that you have my sympathy. If you learn anything more about this problem that I ought to know, you give me a call or come to see me, hear?"

Shortly after the Medical Center opened, as Owen had more than half expected, there was an outbreak of McNulty's among the food handlers, the MP guards, even her own staff. Owen had already laid down a policy: no one was to be dismissed simply because he or she had had McNulty's, but every recovered patient, without exception, must undergo a battery of tests like those given to the detainees. Eight or ten people resigned rather than undergo the tests; most of them were second-rankers, but three or four were hard to replace.

Donald Strang collapsed in the corridor on the way to his section in mid-September. When he recovered and came back to work the next day, Owen called him into her office to discuss the testing program.

"Harriet, I haven't got time for this," he said. "I have a full schedule of experiments through March."

"Donald, I sympathize, but in this instance I think we'd better stick to the rules. Will it help if I spread the tests out over ten weeks?"

"I suppose." Strang got up and looked at her; his lips were compressed. "Am I to take this as a vote of no confidence?"

"Certainly not. Donald, sit down a minute; this is important." She waited; Strang sat down and crossed his arms on his chest. She said, "Are you aware of any changes in your attitudes or sympathies?"

"No."

"Then you have nothing to fear from the tests?"

"It's a waste of time."

"No, it isn't, it's valuable data. Are you aware that I've had the disease, too?"

"No."

"Or that I am undergoing the full battery of tests myself, although I'm certainly as busy as you are?"

"No." Strang put his hands on his knees.

"Well, I am, and so far the tests are negative. If you're worried, don't be. Highly motivated people, doing work they believe in, don't quit their jobs and become beach-combers. You know that and I know it. But we have to have the data. True?"

"True," said Strang. He smiled slightly as he got up. "You're very persuasive, Doctor."

"That's my job."

Later she asked Mitzi for the records. One lab

assistant in Section Eight had tested borderline and had been dismissed. There had been eight patients among the food handlers. Of the five they had been able to get to come in for testing afterward, three had shown deviant attitudes, but there was no baseline measurement and the data were useless. Among the Marine guards there had been twelve patients; Mattison had insisted on rotating them out of CV and they had not been available for testing. The most she had been able to get from him was a promise to inform her if any disciplinary problems turned up among that group later.

One thing still worried her: among the staff and employees, McNulty's patients could form a chain along which the parasite could move without revealing itself. People who had had the disease once apparently didn't collapse when they got it again. There were anecdotal reports of a tingling sensation at the moment the parasite changed hosts; Owen had experienced it herself more than once—so often, in fact, that she could not avoid the suspicion that the parasite was visiting her over and over. She tried to follow the five-foot isolation rule, but it was impossible. There were always times when she had to shake someone's hand, or give something to a waiter. It would have been very easy to become fanatical and obsessive about protecting herself; but then, perhaps, the parasite would have accomplished its object. Owen fought her battle every day, and won.

After dinner Monday night there was a sudden blast of sound from the P.A. in the corridors. "Attention, all detainees. Turn on your TVs or holos for an important announcement. Attention, all detainees—"

They clustered around the holos in the mall. The

commercial broadcasts abruptly vanished; in the tanks, they saw the disembodied head of a gray-haired woman. "Ladies and gentlemen," her voice said, "I'm Harriet Cleaver Owen, and I'm in charge of the research staff of the Medical Detention Center. Let me try to answer some of the questions that may be on your minds. To begin with, we're going to give you a series of written and physical examinations to find out just what we're dealing with, and that will be the first assignment for everybody. These examinations will begin tomorrow morning at nine o'clock in the Main Deck mall. Please consult the list that will appear in the screen or tank as soon as I have finished speaking. If your name is on it, please report to the mall at the time given. Parents with children under the age of twelve, please make arrangements to leave the children with your spouse, or with a neighbor, during the interview. The children will be interviewed later. If you cannot appear on time for your interview, please apply for an excuse from my office on the Signal Deck.

"Now an important note. Please listen carefully. If you see anyone suddenly collapse, that may be a symptom of McNulty's Disease. If you were more than five feet away from the victim at the time, leave the area immediately. If you were closer than five feet, stay where you are. Call the emergency number and wait until the medics arrive. Don't be alarmed if the victim is a relative or close friend. As you know, McNulty's is not life-threatening. After a semiconscious period of about eight hours, the victim will be as good as new. Thank you for your patience."

There was a buzz of conversation, and people crowded around the holos. McNulty escaped to his room, where he found Morrison already looking at the appointment list on the screen. They were both scheduled for nine o'clock the next morning.

"Are you going to go?" McNulty asked.

"Sure. What about you?"

"I'm thinking about it."

In fact, McNulty was aware of a deep smoldering anger, an unfamiliar emotion. He thought it might go away, but it was still there the next morning.

Morrison was up early; after he had left, McNulty put his clothes on and went over to the mall to see what was happening.

The shop doors were open now, with an MP standing guard at each. A few people were standing around watching, like McNulty. One of them came over to him with a sheaf of papers in his hand. "Will you sign this petition, sir?"

"What is it?" McNulty looked over the top sheet.

The undersigned, prisoners illegally detained without a hearing, make the following demands:

1. Free unrestricted use of telephones and networks for communication both internally and externally.
2. The right to visit each other in all parts of the vessel.
3. The right to receive parcels and visitors from the outside.
4. Formal notice of the reasons for our detention with right of appeal.

Until these demands are met, the undersigned will refuse to cooperate with the prison administration in any way.

* * *

On the following sheets there were hundreds of signatures. McNulty added his. "How's it working?" he asked.

The man nodded toward the open shop doors. "Only about twenty people went in there at nine this morning. This isn't Russia. They'll have to listen to us."

When Morrison came back just before lunchtime, McNulty asked him what the tests had been like. "Oh, nothing much," Morrison said. "Medical checkup, then one of those computer exams. What do you like to eat, did you ever wet the bed when you were a child, and so on. Nothing to it."

McNulty went back to the mall that afternoon and watched. The proportion of men and women seemed to be different; when he looked more closely, he saw several people with wedding rings. That didn't necessarily mean anything, but it could mean they were examining everybody in the same place, single people and married couples alike. He hung around for another hour and a half, hoping to see Geller and Barlow, but they did not turn up.

25 The problem of getting Julie and the child out safely, regarded as an exercise, admits of possible solutions under six separate headings, which I will keep, naturally, in my head.

1) Legal: Under their present identities Julie and the child are Australian citizens, but that identity will not

bear close examination; even if it did, diplomatic efforts would be required to get them released. Since Julie was arrested at her mother's house, it would be simple for her to claim her true U.S. citizenship, and then, I suppose, we could try to get her out on a writ of habeas corpus or some such thing, but that would take too long, and might not succeed.

2) Direct methods: A rescue by helicopter, for example, or stealing a lifeboat. Uncertain and risky.

3) Deception: A cloud of possibilities. If it were just Julie, there are half a dozen ways in which I could get her out, but the child is another matter.

4) Sabotage: Forcing a sudden evacuation of CV, thus creating a confused atmosphere in which I could hope to get Julie and the child away. There are several possibilities, including fire and flood, but none that do not involve unacceptable risk.

5) Assassination: I could certainly dispose of one or more of the officials in charge, but it is not clear how that would give the desired result.

6) Bribery: In other circumstances that might have been the simplest and surest approach, but here it is uncertain.

All these avenues except the first necessarily involve my gaining access to Sea Venture. Here there are two possibilities: First, surrendering myself as a McNulty's patient, either as Robert Ames or in some other persona. That has the appeal of simplicity, and the additional benefit of reuniting me immediately with Julie and the child, but I suspect it for that very reason, and because any plan I invent may require me to move freely in and out of Sea Venture. Second, obtaining employment aboard CV in some menial capacity.

The last option seemed to Stevens much more likely
than any of the others. In order to use it he would need
documents other than the ones he was carrying; he had
several sets of papers, but they were all English or
Australian. Therefore he did not go directly to San
Francisco but flew to Chicago, where he went into a
downtown bank, presented a key, and was admitted to
the safe-deposit vault. "Well, Mr. Coover," the attendant
said, "we haven't seen *you* in a long time."

"I've been in Europe."

"That sounds exciting." She took his key, inserted it
in the box along with hers, and slid the box out. "Do you
want to take it to a booth?"

"No, it's all right, I'll just be a moment." Stevens
removed the contents of the box and put them in his
briefcase, making a mental note to let this account lapse
along with the Coover identity.

In the morning he flew to San Francisco, where he
took a room in a hotel not far from the waterfront. From
his twentieth-story window, using field glasses, he could
see the unmistakable shape and bulk of Sea Venture
blazing white beyond a pier on Treasure Island.

After lunch he walked along the dockfront until he
found a sign advertising harbor cruises. The departures
were hourly. Stevens bought a ticket and went to
Fisherman's Wharf, where he bought a white plastic
fishing hat, a T-shirt that read, "I ♥ SF," and a Toshiba
SLR minicam with a long lens, more suitable for his
purpose than the field glasses. He rested in his hotel room
until three-thirty, then went back to the harbor, where he
lined up with a dozen other tourists for the four-o'clock
cruise.

". . . And on the right," said the talker, "you can see

the famous Sea Venture, now the Medical Detention Center for victims of McNulty's Disease, moored at the Treasure Island Naval Base. Sea Venture has been docked here since nineteen ninety-nine, when it returned from its last voyage around the Pacific." Stevens obediently pointed his camera and clicked away. On the return leg they passed CV again, and now, through the Toshiba lens, Stevens was able to see the open door forward at the Main Deck level, and a few people moving down the stairway.

On the following day Stevens rose early and trained the Toshiba lens on Treasure Island. At six-thirty, he saw people with handcarts begin collecting at the gray-painted barrier to pass through the checkpoint. The handcarts contained freezer packs and cartons; evidently this was the kitchen crew. Stevens counted more than a hundred men and women. At seven-thirty a smaller group began to form, younger, a little better dressed, some of them carrying briefcases. He saw them board at a quarter to eight. Another group boarded an hour later, and at ten o'clock a detachment of Marine MPs came ashore, evidently on liberty. Another shipment of cartons and boxes went through at ten-thirty.

As Robert Ames, he called the Medical Detention Center every day. The computer always gave him the same answer: Mrs. Ames and her daughter were in good health; no visitors were allowed at present.

Dissatisfied with the holo in his room, Stevens bought a new Sanyo and connected it to the hotel cable. The Sanyo had complete search and recording functions; he set it to record any mention of Sea Venture, the Medical Detention Center, or McNulty's disease. He checked the recording every day, but there was surprisingly little. The news was all about the coming election, the volcanic eruption in Indonesia, the wars in Africa and Iran.

He called the Medical Detention Center and got the usual computer image.

"I would like to inquire about employment opportunities in the Detention Center," he said.

"One moment. Employment opportunities in the Medical Detention Center are made available through the Federal Employment Agency in San Francisco. Are there any further questions?"

"No."

"Thank you for calling the Med—"

The government employment office was on Telegraph Avenue, in a district of decaying shop fronts. High on a wall, in black spray-paint letters, someone had written, "FUSOB." Shabbily dressed people, mostly men, were standing on the littered sidewalk, listening to three orators standing on boxes. As Stevens passed, he heard one of them shout, "Why should these machines be taking our jobs away? Taking the bread out of our mouths—"

Inside, there were more men and women in a cavernous space illuminated by long fluorescents hanging crooked from the ceiling. Stevens saw a sign over a row of terminals: FILL OUT YOUR APPLICATION HERE. Most of the terminals were vacant. The room was crowded, but nobody seemed to be doing anything. There was an odor of sweat and deodorants, and something else, perhaps despair. It had been years since Stevens had been in such a place, and his immediate instinct was to get out.

Instead, he took a vacant terminal and filled in the data of one of his personae. Under "employment skills"

he typed, "Food handler" and "custodial engineer."
Under "Previous experience" he put the names of five
companies, all in New York and New Jersey.

The terminal prompted him: NOW TAKE A NUMBER
FROM THE DISPENSER. WHEN YOUR NUMBER IS CALLED, GO TO
THE TERMINALS ACROSS THE ROOM AND ENTER YOUR SOCIAL
SECURITY NUMBER.

Stevens looked for the dispenser, found it, and took
a red plastic card. The number was 520. He sat down on
a bench beside a woman in a flowered muumuu who was
knitting something out of purple wool. She gave him a
friendly smile. "Your first time here?"

"Yes. It's a little unfamiliar."

"Well, you'll get used to it."

"Number one hundred and two," said a mechanical
voice. "Number fifty-three. Number seventeen . . ."
People were getting up, moving toward the far side of the
room.

"Does it take long to get a job?" Stevens asked
politely.

"Sometimes it does. I was talking to a lady here
yesterday, she was only here a week and she got one."

"How long have you been here?" he asked.

"Since the first of August."

Two months. "But when your number is called,
what happens then?"

"You go over to one of those terminals"—she
pointed with her needles—"and put in your social
security number. Then they tell you if there's any jobs
today."

"And if there aren't, you come back tomorrow?"

"That's right."

Stevens thanked her and stood up. He wandered

over to the far side of the room and stood watching the
people who came up to the terminals. After a time one of
the terminals emitted a printout, which a man seized
and put in his pocket.

Stevens followed him through the crowd and
touched him on the arm. "Pardon me," he said. "Will
you let me look at your printout for fifty dollars?"

"You just want to look?"

"That's right." Stevens held out a folded bill.

"You try to grab it, I sock you."

"Understood."

The man took the bill, then unfolded the printout
and held it open with both hands. The printout read:
WILLIAM F. GORMAN, 987-50-1920. REFERRAL: FLOOR SWEEP-
ER TECHNICIAN, SUNSET ELECTRONICS. Then an address in
Berkeley.

Having found out what he wanted to know, Stevens
walked away and made a circuit of the room to make
sure he had not missed some alcove containing a human
employee. There was none; the business of the agency
was conducted entirely by computers. He went back to
the lobby and found a double door leading to an
elevator. Beside the elevator was a directory:

ADMINISTRATION 301
PROCESSING   208

Stevens took the elevator to the second floor, and
found himself in a sketchy foyer beyond which he could
see banks of computers and piles of printouts. After a
moment a stout woman crossed the room; she glanced up,
saw him, and came nearer. "Yes, can I help you?"

"Good morning. I was wondering, do you have any
job openings in this department?"

"If we did, you'd get them downstairs," she said. She smiled briefly. "New approach, anyway."

Stevens thanked her and left. Downstairs, he explored the hall past the elevator until he found an exit on a side street. There was a lunchroom across the way. Stevens went in, ordered coffee, and waited patiently until twelve-thirty, when the woman emerged. For a moment he thought she was heading for the lunchroom, but she turned and went past. Stevens paid his bill and followed her. Two blocks down the street, she entered a Russian restaurant. Through the window he saw her taking a booth by herself.

Stevens walked down the street and back, giving her time to get settled. When he walked into the restaurant, she was taking her first bite of a sandwich.

He sat down. "Please don't be alarmed," he said. "I have a business proposition for you." He showed her a fan of bills and then put them away.

She swallowed, looking annoyed. "What do you want?"

"A job in the Medical Detention Center, and I'm willing to pay for it. Would you consider two thousand dollars?"

She took another bite of the sandwich, chewed and swallowed. "I might, but I don't get it. What kind of a job do you think you could get that would pay you back that kind of money?"

"Food technician, custodial engineer, anything."

"Those are entry level jobs. Do you have a food management degree or anything like that?"

"No. I don't care about the wages. Will you do it?"

"Only if I understand it."

Stevens said, "My wife is a prisoner there and I have to see her, it's very important."

She considered that, and wiped her mouth with a paper napkin. "Why don't you turn yourself in? Tell them you've had the disease too."

"I have had it, but—may I tell you the truth?"

She looked interested and pleased. "Good idea."

"I am wanted by the authorities for a felony—nothing serious—I stole some money. Believe me, the insurance company paid for it and no one was hurt, but if I go to the police now and try to get into the Medical Center, they will put me in jail instead." He smiled and spread his hands. "So you see, I've told you everything, and I trust you. Because I know you are a good person, and because only you can help me."

"Uh-huh." She looked at him in silence for a moment. "All right. One thousand now and the rest when you get the job. After that you're on your own."

Stevens paid her the money. "How long will it take?"

"Hard to say. Could be next month, could be tomorrow."

"Personality," looked at from the inside, consists of the things we do without knowing we are going to do them, and without knowing why.
—JAN ERIC MUHLHAUSER

26 Nat Frankensteen was in Sea Venture because his wife Eleanor was a former McNulty's victim. They were from Cincinnati, where Nat worked as a junior market analyst for Remco. He was twenty-eight, she was two years younger; they had been married a year and had a child on the way. Eleanor had had her attack during a Florida vacation the previous winter, and they both decided to keep quiet about it, but the police came for them anyway. It was Nat's opinion that her sister in Coral Gables, who had never liked him, had blown the whistle. Anyhow, here they both were, although there was no sense to that at all; he had left messages on the phone asking them to release him, but had never got an answer. Eleanor, who was crying a lot lately, took the attitude that he wanted to desert her, and it didn't do any good to argue that they weren't going to let him go anyway, so what was the difference? She said the point was that he wanted to go, and that if he loved her he wouldn't. So they went around that for a while, and Nat said he didn't want to go, it was just the unfairness of it, and besides if he was outside he could be working with a lawyer or something to get her out, but the fact was, was he was worried about his job. The entry requirements at Remco were stiff, they were very strong on dedication and loyalty, and there were mandatory reevaluations of midlevel employees every six months. If they thought he had McNulty's, they might have fired him already, and then what good would it do if he came back later with some kind of records that showed he hadn't?

Then there was all that stuff about refusing to take the tests. Some guy had come up to them with a petition, and Ellie had wanted to sign it, but Nat hustled her away and said, "Look, use your head for once. The quicker we get through, the quicker we get out of here, can you understand that, bird-brain?"

So they both took the tests, which were the same stuff Nat had had for years in school and at work, but Ellie, who worked in a florist's shop and had never been what you would really call a mainstream person, hated every minute of it. So it was a relief in a way when they told him he had been selected for special testing in the lab section, where he would have to stay by himself for up to two or three days. That he could use. In fact, the more Ellie said their marriage had been a mistake, the more he agreed with her for once. She was fed up, and he was fed up too; all they did was yell at each other, and Nat couldn't bear the thought that it was going to be like this for the next thirty or forty years.

So he went down to the lab section, and showed his pass, and they led him down the corridor into a room where a dark-haired young woman was sitting in a steel cage. There was another empty cage in front of it, and the MPs shoved him in there and slammed the door. "Hey!" he said, but they were already walking away.

Then he turned to look at the young woman, who was wearing some kind of airline uniform. She took a couple of steps toward him, and Nat moved up to the bars to get a better look at her. "What's this all about?" he started to say, but he only got halfway through, because her eyes rolled up and she went limp all over. She bounced off the bars as she fell, and lay on the floor with her legs every which way.

After a while the two MPs came back, and this time they were each carrying a metal pole. They unlocked his cage, snagged him around the waist with the gadgets on the end of the poles, and hauled him out into the corridor again.

In the room they took him to there was a black couch and a machine with dials and wires, and a holotank against the wall. In the tank he saw the head and shoulders of a guy about his own age. "Hello, Mr.

Frankensteen," said the guy. "My name is Dr. Meyer. Are you feeling okay?"

"I guess so."

"Well, Mr. Frankensteen, I want you to know nothing bad is going to happen to you, so don't be alarmed. The only reason we're isolating you this way is that we know you're carrying the agent of McNulty's Disease, and we can't let you get too close to anybody until we've done some tests."

"What kind of tests?"

"First we're going to do an EEG. Have you ever had that done?"

"No."

"Well, it's a test where we measure the electrical activity of the brain. It's absolutely painless. All you have to do is put those electrodes on your head and lie down on the couch, and it'll be over in five minutes."

As soon as she was allowed to use the phone, Julie had tried to call her mother. The computer had informed her that her mother was not at home. Finally a human being appeared in the tank, Julie's aunt Edna, whom she hadn't seen in years, and who looked shockingly withered now.

"Your mother's in the hospital," the old woman said. "Getting better. No thanks to you."

The image disappeared, and when Julie called back, all she got was the computer.

Then there was Kim. Ever since they had been brought to CV, there had been something different about her. She was more subdued than ever, or maybe that wasn't quite the word; more solemn? She didn't act frightened or unhappy, but her wild humor was gone. She had stopped asking about her father, and seemed indifferent when Julie mentioned him. She was behaving almost like an adult; she came to Julie for hugs more often than before, but Julie had the peculiar feeling that she did it to give comfort.

She had been hoping for a change after Kim started in preschool. "Do you like the children here?" she asked one morning. What she meant was "Do the children like you?"

"Some of them," said Kim, "but they're all babies."

"How old are the babies?"

"Three."

Julie tried not to smile. "But don't you like any of the children your own age?"

"No. They don't like me. But it's all right, Mommy, because I have the nice babies to play with."

There it was again, and in a different school. In Australia she thought she had understood it, because the place was so class-ridden and sexist, but how to explain it here?

She talked to the teacher, Miss Levin, a serious young woman with a nervous smile. "Well," Levin said, "it is true that Kim doesn't play much with the four-year-olds in this group. She seems to be a perfectly well-adjusted child, though; mature for her age, in fact. I really don't think it's anything to worry about. If you want, I could have her transferred to another class."

"No, don't do that."

Julie tried to dismiss the problem, but she couldn't. What was the matter with her strange wonderful child?

27 Thursday after lunch, when Frankensteen was through with the psych test, they told him to go into the next room. There was a holotank in there, a big one. In the tank he saw a woman in a white coat, standing beside an easel with some kind of chart on it. Under the easel was a black box with a dial.

"Hello, Mr. Frankensteen," said her voice, "I'm Dorothy Italiano. Will you sit down in the chair, please, and hold those two cylinders?"

He looked at the chair. There were two things on the arms that looked like shiny tin cans, with wires trailing out of them.

"You're not going to electrocute me, are you?"

She smiled. "No, those are just sensors. You won't feel any current. Just sit comfortably and hold them in your hands. Don't squeeze, just hold them comfortably. Now, Nat—can I call you Nat?—we'd like to find out if you can communicate by raising the skin potential in the palms of your hands. And in order to do that, we'd like to say that raising the potential means 'yes,' and no response means 'no.' Is that all right? Do you agree?"

The needle swung over. "Hey," said Frankensteen. He was surprised, because he hadn't felt anything or done anything, and in fact he hadn't even understood the question.

"Fine. Now we'd like you to answer some questions about your previous host. We'll do this by yes-no at first, and then we'll try an alphabet system. And one more rule, if we're using yes-no and you want to go to the alphabet, or vice versa, you can indicate that by two yesses one after another. Is that all clear?"

Yes.

"All right, now, is your previous host a woman?"

Yes.

"This is spooky," said Frankensteen with a nervous laugh. "I'm not doing that."

"Just watch, then, and don't say anything, okay? Now, is she married?"

Yes.

"Is her husband dark-haired?"

No.

"Does he have blue eyes?"

No.

"Did she complete college?"

Yes.

"Now let's go to the alphabet, and I'll ask you to spell the name of the college she attended. You notice here the letters are arranged in six blocks of four, plus one block of three, the X, Z, and the 'end' sign. I'll point to these blocks in turn, and you give me a yes when I'm pointing to the right block, and another yes when I'm pointing to the right letter." She began to move her pointer across the card. After a moment the pulses began. They spelled out:

K-A-N-S-A-S S-T-A-T-E End.

"Nat, did you know that?"

"No."

"Just one more of this type. Back to yes-no for this one. Does she have brothers or sisters?"

Yes.

"Spell the name of one of them, please."

B-R-Y-A-N End.

The woman dropped the tip of her pointer. As she was about to speak, the needle swung over twice, then twice more.

"What does that mean? You want to go to yes-no and then back to the alphabet? Do you have more to say?

Yes.

"All right." She returned the pointer to the chart. The pulses spelled:

H-E D-I-E-D W-H-E-N H-E W-A-S F-O-U-R End.

"That's interesting," said Strang at the evening conference, "but it doesn't have any validity, of course."

Italiano said, "We checked that information out with Ms. Saunders. Her husband has blond hair and brown eyes. She went to Kansas State, and she had a brother named Bryan with a Y who died when he was four. There was no known contact between Saunders and Frankensteen except their one meeting in the detention room, and they didn't exchange any information then."

"Okay, but the freak literature is full of things where people have given correct answers to questions like that under hypnosis and so on. Where's the evidence that you're getting this from some hypothetical alien intelligence in Frankensteen's brain? All you can say is that he gave the right answers."

"Where did he get them?"

"I don't know, and I don't have to know. This whole line of inquiry is a waste of time, and I think it should be dropped."

"I think it should be continued," said Italiano. "It's probably true that we're never going to get any evidence that will satisfy Dr. Strang, but we may get something that will lead to a hypothesis we can test."

"About what?"

"About the parasite's intentions. Why is it doing what it's doing? What does it want?"

"Intentions," muttered Strang.

"Donald, do you deny that the parasite shows purposeful behavior?"

"Sure I do."

"All right, suppose we find out that it does show behavior that we would call purposeful in a human being, and suppose we can modify that behavior in some way. Then it won't matter whether we call it purposeful behavior or not, will it? This is really a philosophical argument, and I'm impatient with that."

"Me too. I'm going back to my office."

Owen asked Italiano to stay after the others left. "You know, Donald is right about one thing," she said. "You haven't really demonstrated that the answers you got came from the parasite. There have been similar things in hypnotic subjects, isn't that true?"

"Sure it's true, and in automatic writing and the Ouija board, but there you expect more garbage. I have other experiments in mind. I know they won't convince Donald, but if they lead to a testable hypothesis, or even give us a clue about what this thing is and what it wants, that's all I care about. You know, he was right about one more thing."

"What's that?"

"It's *interesting.* Isn't it? It's really interesting."

In the occasional moments when she had time for reflection, Owen sometimes examined herself for signs of altered personality, like a woman feeling for lumps. She could not say certainly that there were none. Her appointment of Dorothy Italiano was perhaps a little dubious; would she have done that before? Italiano was an irritant in the group, a discordant factor, but on the other hand she brought a viewpoint which sometimes broadened the discussion in ways Owen herself would not have thought of.

Mentally and physically, she appeared to herself to be essentially unchanged. She was feeling well and alert, even though the job was more demanding than any she had ever had. She had had no asthma attacks for more than a year. Nowadays she seldom thought about her parents, and then without bitterness.

There was another thing. She had been taught to believe that asthma was *never* psychogenic or psychosomatic, and yet she knew that the frequency and severity of her attacks had a high positive correlation with her negative feelings toward parents and superiors. She knew very well that she was still repressing a great deal, but it was a very different thing now that she was her own boss and the boss of others.

She was lucky to have been unaffected by the parasite, perhaps because her orientation and goals had always been realistic. There were others, certainly, who had been equally unaffected. It was possible that the research she was doing would identify and explain them.

What it came down to was that only she could be the judge of her own stability and competence. She clung to that.

The third day, when they brought him into the room, there was a white rat in a cage on a table, and some kind of scientific gadget on the end of a long jointed pole sticking out of the wall. "Sit down here, Mr. Frankensteen," said a voice from the holo on the desk.

The thing at the end of the pole swiveled around as he moved, staying between him and the rat, and he thought that was funny. "What is that thing?" he said.

"Just a monitoring instrument. Now today, Mr. Frankensteen, we're going to give you a test called the Minnesota Multiphasic Personality Inventory."

"I had that already," he said.

"I know you have, Mr. Frankensteen, but we're going to do it again. Don't try to remember the answers you gave before, just take each one and give whatever you think the answer is now."

That night when they took him back to his cage, the rat was there too.

At the staff meeting Monday morning, Owen said, "First some good news and bad news. The good news is that we have five more active hosts on the way. The bad news is that Justice is unwilling to pursue the capture program beyond this point because of the protests they've been getting. The airline unions say they will strike if any more of their people are forcibly detained, and apparently they're being quite tough about it."

"They've struck before," said Strang.

"Yes, but of course you realize how damaging the publicity might be. That would be embarrassing to the administration, and it would endanger the program. So I think we're going to have to live with this, unless we can come up with another high-risk group of people who can be captured quietly—that is, not in any public place. Suggestions?"

They were silent a moment. "What about the cabdrivers?" Cunningham asked tentatively. "They are mostly independent, aren't they?"

"Yes, but as a rule they are active hosts only during the time it takes to transport a passenger to the airport. We'd have to use roadblocks or something of that kind to capture one, and it just isn't feasible. By the time they arrive at the airport the active host is already the passenger, and that gets us into the problem of capture in a public place again."

"Let's think about this," said Meyer. "What happens at the other end? An active host gets into a cab, transfers to the driver, and collapses. So what does the driver do? Does he call an ambulance, or drive to the nearest hospital, or what?"

"Usually the ambulance, or a fire department rescue team. Depends on where it happens."

"All right, suppose it's the ambulance. Couldn't we monitor those calls, arrive on the scene when the ambulance does, and take the driver before he can infect anybody else?"

"That's a good idea, and I'll suggest it, but right at this moment I doubt whether Justice will be willing to listen. We'll see. We may have to make do with six active hosts, unless the animal program gives us something. Jerry, what can you tell us about that?"

Plotkin shuffled some holocards. "Well, the first thing is to find out if we can get the parasite to go into a laboratory animal, in this case a rat."

"One rat?" Cunningham asked.

"Yes, because we need to know exactly where the parasite is at all times, or we can't take adequate precautions. We have some later experiments scheduled to see whether it shows a preference for one kind of animal over another, and so on, but the important thing right now is just to demonstrate the transfer. Because if we can get it to go into an animal host, then that's one possible way of getting rid of it."

"How is that going?" Strang asked.

"Too soon to say. On Sea Venture the parasite seemed to have a maximum tolerance of four days in one host. Ordinarily it will change hosts oftener than that, but in this case we think it may be inhibited against going into an animal host because of what happened to it on CV."

"You think it remembers?"

"Well, that's one of the things we hope to find out."

Italiano seemed to rouse herself. "Jerry, is that a female rat?"

"Yes, it is, and it's due to go into estrus next week."

"Okay, so you're going to try to breed it."

"Yes. In a sense we're playing with too many variables here. We don't know if the parasite will behave the same way in humans after being in an animal host, for instance. But our big problem right now is the shortage of experimental parasites. If we can get it to reproduce in rats, then we'll have all we want."

"How long would that take?"

"Gestation in rats is about twenty days, and the litters run from four to ten. We still have to find out if the parasite can reproduce itself in multiple births, but even if it can't, we'd have two parasites instead of one in twenty days. So, even in the worst case, if we can breed the parasite in rats at all, we'd have, let's see, fourteen in forty-eight days."

"How do you figure that, Jerry?" Cunningham asked.

"It may take less time than that, of course, if the parasite becomes mobile before the full term, but to be conservative, say twenty days, and also that each parasite changes hosts every four days. That's the maximum in man; it may be much shorter in rats. Okay, so then you get a chain where one rat gives birth after twenty days, the next on the twenty-fourth day, next on the twenty-eighth, so for a while you're getting one new parasite every four days. Then beginning on the forty-fourth day you're getting three every four days, then five, then seven, and so on. To put it in more scientific terms, at the end of a year you're up to your tuchus in parasites."

The subject's name was Corinne Balter; she was eighteen, small and rather attractive. Italiano said, "Today we're going to see if we can communicate directly with the parasite by using the yes-no and alphabet system. You remember how we did that before?"

"Yes, but I don't know what you mean communicate directly."

"It doesn't matter. Just think of it as a game. Now are you comfortable? Okay, let's begin. The first question is, 'Are you inside Corinne's mind?' "

Yes.

"Alphabet now. Where did you come from?"

As she ran the pointer over the chart, the pulses spelled out: M-O-T-H-E-R. End.

"I don't understand. You came from Corinne's mother?"

No.

"Whose mother, then?"

M-I-N-E. End.

"Do you mean the original parasite—the one on Sea Venture?"

Yes.

"Well, where did it come from, then?"

D-O-N-T K-N-O-W.

"Do you know how it came here?"

No.

Italiano sighed. "Let's try something else. Are you aware that there have been some personality changes in people when you've been in their minds?"

Yes.

"What is the reason for that?"

M-A-K-E Y-O-U B-E-T-T-E-R. End.

"Better in what way?"

N-O-T S-O S-I-L-L-Y. End.

"That's just garbage," said Strang. "It's mush. You could get the same stuff from a séance." He shook his head. "I honestly don't see why we're wasting our time."

"I admit the content is poor," Italiano said. "One reason may be that the subject is relatively uneducated and doesn't have the vocabulary to express the concepts. If that's the case, we may get different answers from another subject."

Strang threw his pencil down. "What will that *prove?*"

"Maybe nothing. This is an unknown field. I don't know what we're going to find in it, and neither do you."

"Shall we move along?" said Owen sweetly.

Wednesday morning, in the lobby, McNulty passed a group of people in close conversation. One of them was the young man who had been handing out petitions earlier; another was an elderly Japanese American who stood smiling faintly and smoking a cigarette in a long holder. "No, I don't think so," McNulty heard him say. He paused to listen.

"Why not?" the young man asked.

"I was at Tulelake in the forties. It was a lot worse than this. No privacy. Just these little cubicles with curtains over the front. Heat, dust—the dust came right through the cracks in the walls. You couldn't keep anything clean."

"So what do you think we should do?"

"Well, everybody has to make up their own mind. You want to go on strike, okay, but I don't think it will do any good."

"Did you ever try that?"

"No. See, we were in a funny position. They rounded us up during the war because they said we were disloyal. We knew we weren't, but what were we going to do about it? If we would have resisted, then they could have said, 'See, we were right.' So we had to go along with it to prove we were loyal Americans. And I think it's the same thing here. They put us in detention because they say maybe the virus has made us disloyal. So if we don't go along with it, that proves they're right. It's different, because it isn't just Japanese Americans now, but it's the same. We did the only thing we could, we went along with it, and after a couple of years they let us go."

"But you lost your homes, your farms—"

"Sure. But we were alive."

"I think I agree with Mr. Yamamoto," said a stocky woman in her forties. "This can't last forever—I mean, this is an illegal detention, and they're going to have to let us go."

The man beside her cleared his throat. "My field is business law," he said apologetically, "but I'd say the detention is legal under the state of emergency. You have to remember something can be very bad and still be legal.

I expect there will be judicial review, but that could take years to work through the courts."

"What about Congress?" the woman wanted to know.

"Well, theoretically they could overturn the emergency regulations, but in the mood the country is in, I don't think they will. Did any of you catch the news about McNulty's patients being assaulted in Kansas City? Maybe we're safer in here."

The lunch bell rang; the group broke up and began to move toward the cafeteria. McNulty found himself walking beside Yamamoto, who smiled and nodded. McNulty took a chance and introduced himself. "You look familiar, but I can't quite— Were you one of my patients?"

"Yes, on Sea Venture. Min Yamamoto."

"Oh, sure. How have you been?"

"Not too bad, considering."

They took their trays to the same table. McNulty said, "That was the Japanese-American internment you were talking about before?"

"That's right. Nineteen forty-two to forty-four."

"Most people don't even realize it ever happened."

"No. They probably won't remember this one either." Yamamoto forked up an anonymous piece of meat from his goulash and looked at it. "I was telling them out there, even the food is better than what we had. I remember they served us very soft sticky rice, like rice pudding, which we weren't used to. And there were strips of flypaper over the tables, and we used to sit and watch pieces of these dead flies fall off into the rice." He put the forkful in his mouth and chewed.

"That must have been hard," said McNulty.

"It was worst for the older kids. They couldn't

understand that we hadn't done anything wrong. They had softball teams, you know, and they gave themselves names like the Nothings, or the Cockroaches."

McNulty, who also had the goulash, looked at it and put his fork down. "Why do you think these things happen?"

Yamamoto did not reply for a moment. Then he said, "I think it's fear. A long time ago, I noticed that whenever I got angry, it was because I was afraid. Then, from that, I could look at whatever I was afraid of, and maybe do something about it. Not easy. When you're afraid, you might freeze up. So I think most people get angry instead, because at least when you're angry you can do something. And people are very afraid now."

28 On Thursday Jerry Plotkin said, "We were hoping something would happen by the fourth or fifth day, but it hasn't. What I'm asking myself is, is there some difference in the tolerance of human hosts? We already know that the hosts collapse for about nine hours, not eight days the way it was on Sea Venture, so it might be reasonable to assume that they can tolerate the parasite for a longer period. If so, we have to find out what that period is."

"Any sign of stress?" Meyer asked.

"Nothing that can't be attributed to the experimental situation. We've monitored his blood pressure and heartbeat, and we're taking a daily EEG. But what it looks like is that we're not going to get the transfer into a rat until we do something that drives the parasite out."

"Such as?"

"Well, there are a few obvious things we haven't tried yet. One of them is pain; then there's hyperthermia, and drugs, but that's a long program. My feeling about it is that we really do need to know how long the host can tolerate the parasite, but demonstrating the transfer into a lab animal is really more important right now, and I think we should go for whatever offers the best prospect of quick results."

"That would be aversion?"

"That's right. There may be something in drugs that would work, but it will take hundreds of hours to test just the most likely ones, and some of them would invalidate the results of other experiments."

"So what do you have in mind?"

"Local application of heat. That's standardized— that's how the original work was done on quantifying pain."

Italiano asked, "What is the unit of pain, Jerry?"

"It's called a dol, from the Latin *dolor.*"

"So you're going to burn him till he screams?"

Plotkin looked disgusted. "We're not going to burn him at all; we're going to use a heat lamp on a measured area of his skin. He probably won't scream."

"Well, he will, though, if you crank up the pain high enough. How high are you prepared to go, by the way?"

"This isn't a productive discussion," said Plotkin. "Dr. Owen?"

Owen looked thoughtful. "Jerry, have you considered other alternatives? What about something that would induce an asthma attack? That isn't damaging to the subject in the short run, but it can cause intense anxiety."

"I'm willing, but I just don't think it would get us the data we need. Even if we find out an asthmatic attack will work, or some disorienting drug, we're going to have to come back to pain sooner or later, just because it's quantifiable and easily administered."

"All right, I think that's persuasive, Jerry. Of course there does have to be an upper limit."

"Sure. Ten dols is about as much as most people can stand. We can cut it off at, say, eight."

The agreement was that Stevens would call Processing each day at four o'clock exactly. If she did not answer by the fourth ring, he was to punch off. When she did answer, she would say, "Wrong code." Then he was to go to a terminal in the main hall and enter his social security number.

At the beginning of the second week Stevens let the phone ring seven times. The tank remained empty, but he heard her voice: "Employment, processing."

"Soon?" Stevens asked.

The phone went dead.

Stevens waited a few days more, calling every day at four o'clock. Then he got a bus schedule from the hotel desk and studied it. On Saturday afternoon he went to a hardware store on Market Street and bought a piece of pipe fourteen inches long. At three-ten, carrying the pipe neatly wrapped in paper like a calendar, he boarded the bus that had left Treasure Island at two forty-five. The bus was full of people whose faces he recognized from the cube of snapshots he had taken. Six or seven got off in the Tenderloin; Stevens followed three men who went into a bar together. After midnight they separated. Stevens followed the one who was by himself, a burly man in a blue jacket. As the man stood waiting for a light to change, Stevens swung the wrapped pipe sideways. The man cried out and fell into the gutter.

Stevens left the pipe in a trash basket on the corner and went home. On Monday he called Processing at four o'clock as usual. The phone rang four times; he punched off. That afternoon he went to the Employment Office and watched her come out. He followed her to the same restaurant, went in and sat down. Her face turned grey.

"There was an opening on CV after Saturday night," he said.

"Somebody else got it," she said. "I couldn't help it; it was already in the program."

"Do you know why there was an opening?" he asked.

"No."

"One of the workers had his kneecap broken." After a moment he said, "Do you know who broke his kneecap?"

She did not answer. Stevens got up and left.

On Tuesday he bought another piece of pipe and got on the same bus. He followed another kitchen worker and hit him in the knee. On Wednesday the phone rang twice. "Wrong code," her voice said. Stevens went down to the employment office, got a printout from the machine. At seven o'clock the next morning he was on CV.

When they brought him and the caged rat into the lab room Saturday morning, Plotkin was in the holo, and he said, "Now, Mr. Frankensteen, after we finish the standard tests this morning, I'm going to give you an opportunity to take part in a different kind of experiment. I'm going to tell you about it now, and then I want you to think it over until after lunch. You see that apparatus to your left?"

Nat looked. It was a black machine on a swivel. It looked vaguely menacing, like some of the things you saw in doctors' offices.

"What we want to do with that apparatus is to determine your tolerance for discomfort, and see if you can stand enough to make the parasite leave you for another host."

"What kind of discomfort?"

"Heat from that lamp. We'll start with a very low setting and go up gradually, with rest periods in between. And if you complete this series of trials successfully, Mr. Frankensteen, that is if the parasite does leave you as a consequence of it, you and your wife will be released from custody."

On Sunday, when McNulty had been a prisoner for eighteen days, there was another announcement on the P.A. "Attention, all detainees. Please go to your TVs or holos for an important announcement."

McNulty and Morrison watched the screen in their stateroom. It was Dr. Owen again. She said, "During the past week we have had a number of complaints about unduly restrictive rules and regulations. I'm glad to be able to tell you that beginning right now these rules will be lifted for everyone who cooperates in our testing program. In other words, you will be able to circulate freely throughout Sea Venture and visit your friends, you can call them on the phone if you wish, and you can make calls to your friends and associates on the outside. For those of you who have not kept your scheduled appointments for testing until now, a revised schedule will appear on the screen as soon as I have finished speaking. Thank you for your cooperation."

"Well, not bad," said Morrison. They watched the screen. McNulty's name appeared on the list for Monday at nine o'clock. "There you are. Going to go this time?" Morrison asked.

"Guess so." McNulty's hunger for communication with the outside world was so intense that he wished for a moment he had taken the tests before. But if he had, if everybody had, would they have bothered to make any concessions?

The waitress smiled as she approached the two young women in the staff dining room. "Here's your coffee."

"Wonderful," said the brown-haired one. They both looked baggy-eyed, the way the scientists always did in the morning. As she poured the coffee, she slipped out and into the dark-haired one, and found herself thinking, Got to get more sleep, but damn, the work is so interesting. She was Lelia Adler, she worked under Dr. Strang in the lab. Her companion, Sally Townsend, picked up her coffee cup and drank greedily.

"The usual?" asked the waitress.

"Yes. No, I think I'll have a Danish instead of toast."

"Gotcha." The waitress left with her tray under her arm.

The observer heard Townsend saying, "Did I tell you about Italiano?"

"No, what now?"

"Well, you know she does these experiments with a lie detector, trying to communicate with the parasite?"

"Uh-huh."

"Okay, the latest is; she asked the parasite where it came from, and it said it didn't know."

"Safe answer." She picked up a breadstick and munched it, thinking, They used to be better than this.

"Right, so why didn't the subject make up something? You know, 'I came from Aldebaran,' or whatever?"

"I don't know."

"It's anomalous, because typically subjects in these kinds of experiments will confabulate like crazy."

"So?"

"Well, maybe that's the right answer. Suppose when the new parasites are born, they're tabula rasa. No inherited knowledge. Maybe the original parasite meant to come back and teach the babies, but it couldn't because we dumped it in the ocean."

"Sally, it's eight-thirty in the morning. What's your point?"

"Okay, just suppose that the original parasite had some standard way of dealing with the hosts—to make them more docile, or more efficient, or whatever. The new generation doesn't know any of that, so they've got to wing it. And listen, this is what I think is scary. All they know is what they get from our minds. Suppose they pick up some system, Marxism or Scientology, and start trying to convert everybody, without knowing it won't work?"

29 At nine o'clock on Monday McNulty found himself part of a group of about fifty people in the mall. He sensed a mood of apprehension coupled with a paradoxical hope; it reminded him of registration day. Something was going to happen, maybe good, maybe not, but it was better than nothing. He felt more than ever as if he were back in college, entering the maw of a vast machine that would manipulate him according to its own Olympian desires and spew him out at the other end. He had buried that whole experience because it was done with and he knew he would never have to go through it again; now that it was starting over he felt worse than he had felt as an undergraduate, he felt diminished, as if all his hard-won maturity had been taken away from him.

He followed the crowd through one of the open doors into a place that looked like a classroom. Up in front a young man in a white lab coat was sitting at a desk. McNulty found a place in the back row. On the desk in front of him was an institutional terminal that looked as if it had had hard use. The display on the screen read: "Thank you for your cooperation in filling out the Emergency Medical Information Form. Please answer every question. Do not leave any answer spaces blank. If you need assistance, press the 'Help' button.

"Now begin by pressing 'C.' To review your answers, press 'R.'"

McNulty pressed "C." All around him a rattle of keys was beginning, like rain on a distant roof.

The questionnaire began with the usual things: name, sex, age, occupation, citizenship, race, marital status, sexual preference. Serious illnesses, with dates. Then there was some new stuff.

"Are you a victim of McNulty's Disease? If Y, state place, date, and time of the attack.

"Did another person collapse in your presence before the onset of the attack? If Y, state the interval between the two occurrences (that is, how long after someone else collapsed did you yourself collapse). If the interval was less than 1 day, give your answer in hours. If the interval was more than 1 day, give your answer in days."

McNulty did his best with the date; it was sometime in May, 1999. He put N after the second question.

"How many other persons besides yourself were near the person who collapsed? Give their names, occupations, and marital status if known, their sex (M or F), approximate ages, and physical descriptions. Were any of these people nearer than you to the person who collapsed? If Y, put an asterisk (*) beside each of their entries."

Then a long series: "List foods you ate within twelve hours before the attack. List drugs, including recreational drugs (including tobacco and alcohol), you ingested within twelve hours before the attack. List places you visited within twelve hours of the attack. List medications you took within twenty-four hours of the attack. List any remarkable incidents that occurred before the attack. List any peculiar thoughts or experiences that occurred to you before the attack." Then:

"Have you noticed any changes in yourself as a result of McNulty's Disease? If Y, please specify. Have any other members of your family had McNulty's Disease? If Y, list their names and approximate dates of illness. Have you observed any change in others as a result of McNulty's Disease?"

They were asking for an essay. If he tried to write down all he knew or had heard about former patients, he would be here all day and he would probably overload the file. Remembering all the questionnaires he had made patients fill out, McNulty tried to be reasonable, but he couldn't help it, he felt that his privacy was being invaded by an arrogant authority. Finally he wrote: "A little more tolerance toward offbeat therapies. Some marital break-ups and career changes."

Then: "Are you now or have you ever been a member of any organization declared subversive by the Attorney General?" Probably not.

"Have you ever been convicted of a felony? If Y, list convictions, dates, and places where felonies occurred.

"Have you ever been imprisoned or incarcerated in a mental institution? If Y, give names of institutions and dates of imprisonment or incarceration.

"Have you ever traveled to foreign countries? If Y, list below dates, foreign destinations, and reasons for travel." Mexico, Canada a couple of times, the Virgin Islands once. What about Sea Venture, was that travel to foreign countries? He put it down: Philippines, Hong Kong, Japan.

At the bottom of the second screen he read:

"WARNING: It is a criminal offense to give false information to any agency of the Federal Government. The maximum penalty for each such offense is a $20,000 fine and five years in prison.

"When you have completed this form, press 'E' and go to the attendant in the mall for further instructions."

Outside in the mall, the attendant handed him a numbered red card and said, "Wait outside the examination rooms, down there."

Half a dozen people were already sitting on benches outside doors marked "A," "B," "C," and "D." McNulty sat down. A woman came out of room "D," followed by a nurse who called, "Number twelve." A tall black man got up and went in. After a long time a man came out of room "C"; a nurse called, "Number eleven." That was McNulty; he went in.

The nurse was in her fifties, stout and cheerful. "Let's just get you on the scale," she said. She looked at the readout and pressed a button, then swung the arm over and got McNulty's height. "All righty, now if you'll just take your shirt off and get up on the table, doctor will be with you in a minute."

The doctor came in, young, bald, fat-faced, with an insincere smile. McNulty recognized the type and disliked him instantly. "Hello, I'm Dr. Fabian," he said, giving McNulty a moist handshake. He sat down at his desk and looked at the screen. *"Well,* you're a medical man," he said. "McNulty? Are you the one who—?"

"That's right."

"Well, this is an honor, Doctor."

"Not for me," said McNulty before he could stop himself.

"No—no—I guess not. Well—" Fabian looked at the screen again. "I see you had hepatitis A in nineteen ninety-three. Any residual problems with that?"

"No, I don't think so."

"Okay, let's listen to your chest."

The examination was brief but reasonably thorough.

As McNulty was buttoning up his shirt, Fabian said, "Say, Doctor, maybe when things settle down here, I and you could get together for lunch or a drink. Sure are a lot of questions I'd like to ask you."

"Let's see how it goes," McNulty said.

In the mall, the attendant motioned him toward another set of rooms. "Wait down there."

It was the same bunch again, minus a few. When his number was called, McNulty went into Room "E." A slender dark-mustached young man was waiting for him. "I'm Dr. Scorsi," he said. He seated himself behind his desk, looked at the screen. "Um-hm, um-hm," he said. "No history of mental illness?"

"No."

"What about depression?"

"I'm depressed right now. Not clinical."

"Why are you depressed?" Scorsi asked, leaning back and folding his hands.

"Situational."

"Yes, that's not surprising. Let's talk about your childhood. Were you brought up by both parents?"

"Yes."

"Parents get along okay, or did they quarrel?"

"They were good people."

"Uh-huh. Any brothers or sisters?"

"One brother. He was killed in an auto accident in nineteen seventy-five."

"How did that make you feel?"

"Crummy."

Scorsi put his hands on the keyboard, tapped a few strokes. McNulty could imagine the comment. *Uncommunicative, hostile.* And he was getting hostile, he couldn't help it. He had seen this sometimes in his own patients and had tried to cope with it by being as open with them as he could; it didn't always work, and it wasn't going to work this time with Scorsi.

"Now, about your experiences after you had McNulty's Disease, Doctor—" Scorsi looked at the screen again. "I didn't notice before, your name is McNulty too. Are you—"

"Yes."

Scorsi sat up straighter. "Well, that must have been an interesting experience. When you got the disease yourself, were you anticipating some changes afterward?"

"I thought about it."

"And?"

McNulty told him just enough to keep from being put down as a possible psycho at one end or a neurotic at the other. "Very interesting," Scorsi said. "All right, Doctor, that's all for now, but we'll be seeing each other again."

"Mind if I ask what your background is?"

Scorsi looked a little disconcerted. "Chicago Medical School. I did a psychiatric residency in Kalamazoo General."

"Board certified?"

"No."

McNulty nodded and left. After all, what could you expect, when there was a shortage of doctors and they had to throw together a program like this? Dregs of the profession, and you would be lucky if you didn't get somebody incompetent enough to be dangerous.

The attendant took McNulty's number card, glanced at a list, and handed him a slip of paper. It read, "Please report to Room 30, Signal Deck, at 11:00 A.M., Sept. 27, 2004."

McNulty's heart jumped a little. He looked at his watch; it was ten-forty. He moved toward the elevator, walking fast, even though it was only a few yards away. He hadn't felt like this in twenty-five years—deep anxiety, depression, sudden hope, and none of it under his control. It was like going to find out what your grades were, or whether you were going to get into the residency program you wanted. Up there somewhere were the people who could give you what you needed, and they didn't have to do it.

The MP at the elevator looked at his card and waved him in. Another MP looked at it when he emerged, and pointed him down the corridor. He wound up in the administrative reception area, facing another MP and a big sign that said, NO ADMITTANCE WITHOUT AUTHORIZATION. The MP looked at the time on his card and motioned him to wait.

When he had been standing there a few minutes, he heard someone calling his name. He turned around and saw Geller and Barlow walking toward him. "You get an invitation too?" Geller asked.

"Boy, am I glad to see you!" McNulty said. He hugged Barlow, then Geller. They were smiling, but they looked tired. "How did you get along with your psychiatrist?" Barlow asked.

"Oh, well, not so bad." Closing ranks; you always tried not to run down another doctor.

"Mine was a sniv. Chewed his pen and drooled."

"Overcome by your sexual magnetism," Geller said.

"Shut up," she suggested.

At eleven o'clock the MP let them in. They showed their passes again to the receptionist in Room 30; he leaned over his desk, murmured something, glanced up. "Please sit down. Dr. Owen will be with you in a moment."

They looked at each other without speaking. After a while the receptionist glanced at his desk again. "You may go in now."

They filed through the doorway, Barlow first, then Geller and McNulty. Dr. Owen was sitting behind a long rosewood desk. She smiled. "Good morning. Please sit down, won't you?"

The only chairs were against the wall, a considerable distance from Owen. McNulty was aware of the sounds of Geller's and Barlow's bottoms settling into the padded seats. He saw the framed diplomas on the walls, and Owen's gray hair haloed by the porthole behind her.

"To begin with," she said, "I want to tell you that I know how you must be feeling, to be brought here like this. I'm afraid it was necessary, but I understand if you're feeling a certain amount of hostility. Would anyone like to comment?"

"How long are you going to keep us here?" Geller demanded.

"That depends on the results of the program. Most of the subjects can probably be released very soon, within a month or two, but I can't make any promises."

"All right, what exactly are you hoping to accomplish?" asked Barlow.

"Now *that's* interesting. First of all, we're going to collect data for statistical studies of McNulty's victims. We want to know whether certain people are more at risk, certain age groups or racial groups or whatever. Are some people naturally immune? If so, we want to know why.

"Then we want to do a study of behavioral and attitudinal differences between McNulty's patients and the general population. We know there are some changes; how serious are they? Next, we want to do EEG studies to see if recovered patients can be identified in that way, and

we want to do similar studies on people who are infected
at the time. Animal hosts, too, for comparison. Then it
gets a little far out. We want to know if there's any way of
detecting the parasite while it is in transit between hosts,
with the object of inhibiting it or destroying it. In another
section, we plan to investigate the allegations that the
parasite is intelligent, by trying to find some means of
communicating with it. There's more, but I think I've
been talking long enough.

"Now the point of all this, and the reason I asked you
to come here, is that you can all be of enormous help to
us. Dr. McNulty, I don't need to tell you that your advice
will be valuable because you were the first to observe the
disease and have experienced it yourself. Ms. Barlow, I've
read your papers on swimmer's itch and they're very
impressive—yours too, of course, Mr. Geller."

McNulty said, "Dr. Owen, when I met you that day
in Sea Venture, you already knew what you were going to
do, didn't you?"

"Yes, I'm afraid that's true."

Geller leaned forward. "Did it ever cross your mind
that you could have got your data just by sending out
questionnaires?"

"Yes, it did, and the answer was no. You may have
your own opinion about this program, and I respect that,
but you have to realize that the program is going forward
no matter what you and I say in this room. The President
has authorized it, it is funded, I'm in charge of it, and it is
going to get done."

"Great. Why should we help you?"

"Three reasons. First, it will be more interesting for
you to be part of the scientific team rather than just
guinea pigs. Second, we can offer you compensation of
various kinds—not just money, although we can pay you

a salary, but housing privileges, passes to town perhaps, little things that will make your life more pleasant. Third, you will be taking part in a study that could turn out to be very important to the whole world."

"What if it isn't?" Barlow asked. "What if it turns out the symbiote is benign?"

"Then we'll have spent a lot of the taxpayers' money and disrupted the lives of a lot of people for a negative result. That happens." She glanced at her desk. "I'm afraid you're going to have to excuse me in a moment, but first let me say that if you accept this offer, you can resign at any time. Try it; if you don't like it you can quit. Do you want some time to think it over?"

Barlow said, "You mentioned housing privileges. What does that mean, exactly?"

"Cooperating detainees with children are being moved into the perm section, more or less on a first-come, first-served basis. Some of the larger apartments have already been taken, but I'm sure you can find something you like. Ask my secretary for a pass when you leave; you can go over there anytime this afternoon, and move when you're ready."

Geller and Barlow glanced at each other. Barlow said, "All right, on that basis we'll take it."

"Good. Dr. McNulty, you don't have any children with you, but if you think you would like to be in perm, I'm sure we can bend the rules a little."

He hesitated a moment. "Dr. Owen, I've sent you half a dozen messages asking about my wife."

"Yes, I know, and I'm sorry about that, but there just hasn't been time until now. We don't know where your wife is, Doctor. If we find her, or if she gets in touch, I'll let you know immediately."

"All right, I'm in too, but I have a question. You said

something about access to phone service. When does that start?"

"If you'll give me a list of people you'd like to call—family and professional associates—I'll have it set up for you by tomorrow morning. That goes for you, too, of course, Ms. Barlow and Mr. Geller."

"Okay. One more thing, my medical bag has been confiscated. Some of the people in my corridor have been asking me for help. I can't even give them an aspirin."

"They can get aspirins at the clinic. I'm sorry, Doctor, I can't do anything about that right now."

"Well, what about letting me work in the clinic, then?"

"Yes, I think that might be arranged." She turned to the computer beside her on the desk. "Mitzi, alternate scheduling for Dr. Wallace McNulty in the clinic, not to conflict with his test scheduling."

"Tuesdays and Thursdays from sixteen hundred to seventeen hundred," said the baritone computer voice.

"Is that all right, Doctor?"

"Sure."

McNulty went away feeling a little better. He had lied about the pills on the spur of the moment; in fact, he was getting all the aspirin and tranquilizers he wanted from Morrison, who took orders for medicine, snack food, liquor, perfume, pens and pencils, anything small enough to carry in a pocket. Most people didn't have much cash—McNulty had none at all—but Morrison would accept travelers' checks, personal checks with bank-card validation, even IOUs. Where he got the stuff McNulty could not imagine, and Morrison would not say.

Owen thought about it when they were gone. What if the parasite was benign? Then they would have wasted the taxpayers' money. But how many generations of infected human beings would it take to prove the point one way or the other? By the time they got to the second or third generation, would there be anybody alive who could make an unbiased judgment?

But it wasn't benign. It was like AIDS, the full effects wouldn't show up for fifteen or twenty years. Somewhere up there in the future, they would be saying, "If it hadn't been for Dr. Owen . . ." That was what she was working for, after all: not the money, not power, but just doing good work and being *right*.

Geller and Barlow went back to the Main Deck and retrieved their son from the Williams' suite down the hall. "Suite" was what Wanda Williams called it; they had three rooms, one for themselves, one for two teen-age daughters, and one for the two younger children. Geoffrey was awake, but he looked tired and cranky; he ran to Barlow and held her tight when she picked him up.

"Thanks, Wanda," she said.

"No trouble. What's one more?" She gave Barlow a slow, tired smile.

"Okay, but I owe you one."

Geoffrey was a terror for the rest of the afternoon. He would not hold still, would not be read to; he yelled and threw his toys. Geller stood it for five minutes, then went out to the lobby. At three o'clock, after Geoffrey had fallen into an exhausted sleep, he came back with a smiling young man in tow. "This is Jim Corcoran. He's here to show us the apartment."

"Let me see if I can get Wanda to sit again. Excuse me." She went next door, put her head in. "Wanda, I have to go out again for half an hour. I hate to ask you, but could you look in on Geoff once in a while? He's asleep."

"Sure, honey. Where you going this time?"

Barlow hesitated. "There's an apartment we might be able to get. We're going over to look at it. Shouldn't take long."

She saw the minute change in Wanda's expression, and felt obscurely guilty as she went back to their own room. "Ready, folks?" said Corcoran.

They walked aft to the perm entrance and waited while the MP guard opened the door. Inside, the broad square was empty, the air stale. "We haven't finished cleaning up in here yet," said Corcoran.

"What happened to the trees?" Barlow said. Here and there in the dead grass they could see a discolored stump.

"I guess they died." Corcoran led the way across the square to a door with a brass knocker. Under the windows on either side were red-painted planters, empty except for a few withered stalks.

"Who used to live here?"

"Don't know."

"I almost remember. The Livermores, was it—the ones who used to have that little market over on Pacific?"

"What difference does it make?" said Geller. They walked in. The living room was pleasantly furnished with a couch and easy chairs, two desks, lamps, a new holo. They looked into the bedrooms; one was large, one small, just right for Geoffrey.

"Looks fine," Geller said. "Yvonne?"

"Sure."

"All right, folks, that's great. I'll give you the keys now and you can move in whenever you get ready. If you have any problems, let me know." Corcoran waved and left.

Geller locked the door behind them with an air of satisfaction. They were halfway back across the square when Barlow stopped and said, "Maybe this is a mistake."

Geller stared at her. "What do you mean, a mistake?"

"If we move out here, we'll be cut off from everybody in passenger."

"That's dumb. We can spend as much time in passenger as we want."

"You know what I mean. If we do this, it's going to be obvious that we've sold out, gone over to the other side. Nobody will even talk to us."

"Yvonne, it's two goddamn bedrooms and a living room. We can have some privacy again."

"All right, but who's going to baby-sit? One of us will be stuck in there all the time, we'll never be able to go out together. I have a lousy feeling about it, Randy."

"So have a lousy feeling about it. Trust me, Yvonne."

The scientist, who examines everything, should look at himself. Tentatively I would define him as a discovery-producing animal whose products fall from him as naturally and as thoughtlessly as a hen produces eggs. Like the hen, he is largely indifferent to the use made of his products. Scientists are mostly not in favor of atom bombs, of course, and hens presumably dislike omelettes; but both are realists and go along with the conditions they find.

—ROBERT SHECKLEY

30 McNulty's name was again on the list for nine o'clock next morning. At eight-thirty he called Owen's office and got a computer image. "Administration, can I help you?"

"My name is Wallace McNulty. Can you tell me if the arrangements have been made for me to make some phone calls today?"

"One moment. I'm sorry, I do not have that information."

"Can I talk to a human being?"

"I'm sorry, no human being is available just now."

"Let me talk to Dr. Owen or her secretary."

"I'm sorry, Dr. Owen and her secretary are not available just now."

McNulty punched off harder than he meant to. He thought about it, then went to the elevator and rode up to the Signal Deck, where an MP stopped him. "Pass, please."

"I have an appointment to use the phone in Dr. Owen's office," McNulty said.

"Sorry, you're not on my list."

"Will you call and see if they're expecting me?"

The MP shrugged, took out his phone and spoke into it. He listened, waited, spoke again. "Dr. McNulty, they say they'll be ready for you after your interview this morning."

"Okay." McNulty went back down to the mall and hung around until nine. Geller and Barlow turned up, but the rest of the bunch were different. Inside, the attendant checked their names on a list and sent half of them in one direction, half in the other. McNulty, Geller, and Barlow

190

found themselves in a room lined with red plastic carrels, each with a terminal and a molded plastic chair.

On the screen in front of McNulty was a message that read: "Thank you for taking the Minnesota Multiphasic Personality Inventory. The inventory consists of numbered statements. Read each statement and decide whether it is true as applied to you or false as applied to you. If a statement is TRUE or MOSTLY TRUE, as applied to you, press 'T.' If a statement is FALSE or NOT USUALLY TRUE, as applied to you, press 'F.' If a statement does not apply to you or if it is something you don't know about, press 'C.'

"Remember to give YOUR OWN opinion about yourself. Do not skip any statements if you can avoid it.

"The first statement is:

"1. My hands and feet are usually warm enough."

McNulty sailed through the first thirty-five statements, but number thirty-six made him stop to think.

"36. I have had very peculiar and strange experiences."

Should he answer that one honestly, knowing it would flag him as a psycho? If he lied, would they fine him twenty thousand dollars and put him in jail for five years? The hell with it; he put down a T and went on.

Number forty-three said, "I do not always tell the truth." There was another one: if he said T, they would flag him as a liar, but who could honestly answer F?

Some of the others were not hard to answer, but they bothered him in a different way. "A minister can cure disease by praying and putting his hand on your head." Was that psychopathology, or just honest faith?

"I do not read every editorial in the paper every day." What was that supposed to prove?

"It is safer to trust nobody." How could anybody disagree with that? They didn't say, "It is better to trust nobody." McNulty put down a T, feeling that it was wrong but that F would be wronger.

"I sometimes feel that people in authority over me are being unjust." T, but McNulty had a sense that he was heading for trouble.

There were five hundred and seventy-five statements. When he finished the last one, the computer said, "THANK YOU. NOW GO TO THE ATTENDANT IN THE MALL FOR FURTHER INSTRUCTIONS."

Instead, McNulty went looking for the men's room, where he met Geller. "Answer all the funny questions?" Geller asked.

"Yes."

"I didn't. I pressed B for bullshit about half the time, and the computer kept giving me an error message."

"Maybe it isn't a good idea to make them mad."

"What can they do to me? Put me in prison?" Geller shook his dong at the urinal, zipped up and left. In the hall, the attendant checked his name on the list. "All right, Geller, Room 'F,' down there."

"Thank you," said Geller. "You've been very kind." In Room F he found the shrink he had seen before, Dr. Quinn. "Hello, Mr. Geller. Feeling all right today?"

"Peachy."

"Fine. Just sit down there at the terminal, if you would. Now this morning I'm going to show you some pictures, and I want you to look at them and make up a story about each one. Here's the first picture." In the screen Geller saw the image of a boy, about fourteen, lying in tall grass with his arm around a dog. The dog's eyes were closed; there was no particular expression on the boy's face.

"Just anything that comes to mind," said Quinn.

"Okay. You want me to just say anything that comes to my mind, right?"

"That's right. Just make up a story."

"Well, this kid, his name is Ralph, he lives in Michigan with his father and his stepmother. The old man is okay, but he drinks a lot and when he drinks he likes to set fire to schoolhouses, so you can imagine the home life is not too great. Now the stepmother, Imogene, is a frustrated ballet dancer who keeps leaping around the house all day in her tutu. The only thing the kid has going for him is his dog, Spot. They call him Spot because he loses his bladder control whenever he sits on the furniture. Well, one day in the early summer, a Wednesday, Ralph takes good old Spot out for a walk in the woods. Now Spot is blind in one eye, but he's a hell of a hunter, and when he sees a rabbit in the bushes he takes off and he's gone. The rabbit gets on his blind side and runs away, but Spot won't give up, and the kid is running after him, yelling, 'Pot! Pot!' Kid can't say his S's, so he's yelling, 'Pot! Pot!'" Geller cranked up his voice to full volume on these words, and saw the psychiatrist wince.

"And the dog pays no attention, of course, because he knows that isn't his name, but a bearded guy in raggedy clothes steps out of the woods and says, 'Did I hear you say pot? Just happen to have some right here, sinsemilla, dynamite stuff, only five bucks a joint.' Well, they sit down to dicker, and meanwhile the dog is still running like hell and by now he's over the next ridge."

Geller went on in this vein for about five minutes; Quinn began to show signs of restlessness. "So he wanders into this whorehouse in Tijuana," said Geller, "and who should be there but the same raggedy guy who sold him the joint. 'Hey, *compadre*,' says the guy, whose name is Bertrand, 'hey,' he says, 'come and have a drink.' Well—"

"How does it end?" asked Quinn.

"Damned if I know. Now you've made me lose the thread."

"Maybe we'd better go on to the next picture," the psychiatrist said. A new image appeared on the screen. This one was of a young woman who was draped over a piano with her head turned to look at a man who was bending toward her with a pipe in his mouth.

"Well, there's a coincidence," said Geller. "That's Bertrand, and he's talking to Conchita, one of the whores in this place in Tijuana. Conchita is actually a good girl who wanted to be a nun, but she was sold into white slavery by her wicked stepfather, Ramón, just when she was about to get married to her boyhood sweetheart."

"I thought you said she wanted to be a nun," said Quinn, looking ruffled.

"She did, but then she realized she was in love with this guy, an apprentice bullfighter who had lost his left leg in a streetcar accident. And she realized it was all for the best, because from her earnings in the whorehouse she could save up and buy him a really great computerized leg. Well, she had enough money for the thigh part and the kneecap when one day who should walk in but Bertrand . . . ."

McNulty was through about a quarter to twelve, and he headed for the administration area. This time the MP let him in; he went to Owen's office, where the receptionist pointed to a holo in the corner. McNulty sat down and punched in his lawyer's number.

"Leonard, D'Amato, and Weinstein, can I help you?"

"This is Wallace McNulty. Can I talk to Phil?"

"One moment."

Phil's head appeared in the tank. "Wally, how are you?"

"I'm okay, but I'm worried about Janice. Can you find out—?"

"Wally, I know something about that. She called me three weeks ago and I gave her the name of a civil-rights lawyer, Alvin Miller, in Washington. As far as I know she went to see him. I haven't heard from her since."

"Oh." McNulty thought a moment. "Better give me his number."

"All right. Just a sec." D'Amato glanced down; in a moment the name and number came up in a window. "Got that?"

McNulty punched for a printout. "Okay. Listen, I'm going to try to call my office, but in case I don't get through, will you check and see if everything is all right?"

"I've already done that, Wally. Ewart says to tell you they're keeping things going and not to worry."

"All right, thanks. Another thing, I'd like to give you a power of attorney, just in case. How do we do that?"

"No problem. Wait till you see the recording sign, then just give your name and say, 'I hereby grant Philip M. D'Amato my power of attorney, this day of September twenty-eight, two thousand four.' "

McNulty repeated the formula. D'Amato came on again and said, "Anything else?"

"Yeah, will you get in touch with Janice's relatives and fill them in? One is Mrs. Bruce Ogilvy, in Seattle, the other is Mrs. Tom Delacourt in Laramie."

D'Amato was writing. "You know their phone numbers?"

"No, but they're in the net. Next thing, would you get somebody to check the apartment?"

"I'll do that myself. Anything else?"

"No, I guess that's it."

"All right. Pat sends her love. Take care of yourself now."

McNulty, who had been fidgeting, punched in the Washington number. He got a computer image. "Wellington, Slake, Miller, and Edge," said the smiling face. "May I ask who is calling?"

"I want to talk to Alvin Miller. It's about my wife, Janice McNulty."

"One moment, please."

A broad dark face appeared. "Dr. McNulty, I've been trying to get in touch with you, but without success. I wanted you to know that I discussed with your wife the possibility of filing a writ of habeas corpus in the Supreme Court, and I am in the process of doing that, but I don't want you to count on it. It may take a long time."

McNulty's spirits lifted. "You talked to her, when?"

"Let me see. That was on the tenth."

"Well, have you heard from her since? Do you know where she is?"

"No. I take it she has not been in touch with you either."

"No." Suddenly he felt awful again. "If she— Wait a minute. Is there any way you could find out if they arrested her and took her somewhere else?"

"Only by filing another writ. But as I told you, that is a long process."

"How long?"

"At least a year and a half."

"Christ!"

"Congressional action might be a little quicker. I mentioned that to your wife. But it is very uncertain."

"You mean there's nothing you can do, legally?"

"Nothing but what I have told you. Are you able to

receive phone calls now at the Medical Detention Center?"

"Yes. I mean, I guess so."

"I'll be in touch with you, then, in case I learn anything."

McNulty punched off and sat looking at the empty tank. The anger was coming up again, and he realized that there was fear underneath it. If he refused to cooperate anymore, they would cut off his phone privileges again. For the first time since he was a kid in medical school, he needed somebody to tell him what to do. And there wasn't anybody.

When he got up to leave, the receptionist motioned to him. "Dr. McNulty, Dr. Owen has scheduled a staff meeting for two o'clock and would like you to attend. It will be in the conference room just down the hall."

"Okay. I know where it is."

McNulty went down to the Main Deck and found a deserted corner of one of the lobbies to brood in. He couldn't bear the thought of the cafeteria, but he knew he ought to eat something. He went and looked at the snack machines across the lobby; they were empty, as they had been since he arrived as a prisoner. Why couldn't they at least keep the damned machines filled? He realized what kind of emotional state he was getting himself into; if he had been a patient, he would have prescribed a tranquilizer. In the end he went to the cafeteria after all, got a candy bar and a plastic bulb of milk, and took them back to his stateroom.

At two he went back upstairs, showed his pass to the guard, and walked into the conference room. Owen was there with four men and a dark-haired woman at the long table. "Come in, Doctor," Owen said. "Please sit down.

Dr. McNulty, this is Donald Strang, Carl Meyer, Glen Cunningham, Jerry Plotkin, and Dorothy Italiano." Strang was a man in his forties, dark-skinned, with recent hair transplants marching across his forehead like seedlings in a tree plantation. Meyer was plump and blond, with a meaningless smile; Plotkin and Cunningham were skinny and pale; Italiano had a monobrow and a fairly distinct mustache.

"Dr. McNulty, we asked you to come here to discuss your experiences—" Owen began.

"Before we get into that," McNulty said, "where is my wife?"

"Doctor, I don't know. I told you that before."

"She went to a lawyer the day after I was brought in here. He hasn't seen her since then, and she hasn't phoned. Has she been arrested and taken somewhere else?"

"To my knowledge, no."

"Well, dammit, that isn't good enough."

Owen put her hands on the table palms up. "Doctor, I understand your natural concern, but what can I do about it? If your wife had been detained as a McNulty's patient or had turned herself in, she would be here."

"What if she was arrested for something else?"

"That might be a different story. Let's think. I can ask the Justice Department to look into it—will that satisfy you?"

"Maybe."

"All right. When we finish here, give my secretary her name, social security number, and so on."

"Let's do that now."

"Right now?"

"Right now."

She looked at him. "Very well." She took her phone

out of her pocket. "Mr. Corcoran, please take down this information, and then I'll tell you what I want you to do with it." She handed the phone to McNulty.

Feeling like a fool, McNulty said, "The name is Janice Werth McNulty. Age thirty-eight, five feet six, red hair, a hundred thirty pounds. No distinguishing marks. Last seen in Washington, D.C., on the tenth. Before that she was in Seattle."

"Social security number?" Owen asked.

"I don't know it. Seven-oh-seven something."

She took the phone back. "Will you get on the phone to Mr. Ybarra at Justice, please, and ask him to find out if Mrs. McNulty is in custody anywhere? Start with federal, then state, county, and local." She paused. "One more thing, Dr. McNulty. If it turns out she is not in custody, do you want the FBI to put out a bulletin?"

McNulty opened his mouth and shut it again. "No."

Owen put the phone away. "All right, now we can get on to the questions we have for you. Would you like a recess first?"

"No, I'm okay. Shoot."

She glanced at Strang, who folded his hands and leaned over the table. "Dr. McNulty, you said that after you had the disease you found yourself becoming more tolerant toward 'offbeat therapies'? Is that right?"

"Well, yeah."

"Have you practiced any offbeat therapies?"

"No. Well, I'm doing a little more dietary stuff now. Sometimes it seems to work."

"So this is mainly just a change in your attitude. Can you tell me why your attitude changed?"

"Maybe because I had the disease."

"But was that how it appeared to you?"

"No, I just started noticing some things that didn't

fit. A patient of mine had a bad acid burn on his arm, a lot of scar tissue, really disfiguring. He spent a year in Ireland, and when he came back the scar had almost disappeared. I asked him what happened, and he said he went to one of the local healers—'bonesetters,' they call them. In the old days I guess they set bones, but they don't any more. Anyway, he said this healer just passed his hand over the scar, didn't even touch it. And he felt a kind of coolness and prickling on his skin. The next day the scar started to shrink. Well, I know this guy, and I saw the scar before and after. So if that isn't a cure, what is it? If it's not conservative medicine, maybe medicine is too conservative. That's all. I don't know the answers."

"Have you noticed any change in your political attitudes?"

"No."

"How do you feel about the present administration?"

"I think it stinks, but I thought so before."

Strang made a note. "Now about the career changes and marital breakups you have observed, how do you feel about that?"

"As far as I can tell, most of them were happier afterward. People who hated their jobs, or their husbands or whatever."

"What if everybody who didn't like their job or their spouse decided to get out?"

McNulty said, "I've thought about that, and it bothers me. But maybe it's the wrong question. You could pick anything and say, 'What if everybody did that?' What if everybody wanted to be a doctor, or an accountant? But they don't, so it isn't a problem. Maybe the right question is, why do people stick with jobs they can't stand or marriages that aren't working? I don't know the answer to that one, either."

After waiting for a few days, McNulty gave in and had himself transferred to the perm section.

In the town park one morning a man came over to him. "Dr. McNulty, do you remember me? I am Jamal Marashi, from Sea Venture."

"Oh, yes." McNulty remembered him very well: he was the one who had hit his wife in the mouth. Five stitches. "How are you, Mr. Marashi? Is your wife here?"

"Yes, she is here, and they have put us together in the same room, even though we are divorced now for more than a year. I have not had peace for a moment. That woman complains constantly. I gave her the divorce, but they have put us in the same room. I want to ask you, Dr. McNulty, can you kindly speak to the authorities? It is not right for us to be in the same room."

McNulty saw another familiar face and escaped with relief. The woman was sitting at the other end of the park, with a child beside her.

She looked around as he approached, smiled with pleasure. "Dr. McNulty! You, too?"

"Afraid so." They shook hands, and McNulty sat down beside her. "Kim," she said to the child, "this is Dr. McNulty—he was my doctor before you were born."

The child looked at him solemnly. "Why?" she said.

"I don't know. Hello, Kim."

"Hello."

McNulty glanced at the wedding ring on the woman's hand. "You're married now. To that young man, what was his name, Stevens?"

She looked embarrassed, or perhaps alarmed. "No, someone else. His name is Robert Ames."

"Is he here with you?"

"No, he was on a trip when—this happened. I don't know where he is now."

McNulty searched for a neutral topic. "Parents okay?"

She looked down, compressed her lips. "My father died recently. My mother became hysterical when the police took me away after the funeral."

"Oh, hell," said McNulty.

31 In the "A" Deck cafeteria, Stevens was put to work unpacking cartons of mashed potatoes, feeding lettuce into the saladmaker, filling plasticware and napkin dispensers, and performing other tasks considered degrading by the more experienced workers. He did all these things cheerfully, showed deference to everyone, and stayed out of the way.

It took him several days to find out where Julie was—in perm, with most of the families and women with children. Then it was necessary to cultivate a woman who worked in perm and arrange a trade in assignments. On Monday he went to work with the early shift in perm.

He saw her at breakfast, with the child. They were with a group of people; Stevens recognized several of them, including Geller and Barlow. She did not see him.

She appeared again the next day at the same time, and took the same breakfasts: French toast for herself, Winkies and milk for the child. On Wednesday Stevens wrote a note: *Don't show surprise or look around. I am here. Write your address on another piece of paper and drop it in the trash when you leave.* He folded the note small, taped it shut, and wrote on the outside, *Julie Prescott.* He left the note in front of the row of Winkies boxes on the carousel.

From the pass-through window behind the counter he saw her pick up the note. He put his head down. When he looked up again, she was at the coffee dispenser. He busied himself with the hashbrown machine until she had had time to go through the line with her tray.

Afterward he saw her put her tray on the conveyor; she had not eaten anything. She dropped a wad of paper in the trash can as she left. When Stevens went out to bus the tables, he picked it up and put it in his pocket. He read it in the lavatory: it said, *118 Oak near Pacific. I love you. Hurry.*

At the staff meeting on Monday, Owen noted with satisfaction certain signs of improved morale. People came in looking well rested and alert; they didn't straggle or slouch in their chairs, didn't talk among themselves, they sat up straight and waited for the meeting to begin.

"I hope you've all had a pleasant weekend," she said. "Carl, let's begin with you today. How are you coming with the EEG?"

"Well, we're refining the Fourier analyses. We have a program now that will recognize a McNulty's EEG pattern with about sixty percent accuracy, but it also gives false positives more than twenty-five percent of the time."

"You need another program to screen out the false positives," said Strang.

"Okay, and we're working on that, but what we really need is more accuracy in the primary program."

"How long do you think it will take?" Owen asked.

"Six months to a year."

"Glen, how are you doing with detection devices?"

"Well, at least we know it can be done. A simple electroscope discharges when the parasite passes within a few centimeters of it on a direct line from one host to another. We were also able to correlate that with visual recordings and get a good estimate of the speed of travel, by the way. It's on the order of ten meters a second."

"And it travels about a hundred twenty centimeters between hosts?"

"We haven't recorded a transfer more than ninety so far."

"So that means roughly that you've got a tenth of a second to attack it in transit."

"That's right, and that includes detection time, aiming, and so on. We have some military fire control systems that will respond well within that time frame, but the problem is detection. One thing we're looking at is a system based on EEG signals at the moment the parasite leaves the host. Those are dramatic—no problem there. What we're thinking of is a miniaturized EEG remote that could be worn as a cap, with a radio link to the weapons system. In a confined situation where you know the parasite is present, you could put one of these devices on everybody and wait for the parasite to move."

"How long do you estimate for that?"

"I'd say at least a year to a working model."

"Could you get there sooner with more staff?"

"Sure."

"All right, let's discuss that later. Anything else? Any Monday morning ideas?"

After a moment Meyer said, "I think we ought to be looking into electroshock. That's quantifiable, and it's harmless under the right supervision. If that happened to work out, we could modify the EEG helmet with a power pack to deliver a jolt to the frontal lobes. That way you'd have the whole thing in one package, and it would even take care of the false positives problem. You get a positive EEG, deliver a jolt, the EEG confirms that the parasite has left, and then you zap it."

Owen nodded thoughtfully. "Glen," she said, "what if you didn't have to come up with a really sophisticated model of the EEG helmet, could you give me something that could be used to screen a fairly large group of people very rapidly?"

"How many people?"

"A hundred or so, and I'd like to be able to do it in not more than twenty minutes."

He scratched his chin. "Well, you could do that with conventional instruments—the only problem would be getting that many EEG machines and the personnel to operate them."

"Can you think of a simpler way? And I want it by next Thursday."

He smiled, flattered. "I'll see what I can do."

Two mornings later Cunningham said, "I think I've got something on that little problem, Harriet. It was Dorothy's skin-potential gadget that gave me the idea." He held up the little box with its two wires ending in shiny metal cylinders. "It's rude and crude, but as far as I can see, it does the same job as a ten-thousand-dollar machine. It isn't scientific, okay, but neither are they. So my idea is, run your subjects through a station where they just hold these contacts and somebody asks them if anybody has collapsed near them recently. If the answer is no, send them on through. The ones that answer yes, probably a small number, can go on to a station where they get a standard EEG, and that way you can process most of them in less than five minutes apiece. I'd say to control the process, from this point on we ought to keep each one isolated, and have guards standing by."

"I think that's brilliant," said Owen. "And Dorothy, hats off to you too. Let's see, the work squads assemble in the forward lobby on the Main Deck and on the Sports Deck in perm. Suppose we set up screens to funnel them through . . ." She looked up. "Jerry, I think we're going to lick the shortage of hosts."

After the tearful reunion, and the best passage at arms he had had with Julie in years, he said, "Where is Kim?"

"I left her with a neighbor. If she knew you were here, she might say something. And besides . . ."

"And besides." He kissed her. "All right. Now let me tell you what is going to happen. I can't come here anymore, it's too dangerous, and passing notes is danger-ous too, so we have to make all our plans now. In a few days we are going to get out of here. When the time comes, you will give Kim a sleeping pill and bring her to the door of the cafeteria kitchen area, past the rest rooms on the right. I will open the door and wheel out a cart with a frozen storage chest on it. In the chest will be an ID card identifying you as a kitchen worker."

"A frozen storage chest? She'll stifle."

"I will cut holes in the chest so that she can breathe. You will take the ID card out of the chest and put it on. You put the child in the chest and close the lid. Then you go to the service elevator and ride up to the Sports Deck.

If anyone asks you any questions, you are a new worker and you are not quite sure what deck you have been working on. Clear so far?"

"Where will you be?"

"I'll be there too. Once we are off CV, we will carry the chest to a truck that will be waiting. Then they will never see us again."

"All right. When?"

"First a dry run. Tomorrow, at exactly four-twenty, be at the door I told you about. Where is it?"

"At the end of the corridor, past the rest rooms."

"I will open the door. I won't speak, but I will see that you are there. What time does Kim come home from school?"

"Two-thirty."

"All right. Today give her one of these pills and watch to see how long it takes to put her to sleep and when she wakes up. Make sure the pill doesn't nauseate her or cause any other symptoms except sleepiness. If everything is all right, tomorrow morning wear something red. Then the dry run. The day after that, unless you see me wearing something blue, you will know we are going to do it that afternoon."

"John, I don't like this."

"I don't either, but it's the best way. Tomorrow, then. At what time?"

"Four-twenty."

The dry run was satisfactory. Stevens finished his chores early and hung back while the others went into the locker room. Precisely at four-twenty he opened the door to the corridor. She was there. He did not speak; he closed the door.

The line out of the elevators across the Sports Deck was moving with unusual slowness today. Up ahead, he could see that pulpboard screens had been arranged to form a passageway on the deck. MPs stood on either side of the entrance. They were admitting workers four at a time.

With three others, Stevens walked into the passage. At the end of it, pulpboard screens formed a little room with four desks. Behind each desk sat a white-coated technician; there was some kind of apparatus on the desks.

"Sit down here," said a guard. Stevens sat, facing a young woman in a white smock, who said, "Pick up those cylinders, please. Just hold them comfortably. Has anyone else collapsed near you recently?"

"No," said Stevens, but he was thinking of the men he had hit in the kneecap.

She gave him a white card. "To the left," she said.

Stevens' brain was working furiously. Evidently this was a crude form of lie detector. Had he been caught? He must assume so.

Others, who had blue cards, were going to the right. Stevens took a chance and tried to follow them, concealing his white card in his hand, but a guard caught him and turned him back. At the end of the left-hand passage he found himself in another pulpboard room with a couch and an electronic device. A technician and four young MPs were standing at the far end of the room. The MPs were carrying aluminum poles with some kind of mechanical device at the end of them.

"Lie down there," said a technician.

"What is this for?" Stevens asked.

"It's just a test to screen out people who have had

McNulty's or might be carriers. Pick up that tube of gel on the table." Following instructions, Stevens applied gel to his forehead, taped contacts to his skin.

"If I don't pass this, can I still work here?" he asked.

"Oh, sure."

A few minutes later the technician said, "Stand up and pull the leads off." He nodded toward the MPs; two of them came forward, and one of them suddenly thrust his pole at Stevens' waist. The other, circling behind him, did the same from the rear. Stevens stood trembling. "Why are you doing this?"

The technician said, "Your test results indicate you are carrying a McNulty's parasite. Next."

They took him down to the lab section and locked him in a cage. The room was full of other cages, a dozen of them occupied by human prisoners, men and women alike. "Welcome to the club," said the man next to him. He introduced himself, and so did the woman on the other side. His name was Max Engelhardt, hers was Elvira Hamm. They were interested to hear that Stevens had been taken from the work crew. That had never happened before, they said. They themselves were volunteers from the detainee population.

"You volunteered for this?" Stevens asked.

Engelhardt shrugged. "Who knew what it was going to be like?"

"What is it like?"

Engelhardt looked away. "Various things. Don't worry."

Dinner was wheeled in on carts; curtains were drawn between the cages (to spare them the sight of each other's table habits?). After dinner Stevens opened the Bible to Romans and read: "Now I beseech you, brethren, mark them which cause divisions and offenses contrary to the doctrine which ye have learned; and avoid them. For they that are such serve not our Lord Jesus Christ, but their own belly; and by good words and fair speeches deceive the hearts of the simple." The lights went out at ten.

The next morning after breakfast the MPs came for Stevens and six others. They locked their poles around his waist and took him down the corridor to a laboratory.

"Good morning, Mr. Bankier," said a voice from the holo across the room. "My name is Dr. Meyer. Will you sit down there, please, and just put the leads from that machine on your forehead the way you did before?"

Over the next couple of weeks, McNulty's hours in the clinic were gradually increased until he was working four hours a day. He was on a rota that included Fabian, Smith, and other MDs from the testing program; none of the other doctors were particularly enthusiastic about the clinic, and one by one they found various excuses to let McNulty fill in.

The ailments he was seeing now were different from his resident-physician days on CV. Then it had been mostly colds, ear infections, an occasional broken bone, and a lot of chronic things in older folks that just needed maintenance therapy. Now he hardly ever saw a cold, but there were a lot of rashes, asthma attacks, gastric pains, insomnia, tricky things because any one of them might be psychosomatic or psychogenic—probably was—but you had to look for a physical cause every time.

People were allowed in shifts onto the Promenade Deck and the Sports Deck for daily exercise. They gathered in each other's rooms and in lobbies for sociability, and in the evenings there were lectures, panel discussions, meetings of Spanish students and gardeners. More and more, though, it seemed to McNulty, people were spending their free time watching holovision. The news channels were heavily patronized. Police had broken up a rally of Wilbornites in Bryant Park after fighting broke out when alleged members of the Freedom Left tried to tear down a swastika banner. Pastor Wilborn himself had been slightly injured. President Draffy, in his monster suit with its plastic gloves and plexy hood, was running for reelection against Richard Rickart. There was a war in Iran and another one in Africa. Three men had been killed putting up the framework of the Space Habitat in orbit, the first construction fatalities in space. There was an interview with one of the widows: "He wanted to be up there. He knew what the risks were," she said.

In early October the first manned expedition to Mars reached its goal. Everyone sat around the holos for that one.

"We take you now to Houston," said the anchor, "where signals from the Mars expedition are being received."

The tank cleared and they saw the face of one of the astronauts, Skip Conroy, who appeared to be wearing his spacesuit without the helmet. The transmission was streaked and grainy. At first there was nothing but static; then they heard: "And I'm going to hope you're reading me, Houston, because it'll be twenty minutes before we can get your reply, so I'll just go on talking. The landing was nominal, right on the money, and systems checks are all in the green, so in a minute now we're going to go EVA, and that's a moment we're all looking forward to. While we're getting ready, we can give you a look at the Martian landscape." The camera swung erratically, swung back, and approached a porthole. Reflected light turned it blank; then they could see a pinkish desert with scattered rocks.

"Ah, Houston, we read you, and so we're going to hope our transmission is still getting through." The camera swung back to Conroy, who was putting on his helmet. It dipped and swayed for a moment; then they could see Conroy opening a hatch in the wall of the spacecraft. The camera followed him as he moved through the opening; now they could see his foreshortened body as it turned and receded down a metal ladder. He stepped onto the rocky soil, looked up at the camera. "That's one more footprint in the soil of another, oops," he said. Spreading his arms for balance, he did a funny little slow-motion backward dance and finally sat down in a cloud of dust. "Another *planet,*" he said.

"Lives of great men all remind us," said Geller, "we can make our lives a race. And, departing, leave behind us sitz-marks in the sands of space."

They were sitting at the kitchen table in Barlow and Geller's apartment, drinking illicit bourbon; McNulty had a beer, which was harder to get than booze because it was bulkier.

"Do you know how much it cost to put that asshole on Mars?" Geller asked.

"No."

"All right, it just happens that I do know, so I'll tell you. From start to finish, it cost a trillion dollars and change. Now you folks may be having a little trouble visualizing a number like that, so I'll help you out. No, don't thank me, it's part of the service. A trillion happens to be about two hundred fifty dollars for every man, woman and child in the world."

"Worth it to me, just in entertainment value," said Barlow.

"Right, but what about a guy with a wife and four kids who doesn't make that much in a year?"

"Randy, you're no fun anymore," said Barlow.

The two Marines brought the prisoner in screaming. He threw himself back and forth in the restraints at the ends of the poles, making it difficult to get him into the chair.

"Mr. Frankensteen, this isn't helping," said Jerry Plotkin from the holoscreen. "Please stop that noise, or we'll have to put the gag in your mouth."

Frankensteen paid no attention. He was red-faced and his mouth was frothy. He was not even shouting words anymore; his voice was that of a wounded animal.

The guards looked at Plotkin's image in the screen. He nodded. "Go ahead."

One of the guards hooked the restraint at the end of his pole around Frankensteen's jaw from behind, forcing his mouth open. The other guard crossed the room and picked up the rubber gag from a table, loaded it into his pole, and got it into Frankensteen's mouth after three tries. The two MPs were white-faced. They left, carrying their poles, and closed the door behind them.

In that part of him that could stand aside, he was sickened and appalled by the man's pain. He dared not go into the rat because he knew that meant death. They would put the rat in a concrete shell. But the man was weakening. Soon he would have to get out of this body or be trapped in it when it died.

They had locked his bare arm onto the chair, and now the jointed pole came swinging over to smear the graphite onto his skin. It was cool, but he felt it as fire. Then the apparatus itself swung over, and the real heat began. "This is number one," said Plotkin's voice.

The man in the holoscreen was out of reach. There was nothing to go to but the little rat in the cage and the faintly humming computer on the table. In despair, he slid out into the gray space toward that alien pattern of energy, and in again where there was no mind, only the quick whispering tickle of scanning circuits. The heat and pain were gone; it could not even hear the voice anymore.

32 Owen asked, "How is the pain experiment coming, Jerry?"

"Not so good. We've been doing two sessions a day for five days, and that's eight days in all that the subject has been infected—that's four days beyond the point where the host *died* on Sea Venture—and we still haven't got a transfer. The subject is not in very good shape. We've got him sedated between sessions, but it's still pretty unpleasant."

"Do you want to discontinue this series and try something else?"

"I'd love to, but I don't see how we *can*. We have to find out how long the parasite can stay in one host, and we have to demonstrate the transfer to an animal if we can, and we really haven't got anything more promising. Either the pain will drive the parasite out or the natural term will, if there is one."

"Jerry, a procedural point," said Italiano. "How sure are we that the parasite is still in this subject?"

Plotkin looked at her. "I don't understand what you're asking. Where else could it be?"

"I don't know, but if I remember, something like that happened on Sea Venture. Dr. Owen, do you recall it? It was the lifeboat thing."

Plotkin stubbed out his cigarette. "I don't consider that a constructive comment," he said. His voice rose slightly. "We've kept that subject isolated. Nobody has been near him except the rat, and we've exposed the rat to another rat after every session."

"What are his EEG readings like?" Strang asked.

"Inconclusive, but there is *no* reason to believe that the parasite isn't in him. Our procedures have been scrupulously careful, we haven't let anything near him, and I resent this line of questioning."

"A suggestion," said Owen. "Let's have a short recess, and then get Dr. McNulty in here. Barlow and Geller too, perhaps. I want to explore what options we have. Jerry, however this turns out, I think we could start over with another subject, don't you? That might actually get us more data."

Plotkin looked at her gratefully and mumbled something. He filed out with the others, lighting another cigarette.

Geller was scheduled for tests, as it turned out, but the other two were free. When they were seated, Owen said, "Thank you both for coming. Dr. McNulty, let's start with you. We've been looking over the information we have about what happened on CV, and there's something that puzzles us. Maybe you can clear it up."

"Okay."

"You collapsed on May second, I believe, and you were stuporous for about eight days."

"So they told me."

"But prior to that, you were not aware that anyone had collapsed near you?"

"No."

"Thinking back, is it possible that someone did collapse within five feet of you without your being aware of it, sometime within the previous three or four days?"

"I don't see how."

"Who was the last patient to collapse before you, do you know?"

"Somebody on the lifeboat—a steward, maybe."

"What lifeboat was that?"

"We were trying to isolate the carrier on a lifeboat, but it got away."

"And did you subsequently infect someone else?"

"Yes. Dan Jacobs. He was in the Control Center at the time, with a bunch of other people, and he collapsed a little later down in his office."

"So there isn't any doubt in your mind that you did have the disease?"

"No."

"But you don't know how you got it."

"That's right."

"Dr. McNulty, you can see why this is worrying us, because if the parasite can sometimes transfer itself to another host without making the previous one collapse, then some of our assumptions about it may be wrong."

"I went back over it at the time, and I couldn't explain it."

"This Dan Jacobs, do you know what became of him?"

"He got off at Manila like everybody else. Where he went from there I don't know."

"One more thing. As I understand it, you tried to isolate the parasite on Sea Venture by drugging the host and locking him up in a stateroom. And he died as a result of that."

"Yes."

"I'm sorry to bring this up, but we have to know. Was he already dead when you reached him or was he still alive?"

"He was convulsing. He might have been clinically dead at that point, if you mean brain dead, but he stopped moving after I got there."

"So you would say he was alive when the parasite left him?"

"Right."

"Thank you, Doctor. Now, Ms. Barlow, one question we've never addressed is just this: why is the parasite limited to four or five feet in moving from one host to another? There might be some physical reason, like the resistance of the air—were you going to speak, Mr. Cunningham?"

"There would be a way to test that," Cunningham said. "Not air, because we can't pressurize a tube and still get the parasite into it, but water. Say a tank with two tubes sticking up, one at each end. The tank is in the middle of a partition, so the parasite can't get to the new subject except by going through the water."

"That's assuming it doesn't have to travel in a direct line between hosts," said Strang.

"True."

"In any event," Owen said, "I wonder if there isn't another explanation, and this is what I'd like your suggestions on, Ms. Barlow. Do you think it's possible that the parasite can't live outside a host for more than a few seconds—that it's time that limits it, rather than distance?"

"That short a time would be very unusual," Barlow said. "But it isn't at all unusual for parasites to take terrible risks. Blood flukes, for instance. The miracidia have to find an intermediate host within twenty-four hours or they die and that's the end of them. When you think about it, they're really very brave."

"You're fond of your blood flukes, aren't you, Ms. Barlow?" said Owen, smiling. "Thank you both; we'll excuse you now."

When the two visitors had left, Meyer said, "I think we ought to do Glen's water experiment. If that works out, we can try some denser liquid, maybe glycerol, and that would be useful data, but it still wouldn't rule out the hypothesis that time outside the host is the limiting factor. Now if *that's* right, all we have to do is isolate a carrier for whatever it takes, fifteen days or whatever, and the parasite will die. Period. The other possibility is, we may find out that the parasite dies with the host if it doesn't get out in time. Okay, then if we kill the host suddenly, there's another dead parasite. I think this problem looks tougher than it is."

Early Sunday morning a man was brought into the hospital with bandaged wrists: Nat Frankensteen, a detainee. McNulty was on call; when he got there he found the patient sedated. The night nurse, a volunteer named Linda Koger, had filled out a slip with the patient's name, and that was all.

"Was he like this when he came in?" McNulty asked.

"Yes, Doctor. One of the medics said they gave him a shot of Thorazine."

The patient, a man about thirty, was wearing green short-sleeved hospital pajamas; his feet were bare. No watch, no rings.

"You get his history from the computer?"

"No, not yet."

"Do that." McNulty removed the bandages, took a couple of stitches, and rebandaged the wrists. The wounds were in the right places but too shallow to do much damage. On the inner surfaces of both forearms there were a number of circular inflamed areas about the size of a dime, some fresh, some almost completely healed; a couple of them were giant blisters full of serum, and the skin around them looked grimy, although the rest of the man's body was fairly clean.

"Here's the history, Doctor."

McNulty went to the computer and read the display. Nat Frankensteen, 28, detainee. Not a McNulty's patient; he was here because he was married to one. Wife also a detainee, no children. One or two childhood diseases; pneumonia in 1990. No record of skin diseases or allergies.

Well, he didn't think there would be. Those spots were too regular, almost perfect circles. What had the young man been doing to himself, or what had somebody else done to him?

The rules are all written by others.
                                        —BUCKMINSTER FULLER

33 Monday morning Plotkin came into Owen's office before the staff meeting and said around his cigarette, "We've got a mess. Frankensteen tried to commit suicide Saturday night."

"Who is Frankensteen? Sit down, Jerry."

"The subject in the pain experiments." Plotkin, whose hands were deep in his pockets, threw himself into a chair. "The MPs had strict orders not to go into his cage, but when they saw him bleeding, they sent for the medics, and the medics took him down to the hospital. Nobody notified me, and I didn't find out about it till this morning."

"Jerry, I don't understand. What did he cut himself with?"

"It's almost unbelievable, but he took apart the Bible in his cage, and apparently he was able to cut his wrists with a little sliver of glue out of the binding. He didn't cut them *deep,* his life certainly wasn't in danger, but who knew he could do it at all?"

"All right, now let's think. Where is Frankensteen, still in the hospital?"

"No, I had them take him back to his cage and sedate him. The two medics, I reported them to Colonel Mattison's office with a request to turn them over to us as detainees, at least until we can determine if they're carrying the parasite. But it's hopeless by now—there's the doctor and a nurse in the hospital, anybody else who could have wandered in, anybody they could have met in the hall . . ."

"All right. Who was on duty in the hospital?"

"McNulty. And a nurse named Koger."

"Well, McNulty is a recovered patient, of course. Mitzi, a nurse in the hospital named Koger—her status?"

"Linda Koger, detainee, recovered patient, volunteer nurse."

"There, so as far as they're concerned it really is hopeless, and we might as well not worry about it. The question is, what do we do with Frankensteen?"

"We can't use him in experiments again."

"No, I didn't mean that. If he's suicidal, or disturbed, we haven't really got the facilities to treat him here. I suppose he signed a release?"

"Yes. We told him if the experiment succeeded and the parasite went into a rat, we would release him and his wife."

"Wife here too?" Owen bit her lip. "I begin to see what you mean; this is a mess, isn't it? Jerry, tell me something. I think I remember we talked about limiting the experiment to eight dols. Did you do that?"

"No, I went up to eleven. It wasn't *working* at eight, that's why. As far as consideration for the subject, it would have been better if we went to eleven and got results, than staying down at eight and just going on and *on.*" Plotkin's voice trembled.

"Never mind. That was probably a mistake, but that isn't the point now. Let's say this. I'll get a psychiatric evaluation of Frankensteen, and if he's too disturbed to be sent home, that will probably be the best solution— we'll transfer him to a mental hospital or a psychiatric unit ashore. We'll discharge Mrs. Frankensteen separately, and in that way, if there should be any repercussions, the fact that Frankensteen has been in a mental institution will probably be enough. Jerry, I know you've been under a strain, and I sympathize. Why don't you go home now—take the week off, more if you need it. We'll talk about this later."

"Are you letting me go?"

"No, I'm not, and this has nothing to do with your career. Your contract will be honored, whether or not you decide to come back to work. There won't be *anything* on your record; I can promise you that. Go on home now, Jerry."

"That was stupid," Strang said. "I should have known something was the matter when he asked for exclusive use of that one subject."

"Don't blame yourself, Donald," Owen said. "We don't need to get into a round of mea culpa, we just want to make sure nothing like this happens again. Who do you think should take over the rat experiments?"

"Wes Schultz, Jerry's assistant. He's familiar with the problem, and he's done a good deal of animal work. I'd say give it to him at least temporarily. I'll supervise."

"I always thought he was a jerk, myself," Cunningham said.

"A little charity, Glen. God has a purpose even for people named Jerry."

How long it had been drowsing in the metal box with its long slow resting rhythms it did not know. It had been in many such boxes. It was aware now that there were others beside it in that cold electric space, but it could not touch or feel them. It roused suddenly when a signal penetrated its darkness: 000000000000000000000000000

0000000111111 . . . It flowed down the wire into the child's finger, up into her brain. She was looking at the three red balls on the screen; her finger had just lifted from the illuminated key. She saw that the number of the key and the red number on the screen were the same, and she understood what that meant. Now the next one was going to be four. But she was hardly aware of all this, because she felt her sisters around her and heard their dear voices:

Wonderful to be   Twenty-seven now.
  with you all,   *Amusement*   How many
    hello.   angels can?

   Thirty.   Signs of   Last in,   *Pop.*
      stress now.   good-bye.   One more out
                                  for safety.
                    Pop.

  All right?   All right.   All right.

              very
This one is moderately comfortable. Parent here?
          extremely

                   Yes.
   Compliments.

Wesley Schultz looked like an undergraduate, although he was in his early thirties—tall, awkward, even a trace of acne. He grinned shyly when Strang told him about his promotion. "Hey, you know, I don't want to seem like an eager beaver, but I had an idea this morning about the rat problem."

"Yes?" Strang poured a cup of coffee, added whitener.

"Question: how does the parasite know there is a host to go to? Unless it has some special senses of its own, it must be that the current host knows there is another person in the room. So the current host sees the other person and can tell the distance is right, the parasite decides to go and it makes the transfer."

"O-ho." Strang put his coffee down. "What if the current host is in a dark room, or what if he's blind and deaf?"

"Good point. That's something else to check out. Have we got any blind people?"

"I don't know. If not, I imagine we can get some."

"Okay. Now, in the meantime, suppose we've got a parasite who's been in the current host too long, wants to move. Let's say we put a rat behind a screen. The host doesn't know it's there, so neither does the parasite. Now, just behind the screen we put this wall of nonreflecting glass, like the ones they use in holotanks. A subject walks in, behind the glass which the host can't see, and disappears behind the screen. The parasite moves, goes behind the screen, and there's nothing there but the rat. What's it going to do?"

"Can it move except in straight lines?"

"That's another thing we don't know. According to the detection studies, it always has moved in straight lines, but there never was an obstacle for it to go around. Anyway, is it worth a try?"

"I think so. Let me talk to Owen about setting it up."

Strang started to explain the idea, but Owen interrupted him. "Wait a minute." She turned to the computer on her desk. "Mitzi, give me a bar chart of detainees with physical handicaps, and another for McNulty's victims not in custody."

The charts appeared on the screen. "Talk about blind," Owen said.

"Blind is a term applied to—"

"Cancel. I wasn't speaking to you." She looked up. "It was right in front of me, and I didn't see it. We have all kinds of other disabilities, hearing problems, even a couple of paraplegics, but not a single blind person." She turned to the computer again.

At the boundary of its perception were inputs of machine-language data, program commands and algorithms, retinal images cycling thirty-two times a second, auditory signals filtered and reencoded. At the level on which it existed it was able to perform ten million logical operations during the time consumed by each coherent visual image. The user input consisted of these images and the auditory signals read in conjunction. As each speech gesture was identified and added to the string, it projected multiple string outcomes. By the time the string was within five hundred milliseconds of the end it had projected the actual outcome to within one percent of certainty. Nevertheless, following program commands, it delayed the start of its answering message until five hundred milliseconds after the string was completed.

The reply called for loading data not immediately accessible in its memory, and the projected loading time was in excess of 1.5 seconds; therefore, according to the program, it constructed and began to encode the message, "Just a moment, I'm loading data," even though the real-time articulation of that message would consume 1.8 seconds. The message began going out in the audio synthesizer circuits. During the time required for completion, it was able to perform 57.6 million logical operations. The answer to the question was then available, and after an obligatory delay of five hundred milliseconds it encoded and began to articulate that answer. In the strange world outside the boundary, the figure of Dr. Harriet Cleaver Owen sat and waited to receive it.

"Good morning, Miss Balter," said the face in the holo. "How are you feeling?"

"A little tired. How much longer do I have to stay here?"

"Probably not long. This is your eighteenth day, isn't it?"

"Yes."

They had put her chair in a different place. She was facing a tall gray screen with a narrow doorway behind it, and there was a jointed rod that came out of the ceiling and hung in front of the doorway. "What's that thing for?"

"Just a sensor. Now, Miss Balter—is anything wrong?"

The pressure was mounting, and she closed her eyes for a moment. When she opened them, she saw a man in a white coat walking past the doorway in front of her, and she let go gladly, drifting out into that gray space, remembering the last words she had heard, "Is anything wrong?"

It was the pattern that was wrong, but there was no other, and she slipped in and saw the world blur through the bars of a cage.

Next time he was on duty McNulty looked into the cubicle where Frankensteen had been; it was empty.

According to the records, Fabian had checked him out Monday morning. "Discharged to custody of experimental lab," the note said.

After lunch, when McNulty was going off shift, he found Fabian in the clinic lounge having a Coke. "Say, Harry," McNulty said, "what was the story with that guy who was brought in with abrasions on his wrists?"

"Beats me. They came down to get him Monday about ten o'clock. They had an order from Mattison, and I signed him out."

McNulty decided not to pursue the subject. That afternoon he accessed the library function of the computer and looked up subject and title listings under "Pain." One, a chatty popular work, mentioned a method of measuring pain by the application of heat. There was a reference. He called that up. The book, also called *Pain*, was by H. G. Wolff and S. Wolf, published in 1958. Wolff was a professor of neurology at Cornell Medical School. He had worked out a method of quantifying pain into units he called dols. There was a diagram of his apparatus. The stimulus, heat from a thousand-watt light bulb, was supposed to be concentrated by a lens on an area of 3.5 square centimeters. It was to be applied to the forehead of the subject, according to Wolff's text, but otherwise it sounded like the injuries McNulty had seen.

Next time he had a chance, McNulty tried to call up Frankensteen's records in the med computer. He got a message: ENTER ACCESS CODE.

McNulty sat and looked at the screen for a while. Then he had a wild hunch. He typed in, DOL.

The screen cleared, filled up with lines of type. There it all was: the slit wrists, the shots they had given him, medication for the blisters on his arms. There was also a psychiatric report: *Deeply disturbed, phobic, delusions of persecution.* Then more shots. The last entry was "Discharged to care of Alameda County Hospital."

McNulty made a printout of the whole file, put it in his pocket, and blanked the screen. He called Owen's office and said, "I'd like to make an appointment to use the phone today or tomorrow morning."

"One moment. Outgoing phone service has been temporarily interrupted," said the computer.

McNulty asked around and discovered that in fact nobody was being allowed to make any external phone calls. He could not make out what that meant; was it paranoid to imagine that it was all on account of him?

"Why don't you go and see Morrison?" Barlow asked. "He's the fixit person, isn't he?"

"My gosh, you're right." McNulty went to the mall and found Morrison where he usually hung out, talking confidentially to an elderly man. McNulty hung back until he was finished; then Morrison beckoned him over. "Doc, I haven't seen you in a while. How are things?"

"Not too bad, but I have a little problem. I need to get a message out. Is that possible?"

"Sure. Maybe. Who's it to?"

"I don't know yet." McNulty thought a moment. "Maybe the best thing would be to put two names on it—my wife and her lawyer."

"All right, what's the message?"

"I'd better write it. Have you got a piece of paper?"

Morrison reached into one of his bulging pockets. "Here's a nice notebook. Ten bucks."

"And how much for the message? I might as well write you one IOU."

"That depends. Let me see it first."

"You want to see the message?"

"Sure, if I'm going to get in trouble over it, I want to know."

McNulty hesitated, then opened the notebook and wrote: *To Alvin Miller and Janice McNulty, c/o Alvin Miller.* He didn't know the address, but he could look it up in the net. No, that was no good. He tore up the page and started over. *To Phillip D'Amato.* He added the address. *Get word to Janice through Miller that prisoners here are being tortured with a Wolff apparatus. See a book called* Pain *by H. G. Wolff and S. Wolf. One prisoner recently tried to commit suicide. His name is Nat Frankensteen. Restricted medical records on CV show he was treated for burns. They transferred him to Alameda County Hospital, probably in the psych ward.* He signed it and handed it over.

Morrison's eyebrows went up and his lips pursed in a soundless whistle. "This is heavy stuff, Doc," he said. "I don't know that I ought to get involved in this at all."

"Dave, you've got to do it for me."

After a moment Morrison said, "Right. Two thousand bucks, and that's cheap."

Silently McNulty wrote out an IOU for two thousand and ten dollars. "When can you get it out?"

"Tomorrow."

"Can you guarantee delivery?"

"I can't guarantee anything."

34 On Tuesday morning Owen glanced over her notes and said to Mitzi, "Take a draft research communication. Title, Preliminary results of investigation into compliance and noncompliance of McNulty's victims and nonvictims in the Medical Detention Center of the Emergency Civil Control Administration, San Francisco, California, September 13–27, 2004.

"First paragraph: Beginning on September 13, when the detainee population was complete, we announced examination and testing schedules staggered in such a way that by the end of the week every detainee had had at least one opportunity to comply. A few detainees passed out petitions urging noncompliance. We made no effort to interfere with this activity. At the end of the week we tabulated compliants and noncompliants. Among married couples, each composed of one McNulty's victim and one non-McNulty's, when both partners made the same decision whether or not to comply, the compliance rate was as follows: Husband McNulty's, wife non-McNulty's, compliance 39.2 percent. Wife McNulty's, husband non-McNulty's, compliance 42.1 percent. In couples where the partners made different decisions, the compliance rate for McNulty's victims was 27.8 percent and for non-McNulty's victims, 93 percent. Among single adults, all of whom are McNulty's victims, the compliance rate was 24 percent. This compares with a 95 percent or greater compliance rate in previous studies of internee populations. For example, in the Japanese-

American relocation camps in the forties, compliance was nearly 100 percent with the exception of a small group of internees who had been born in this country but had spent some years in Japan. This group had a very low compliance rate.

"Second paragraph: These results are consistent with earlier studies of dominance in husband-wife decisions, in which it was found that when husband and wife disagreed about some action to be taken by both, the husband persuaded the wife in 51 percent of cases, the wife persuaded the husband in 36 percent of cases, and in only 13 percent of cases did husband and wife take opposing actions. The validity of assumptions concerning husband-wife dominance was confirmed by interviewing a random sample of 53 married couples.

"Add the following graphs and tables. Table 1, numbers and percentages of compliance and noncompliance among married couples in which the husband is McNulty's and the wife is non-McNulty's. Numbers and percentages of couples in which the reverse is true. Numbers and percentages of couples in which both partners are McNulty's, and those in which both partners are non-McNulty's. Figure 1, a bar chart showing compliance and noncompliance of each group as well as the group of single adults."

"Shall I omit the null group?" the computer asked.

"Both partners non-McNulty's? Yes. In the chart, not in the table. New paragraph: After the conclusion of this phase, detainees were told on September 20 that those complying would be granted privileges such as improved housing assignments and access to phone service. Early results are consistent with a compliance rate among single adults of 85 percent, and among married couples, 89 percent.

"New heading: Conclusions. First paragraph:

"A pronounced deviation in compliance of McNulty's victims as compared with other populations is shown by this preliminary study. Acting as a control group, the 48 percent of married persons who are non-McNulty's victims support the inference that McNulty's victims are less likely than non-McNulty's victims to comply with authority in the absence of any direct benefit to themselves." She paused. "Add references and print."

The pages curled noiselessly out of the printer. Owen read them through, made a few corrections. "Now take a letter to Henry Harmon. Dear Hank, The enclosed draft of our first preliminary study certainly bears out the President's view that McNulty's Disease is a possible source of danger to the population.

"New paragraph: Although we are not yet ready to make a formal report of our attitudinal surveys, the following findings are at least suggestive. Among adult McNulty's patients, 65 percent report a change in their political orientation or allegiance after onset of the disease. General approval of the current administration changed from 59 percent to 39 percent.

"New paragraph: As you are already aware, these changes accompany reported changes in social and moral attitudes. Twenty-seven percent of adult McNulty's victims in the Medical Detention Center population report dissolution of marriages or informal relationships after onset of the disease. Thirty-one percent report changing employment, and 23 percent report changing occupations. With best regards."

35 The Governor of the sovereign state of Texas could see from his bullet-proof office window the National Guard soldiers massed in the avenue, and beyond them the marchers with their flags. In the holo beside him he had the same picture from a different angle. Even in the holo, the mob was too far away to see faces, but he knew the type, and they made his blood boil. They were against everything he believed in; they wanted to tear down the sacred fabric of society. Scum and refuse, pinkos, queers and commies. He wished he could hang every one of them personally and one at a time.

The holo sound was turned down to where he could barely hear the voice of the announcer, but he caught the words, "has declared he will take a firm stand against . . ."

There was a phone window at the bottom right, blank at the moment. Then the face of Colonel Harvine slid into view. He looked steadily at the Governor and spoke. "Sir, my men have taken up their positions. What are your orders?"

Three now? Too many? No, stressed but stable. Four
more are waiting.

Here comes decision.   Meanwhile a global topic.
I think he will   Species can't control

tell them to shoot.   population except by
                          famine, war.

                    Can, but won't.
Have tried,   Can we inhibit conception?   Why not let
failed. Would   problem rest
    mean being in every   until we equal
        female host at moment of   population?
    conception.

Might take seventy years.
                    Population now doubling every forty.
                    Means thirteen billion people.
    What others?   Impossible. Another
                              famine first.
Change network to make
    females desire intercourse If they want children, will
    only when not fertile?   calculate dates, conceive
                                anyway.
        True. Make them not
        desire infants, then?   Serious distortion.
                                     Will cause other
                                         imbalances.

He has decided. Call   Here. Here. Here. Here.
    the others.   Heart stopping.
                        Now, all out!   But what is
                                             optimum
Pop. *Pop.* *Pop.* *Pop.* *Pop.* *Pop.* *pop?*

The Governor had opened his mouth as if to speak.
His face was a little more flushed than usual; then it
seemed pale. With a startled look, as if he had suddenly
remembered something, he pitched forward, turning

slightly as he did so. One of the aides shouted, "Get the doctor!" Another knelt beside the body of the Governor and loosened his tie. The Governor seemed to be breathing, but by the time the doctor got there, he was dead.

36 The blond man smiled confidentially out of the tube. "Hello, I'm Fred Ostrow and this is *Think Tank*. Tonight we have with us John F. Persson, the distinguished foreign correspondent"—a gray-haired man who nodded without smiling—"T. Y. Okawa, president of the Wyandotte Foundation, and Barbara Pauling, the author of *Being Everywhere.*" The others smiled and nodded.

"We're here," said Ostrow, "to talk about a rather disturbing and significant development. In a series of recent events, it appears that a number of people have been killed by McNulty's parasites when they were about to commit acts of violence, or, in three cases, to order them committed. The most familiar of these, of course, is Governor Tom Yount of Texas, just last week, but reports have been coming in of parallel events in Nigeria and Afghanistan. In brief, an army colonel in Nigeria collapsed when he was about to give the order to fire at a group of rebel soldiers. On the other side, the rebel commander also collapsed when *he* was about to give the same order. The two sides retired, and there was no bloodshed. In Afghanistan, a provincial governor appeared to be on the point of ordering the execution of fifty prisoners when he was stricken. In each case there was evidence that people around the victims, if I may call them so, had been infected with the McNulty parasite. Now I think you'll all agree with me that it is too early to draw any firm conclusions, but I would just like you to speculate with me. Supposing it is true that the parasites are actually causing the death of people who attempt to injure other people, what will this mean to society? John?"

"Lawfully or unlawfully."

"Yes, that's right, and that's an important point—"

"Yes, it is, because they don't seem to distinguish between a soldier and a murderer. Now we have always made that distinction, but to an alien intelligence, if that's what we're dealing with here, the distinction might not make any sense. And indeed, we might find it hard to explain. Why is it not okay for a civilian to kill somebody, but okay for a soldier to do it?"

Okawa interjected, "They don't care about our laws."

"No, that's probably so. After all, they're really above our law, aren't they?"

"Should we be afraid of them? Ms. Pauling."

"Well, I think it's natural to be afraid of them, because we know so little about them and they're so powerful. But just looking at what they're *doing,* I wonder if we shouldn't be grateful to them instead. Can you imagine what it would be like if nobody could use force or violence against anybody else?"

"I can," said Okawa, "and I'm a little more worried than Barbara. Remember we've always relied on violence or the threat of violence to keep order in society. Does this apply to policemen?"

"Apparently it does, at least there have been two

cases of police officers dying suddenly while attempting to shoot a criminal. I agree with you that this is a problem we should explore. What are we getting into, if we go into a world without violence?"

"Let me suggest a scenario," said Persson. "I'll put this in general terms. Let's say there's a place where all the good agricultural land is owned by a few people, and there are a lot of landless farmers. One morning they say to themselves, let's go take that land. And they just do it, they walk onto the land and say this is yours, this is mine, and they start farming. Now what does the landowner do?"

"He goes to court?"

"All right, and the court upholds his right to his land and issues a dispossess order. Now the sheriff or whoever it is comes out and serves the order. He says you've got to get out. The farmers don't move. Now what?"

There was a little silence.

"Another issue that troubles me," said Okawa, "is the moral dimension. In a sense, you might say that these creatures are making it impossible for us to sin. In that case, what happens to morality? Does it mean anything? Do we have a moral choice anymore, or are we just puppets?"

"Don't you think some people would refrain from killing other people even if they didn't know they'd be punished?" asked Pauling.

"Certainly, but—"

"Well, those people are certainly exercising a moral choice, and so are the other ones, or at least they have been. I mean, if you choose to murder somebody, that's a moral choice, it just happens to be the wrong one."

"Barbara, doesn't it bother you that your kids might grow up being *coerced* into moral behavior, behaving well because of the fear of punishment—knowing there's somebody watching every minute?"

"Yes, it does. But John, think about this a moment. I grew up knowing that if I did certain foolish things, like stepping off the curb into traffic, I would probably be killed. You *know* there are automatic punishments for certain things, and you just don't do them. You don't get careless with hot grease, you don't stick your finger in a light socket, and it never occurs to you that you're being manipulated to behave correctly or that you've lost any moral choice, you just know that's the way it is. So I just don't see there's any big difference here, and one more thing. My son is probably not going to have to go to war, and my daughters probably are not going to get raped and murdered. I don't care whether the men who might have raped and murdered them have lost their moral choice. I'm glad."

"Isn't there one difference?" asked Persson.

"What's that?"

"You don't stick your finger in a light socket because you know the laws of the universe will punish you. But now it seems you won't hit anybody with a hatchet because some alien creature will punish you if you do."

"Our new masters?" said Okawa.

After a while Draffy began to realize that his mind was changing about some things. Or not changing exactly but just a different slant. Well, there was a certain amout of B.S. in everything, wasn't there? Maybe he hadn't noticed so much before, but it didn't make any difference, because he was committed to the principles that had made the country great and got him elected, and if he reneged on any of that where the hell would he go?

One thing he knew, the parasite had to be stopped. If

it could give him even the shadow of a doubt, why, look at all the dim bulbs in the country who might be knocked over by it! He was delighted at the progress being made at the Medical Detention Center. He particularly liked the prototype detection devices which had been sent to the White House. As soon as the remodeling was done, he was going to have them installed in the anteroom to the Oval Office and the foyer outside his private quarters. When he knew that everybody who came near him had been screened, he would feel a lot safer. Yes, he had had the disease once, but what if he got it again? What if they *came after him* to change his mind? And of course he knew they would; that was obvious.

One afternoon he woke up from his nap boiling mad. It was as if something had happened during his sleep, as if they had almost got him. He dressed and called Buz and Larry into the office. "Draft me an emergency decree," he said. "Any woman that's pregnant, if she can show the virus was in her when she got that way, she can have an abortion for the asking. Then I want another one, where we can examine hospital records and if *we* find out there's reason to believe a woman is carrying the virus, we can go to court and get an order for abortion. Third thing, I want an order setting up a national system of clinics, or whatever you want to call them, to examine kids under the age of four for signs of virus behavior. Kind of thing they've been finding on CV—little bastards don't play with other kids, so on." Buz started to speak, but Draffy overrode him. "And when we find those kids I want them put on CV for study or any damn thing, I don't care what, but I don't want them to come out."

"Chief, that might be going a little bit far."

The President turned to him. "Buz, this is the survival of America we're talking about."

"I know that, Chief, and you're right, of course. All I'm thinking is, do we want to sit down and consider, are there things, like killing unborn children, that we'd say, well, we draw the line here, that's not the kind of thing—"

Draffy stopped him. "All right, I know, I know. Forced abortion and so on. Believe me, Buz, it's the *last* thing in the world I would ever *want* to do. My God, you know that. But look at it from my position. Am I going to go down in history as the guy who saved the country by nipping this goddamn thing in the bud, never mind if I had to get a little bit rough? Or am I going to be the one who sat back and said, well, I'm too squeamish, let them take over. Suppose I did that, who the hell do you think would write the histories?" He was beginning to shake; his eyes were bloodshot and bulging. He struck the table with his fist. "*They* would, and they'd write whatever they damn please, because it would be all over with America!"

"Chief, you're right, you're absolutely right," said Buz. He laid a hand on Draffy's arm. "Easy, Chief, easy. Get Oliver in here," he said to Larry.

"Well, I'm just—so—" Draffy's face turned redder; his eyes clenched shut and moisture brimmed over the lids. "I have to carry the whole damn—"

"I know it, Chief, it isn't fair, but you'll come through. You always have and you always will."

Oliver Grummond entered and put his black bag on the desk. "Get his jacket off," he said. "Little too much tension again?" he asked the President. Draffy nodded, unable to speak. Buz was taking the jacket away; Larry rolled up the President's sleeve, patted his shoulder and then stood aside. Grummond held up a syringe.

Larry and Buz had a private skull session over drinks and sandwiches in Larry's office a little after eight. They had both been busy putting out fires all afternoon, and they were tired. "Old man's going overboard about this thing," Buz said gloomily. "Had a lot on his mind."

"No, I don't think so," said Larry. He was the younger of the two; he had been a successful ad writer before he went into government.

"How do you mean?"

"Well, think about it. We have all these ways of kidding people that they like their jobs, or if they don't, it's because they're freaky and they wouldn't like any other job any better, and anyhow they're going to think of some scheme to get rich as soon as they get around to it, and besides if they quit those jobs they wouldn't be able to afford all the goodies they want, and so on. Little stories that we keep telling them so they can get up in the morning."

"You're saying they don't like to work for a living, right? What else is new?"

"No, I'm saying people who have had McNulty's don't seem to believe those stories anymore. There's some kind of change that happens in their heads. Maybe the parasite just calls their attention to something they knew all along. Look at this."

He delved into his briefcase, came up with a print-out. "Voluntary job changes for the first six months of twenty ought-four are up seven percent over last year. And that's only people who couldn't manage to get fired to collect unemployment. The real figure must be at least twelve percent, and remember, this is in the trough of a growth adjustment. If times were good, God only knows what the rate would be."

"I still don't see it. Suppose they quit their jobs— they still have to eat, don't they? So there's a higher turnover. A nuisance, so what."

"No, you don't see it, do you?" Larry said. "All right, never mind. But here's another question to think about. How many *other* stories do we tell people to keep them happy?"

Later that night Draffy invited Buz to the Lincoln Sitting Room, where he usually spent his evenings. He poured Buz a bourbon. He had already had two or three before he decided to call Buz, and he was feeling them a little, although fully in command, of course.

"Don't tell anybody I broke down," he said.

"I won't, Chief."

"Dick Nixon broke down and cried, and they crucified him. I never forgave those sons of bitches. Never." He took a pull at his bourbon. "Fact is, he was a great president. He wasn't afraid to do the right thing even if was unpopular."

"That's right, Chief."

"Know damn well it's right. And *he* knew, and if was right, he did it." His consonants were getting a little indistinct, but he held himself upright and looked at Buz with great earnestness.

"Now, I'm talking to you because I know can trust you. With my life. Trust you with my life, Buz. And I want you to know, I'm not afraid to do the right thing if I have to. What the hell, everybody dies. It's a fact of life. Fact is, we're at war. People get killed in a war. Thousands. Millions. Innocent people get killed, children get killed. Well, once you're dead, what difference does it make?"

"Good question, Chief."

"Damn right. I'm not afraid to die. You know that?"

"I know you're not, Chief."

"In a war, somebody has to die. But, better them than me or you, right?"

"That's right, Chief."
"Let's get down and pray, Buz."

In October the growing crisis in the Middle East gave Draffy the best of reasons to cancel almost all his remaining appearances and stay close to the White House—"taking the high ground," Buz and Larry called it. That was really not the issue, though; Draffy *was* the President and he did have to deal with this situation, which might erupt into war at any moment, a war which he as Commander in Chief would have to direct, and if the Democrats didn't like that, tough titty.

Ever since the civil war broke out in Iran, the Soviets had been threatening to cross the border in support of Colonel Hourani's government, but Draffy had gone eyeball to eyeball with them and had continued to send American advisers, weapons, and supplies to the rebels headed by Colonel Khadouri. Then the damn rebels had captured a Russian out of uniform in their territory. Mad Mike Dougherty was pretty much in the saddle there, but the rebels were Iranians, after all, and they were threatening to shoot the Russian as a spy. There had been a hotline message last week that the Soviet Union would "take severe retaliatory action" if that occurred, and it looked like it was going to. On the one hand, he was right where he wanted to be, on top of a situation that could make him more famous than Roosevelt or Truman, and on the other hand the suspense was making him edgy. His spirits were up and down like a yo-yo, and Grummond had to give him a shot once or twice a week.

In mid-October the female rat gave birth to a litter of four. "All right," said Strang, "we know the parasite can take a rat as host and we know what happens when it goes from one rat to another. So we're that much farther ahead. But we haven't succeeded in getting it to reproduce in rats, because in the one trial so far it moved into the male before copulation. I won't speculate about the reason—"

"I will," said Italiano.

"Right, you'll tell us the thing doesn't want to reproduce in rats. And that's your privilege, you can believe in purpose and will and all those neat things. All we know is that the parasite moved from the female to the male before copulation. If it does that in other trials, we've got a problem."

"Predicted by the hypothesis of intelligence and volition in the parasite," remarked Italiano. "But don't mind me."

"You know," said Meyer, "whatever this is, whether you want to call it reluctance or what, it might be a damn good thing. Can you imagine how fast the parasite population would be growing if it could reproduce naturally in *rats?*"

Resolutely ignoring both of them, Strang went on, "One obvious possibility would be artificial insemination, but that would mean we'd have to come up with some remote control device to keep the parasite from infecting the human operator. So that brings us down to the crunch. We've got to infect both the male and the female, and that means risking one more parasite in an animal host."

"There is one other possibility," Italiano murmured, gazing at the wall.

The others looked at her. "Well, what?" Strang said impatiently.

"Use a human host as the operator. Then there's no

place for the parasite to go except into the human host, who already has one. It can't be that hard to put an eyedropper up the vaginal canal of a rat. There might even be someone among the non-McNulty's subjects who's had lab training with animals. Just a suggestion."

"All right, that's a possibility," Strang said after a moment, looking at his folded hands. "Two things I don't like about it. One, you seem to be assuming that two parasites can't occupy the same host. I don't know why you make that assumption. If it's false, the rat experiment is ruined. Even if it's true, it would muck up the data even more than it is now. We wouldn't know if there had been a mutual transfer between the rat and the human subject, and there goes any chance of separating the two sets of data."

"It's gone already," said Italiano. "We have no way of knowing if the parasites we're working with have previously used animal hosts or not."

"According to you, they'd never use an animal host, because they remember what happened on CV."

"That was in a different situation—"

"Dorothy, and Donald," said Owen, "I think this bickering has gone on long enough."

"Well, damn it," Strang said, "it's an important issue. If we start introducing imaginary entities at this stage, we're right back to bodily humors and phlogiston."

Italiano pointedly did not reply.

"What I like about this debate is that it's often stimulating," Owen said. "Obviously the two of you have viewpoints that will never be reconciled, but that's okay as long as we all listen to each other and don't quarrel. I think you two should have dinner together. That isn't an order, just a suggestion." Strang and Italiano exchanged a startled look. Several others were smiling. "Now, back to our topic. We're all on edge because of the shortage of parasite subjects, but the breeding program is designed to cure that, and I think we have to pursue it. Dorothy, your idea has merit, and in fact it would be fascinating to find out whether two parasites can occupy the same host, but I don't think we can afford the delay. You're right that we can't be sure we have parasites who have never been in animal hosts. Let's put that line of research aside for the time being. Donald, you're right that we don't have to assume volition and purpose as long as we observe behavior correctly. So let's go forward with another rat host. That will give us some indication of repeatability, which we need anyhow." Heads were nodding around the table. "Wes," she went on, "if you get one successful copulation between infected rats, how many more would you like to do now, just to be on the safe side?"

Schultz said, "Well, two or three. Say three. Then we could reinfect the human subjects?"

"That's what I had in mind. All right, that sounds good to me. Thank you, everybody."

Strang approached her in the hall that afternoon. "I think Owen is right about dinner. What about tonight, is that too soon?"

"No, I can make it."

They went to a Hungarian restaurant on the waterfront; there were shaded lamps on the tables, and the wine was excellent. They were cautious with each other at first; they talked about their childhoods, where they had lived, where they had gone to school. Strang was the oldest of three brothers. The other two were a lawyer and an astronaut. Italiano came from a family of women—six daughters, all of whom had become academics of some kind. They had some tastes in common: Scarlatti, Italian ice cream, old Woody Allen movies.

"To me," Italiano said over coffee, "the idea that the parasite is intelligent is just a hypothesis, but you seem to see it as almost heretical."

"Loaded words," said Strang. "I don't think this is a religious question, I just believe in an orderly universe."

"So do the tribal Africans."

"How's that?"

"They don't believe anything happens by chance. If somebody gets sick or dies, it has to be witchcraft."

"Ignorance."

"All right, but Donald, when you look back at the scientists of a hundred years ago, weren't they ignorant? How are scientists a century from now going to feel about you and me?"

"Not my problem. If it turns out this is an invisible intelligent parasite and you can prove that by scientific means, okay, fine, I'll trust the evidence."

"How much evidence would I have to have to convince you?"

"Overwhelming. All right, I'm too skeptical, but you're too easy. You remember the stuff you got from your subject about why the parasite is here? 'To make you better'? Even supposing that's evidence, granting that for a minute, it might not mean what you think. If a pig was bright enough to ask you why you're fattening it up, what would you say?"

Later, after he had touched her hand, he said, "One problem I have is methodological. Is it okay for me to say that?"

"Sure."

"All right, if you want these experiments to be taken seriously, you've got to be more careful to exclude error.

When you use the pointer to spell out words, you could be giving the subject unconscious cues in tone of voice and body language."

"Making up the message and feeding it to the subject?"

Strang waved that away. "Anyhow, this is all I'm saying. Get the computer to write you a program for the alphabet chart, with a cursor that isn't under your control. You can make it accept the input from the skin potential gadget and display the message as it goes along, and then you'd have a record that couldn't have been tampered with, and people like me will have a lot harder time shooting down your results."

"You know, that's very generous," Italiano said after a moment.

"Ahh," he said, dismissing the compliment. "I'll still try to shoot them down, you know. No quarter."

Italiano raised her glass. "I'll drink to that."

After a second failed attempt to reproduce the parasite in rats, Strang's suggestion of artificial insemination was adopted. Cunningham devised a remote manipulator with which the experimenters successfully inseminated an infected female rat in late October. "Now we're getting somewhere," said Wesley Schultz.

Janice McNulty kept traveling. She spent some time in New York talking to media people who at first seemed interested but later did not return her calls.

She phoned Alvin Miller's office every week, and usually got a computer image. One morning, instead, Miller himself appeared in the tank. "Mrs. McNulty, I have a message for you from a family member. I don't want to be more specific."

Her heart began to thump. "Can you read it to me?"

"No. I believe you had better come to my office and see it. Can you be in Washington tomorrow?"

"Yes."

Tears blurred her eyes when she read McNulty's note.

"Is that your husband's handwriting?" Miller asked.

"Yes. Does this change anything?"

"Not necessarily, or not right now. It may have an influence on the outcome eventually."

Janice put the note in her purse. "I'm going to see Senator Gottlieb again. Thank you. I'll be in touch."

She found Gottlieb at home in Atlanta and showed him the note.

"Little lady, I'd like to help you, but what can I do? The Congress goes into recess in November. We won't be back till January."

"I understand that, but those people are being tormented right now. Couldn't you send somebody to investigate, at least?"

The Senator sighed and took off his glasses; without them his eyes looked naked and tired. "Well, it's hard to say no to you, ma'am. You know that, don't you? All right, I'll see what I can do. And don't you fret now; we'll get that husband of yours out of there as quick as we can."

On Friday afternoon McNulty's phone rang. It was Barlow. "Wally, turn on the NBC news, quick."

He fumbled with the controls. In the tank, he saw a familiar face; he could not quite take it in until he heard the reporter say, "Mrs. McNulty, you've been—"

He punched for replay.

The anchor looked at him earnestly and said, "Janice McNulty, the wife of Dr. Wallace McNulty and herself a McNulty's victim, surrendered to federal marshals in Washington today, charging that detainees aboard the converted ocean vessel Sea Venture are being tortured by medical researchers."

In the tank he saw Janice, with her hair blowing. She was squinting into the sun, and her nose looked pink. The interviewer said, "Mrs. McNulty, you've been a fugitive for two months. Why are you giving yourself up now?"

"I want this detention to be investigated as soon as possible. Those people are being tortured, and I've given evidence of that to Senator Gottlieb. I think we've forgotten some pretty basic things about this country. We're supposed to have life, liberty, and the pursuit of happiness, but instead we're being turned into helpless guinea pigs."

The interviewer said, "Will you be sent to Sea Venture, to join your husband?"

"I hope so."

The anchor reappeared. "Senator Gottlieb today would not comment on Mrs. McNulty's allegations. In other news—"

Monday morning there was a knock on the door. McNulty opened it and saw an MP standing there. "McNulty?"

"Yes." Then he saw Janice. Somewhere around that time they were in each other's arms, and the MP had gone away.

"Gosh, I missed you," said McNulty. "You're a sight for sore eyes."

"Well, you're not," said Janice. "Oh, Wally, you're so *thin.*"

Dr. Owen now found it possible to attack a problem she had been putting off because of the shortage of parasites for experimental work. It had always been part of her plan to study a subclass of McNulty's patients, the children conceived when their mothers were active hosts, in order to determine whether this second generation differed significantly from the first.

Since the parasite was reproducing in human beings, the number of such children must be equal to the number of parasites; however, by the most optimistic estimate, the probability that one such child was already aboard CV was about unity; moreover, even if there were fifty such children, at present there was no positive way to identify them.

"Mitzi," she said to the computer, "take a memo on a new program, titled 'Human breeding.' Select fifty detainee women with the following characteristics: Between the ages of eighteen and thirty-five. No evidence of infertility. Married or coupled with a male detainee who meets the first two criteria. Each member of a couple is to be infected with a McNulty's parasite just before the beginning of the woman's fertile period and the couples subsequently isolated until—No, that won't do. We've got to infect them temporarily and then reinfect them, so that they can tolerate the parasite longer. Fix that, Mitzi."

"Each member of a couple," the computer's calm voice said, "is to be temporarily infected with a McNulty's parasite, then reinfected and subsequently isolated until—"

"All right. Until pregnancy is established. Women in this program are to be denied all birth-control devices and drugs except oral norgestrel and ethinyl estradiol. End memo. Now an order for the clinic pharmacy: Ten thousand units of norgestrel and ethinyl estradiol, placebo only, in daily-dose dispensers."

The documents curled out into the tray. "One more thing," Owen said. "Calculate the number of additional beds and staff needed in the maternity corridor."

God is not good, or else he could be better.
—MEISTER ECKHART

37 Shortly before noon on November second, a technician at the U.S. Weather Satellite Station in Bethesda noticed a flagged reading in the transmission from the GEOS satellite in polar orbit over the Pacific: there seemed to be a circular bulge in the ocean with its center about nine hundred miles west of Los Angeles. The technician showed the printout to his chief, who decided to seek confirmation from the Geophysical Data Center in Washington. The Center reported that, in fact, a seismic disturbance at that location had been detected; it was estimated to be 8.7 on the Richter Scale.

The Weather Satellite chief fed the data into his computer and asked for estimated times of arrival in Los Angeles, San Diego, San Francisco, Portland, Vancouver, and Honolulu. The ETA in the first two places was almost the same, 1100 hours; in San Francisco it was about twenty minutes later.

"Put out an advisory on the tsunami network," he

said, "and then get me the Navy in California. This could be a real bitch."

That morning, in Owen's office, a phone window blinked in the holo while she was in conference with Melanie Kurtz. "Yes?"

"A call from security."

"All right."

The face of an MP sergeant appeared in the tank. "Dr. Owen, there's a man here who wants to see you. He has credentials from Senator Gottlieb. His name is Raphael P. Bushman."

"Put him on, please."

The face moved aside and was replaced by another. "Dr. Owen, I'm an investigator for Senator Gottlieb's subcommittee. I want to come aboard in order to interview some of your staff and examine the records."

"Well, this is something of a surprise, Mr. Bushman, but of course— Put the guard on again, please."

The face of the MP reappeared. "Give Mr. Bushman a temporary visitor's pass and an escort up to my office," she said. She turned to Kurtz. "Melanie, I'm afraid you're going to have to excuse me. I don't know how long I'll be tied up—give me a call sometime this afternoon."

"All right." Kurtz smiled and left. After a few minutes the phone blinked and Corcoran said, "Mr. Bushman to see you."

"Send him in."

Bushman came in; he was a tall, rather stooped and scholarly-looking man in his thirties. Under other circumstances, Owen realized, she would have liked him instantly.

"Mr. Bushman, please sit down. Forgive me for not shaking hands. We have to take certain precautions."

He looked at the chairs against the wall. "Because of the parasite?" He had a pleasant tenor voice.

"Yes. It's inconvenient and futile, but that's what we have to do."

Bushman sat down, with his briefcase in his lap. "Well, Dr. Owen, you probably know why I'm here. There have been some allegations of inhumane treatment of prisoners, and our committee would like to know more about that."

"We're at your disposal, Mr. Bushman. Let me say that I do know what this is about, and it's partly true. There was an experiment on one subject, conducted by Jerry Plotkin, that went too far. The subject turned out to be unstable; some of his injuries were self-inflicted."

Bushman took a legal pad from the briefcase and made a note. "Where is Mr. Plotkin now?"

"I accepted his resignation as soon as I found out about this. I believe Jerry went back to Boston. I can have my secretary give you his address there."

"Fine. Plotkin is one of the two people I wanted to talk to first. The other is Dr. Wallace McNulty."

"He's here."

"Okay, and then I suppose there's some associate of Plotkin's that I could see?"

"Yes. Wesley Schultz worked with Mr. Plotkin."

"All right. Is there a room here that you could let me use?"

"Yes, certainly. And perhaps you'd like a tour of the laboratories, so you can see for yourself what kind of work we're doing? Excuse me." There was a blinking phone window in the tank. "Yes?"

"Call from Colonel Mattison."

"Put him on."

Mattison's face appeared. "Dr. Owen, there's a tsunami warning. Better turn on your holo. I'm on my way up." The window blanked and disappeared.

"I'm sorry," Owen said, "there seems to be something—Mitzi, get me the weather news."

Standing in front of his map, the GBC weatherman was saying, "Jim, a tsunami is a wave generated by an earthquake or some other movement of the crust under the ocean. We don't call it a tidal wave because that's misleading—it doesn't have anything to do with the tides."

"Oh, God," said Owen. "Mitzi, get me the beginning."

The weatherman disappeared and was replaced by the grave grey head of the morning anchor, James Fellowes. "We have just learned that about an hour ago, approximately eleven-fifty Eastern Standard Time, a tsunami was detected in the Pacific Ocean off San Diego. The Naval High Command has ordered all units in West Coast ports or close offshore to put out to sea, and residents of low-lying areas are being advised to seek higher ground. Predicted arrival time of the tsunami is eleven A.M. Pacific Time. That's two o'clock here in the East. We'll have more on this breaking story."

"Enough, Mitzi," Owen said. "Mr. Bushman, I assure you I didn't arrange this for your benefit." He laughed uneasily and stood up. "But I think," Owen said, "for your own safety, you'd better leave immediately. Mr. Corcoran will arrange for your escort."

"Yes, I suppose you're right."

When he was gone, Owen turned the holo back on. "Where does that name come from, tsunami?" the anchor was saying. "Sounds Japanese."

"Yes, it is, Jim, and they provided the name for it because they've gone through this so often themselves.

Now what *happens* in a tsunami is that you get these waves generated out in the ocean which are really very small, less than a foot in height—so small that you wouldn't even notice them, but they *can* be identified by the GEOS imaging radar."

"That's amazing," said Jim. "To detect that small a difference from, what, two hundred miles up?"

"Or even farther," said the weatherman. "This technology was developed to detect underground nuclear explosions—just another way the space program has spun off things that benefit us in our daily lives."

"Well, so now we know there's a tsunami, because of these little one-foot waves. What makes it so destructive later on?"

"Those are little waves in deep water, Jim. But as the waves approach the shore and the water becomes shallower, the waves get higher." In the screen, they saw a computer simulation of a wave rushing over a sloping bottom. "And that's what causes the tremendous destruction. So, luckily, the warning network has given us plenty of notice and we're hoping for complete evacuation of low-lying areas along the Pacific Coast, but of course we expect a great deal of property damage."

"Nothing to be done about that."

"No, science has just given us the ability to predict events like this, but we can't modify them. These natural forces are just as big as they ever were, and man is pretty small."

She turned as Mattison came in. "Sound down, Mitzi. Colonel, how will this affect us? Should we stay here, or try to get out to sea?"

"I don't know. I tried to call—"

"But you're a naval officer!"

"I'm an officer in the Marine Corps," Mattison said

patiently. "My basic specialty is accounting. I was going to say, I tried to call Navy Operations, but they're going crazy over there. They told me to get off the line. I've got people phoning the Coast Guard and commercial tug operators, but I think that's hopeless too."

"Let me think. Mitzi, do we have anyone aboard who was formerly in the Navy or has nautical experience?"

"I'll check. Thomas M. Gangle. Marjorie M. Hamilton. Steven R. Orr. Leslie Tomms."

"Are these former Naval officers? Give their ranks."

"Gangle, chief machinist's mate. Hamilton, yeoman first class. Orr, seaman first class. Tomms, yeoman first class."

"That's no good," Mattison said.

"What's a yeoman?"

"A clerical worker."

"Well, we have to do *something*. Mitzi, load information about tsunamis if you don't already have it. Load charts of San Francisco Bay and of the Pacific Ocean. A tsunami is approaching from nine hundred miles west of San Diego. It will reach the Bay in one hour. Compare outcomes if we stay moored at Treasure Island or cut ourselves loose." She looked at Mattison. "Can we? Do you know how to do that?"

"Yes."

A chart of the Bay appeared on the flatscreen. "Will you please show me your present location?" said Mitzi's voice.

"Oh!" said Owen in exasperation. She touched the screen. "Here."

"Are you inside a structure?"

"Oh, *damn*. Yes. We are inside a structure called Sea Venture, moored to a floating dock on the northwest side of Treasure Island."

"I'm loading more data. First assumption: Sea Venture remains moored to the floating dock. Outcome, severe damage to Sea Venture and dock." In the holotank, they saw a skeletal diagram of CV tilting over, crushing a skeletal dock and being crushed. "Second assumption: Sea Venture is released from moorings ten minutes from now. When the tsunami arrives, Sea Venture will be six miles west of its present location. Minor damage."

"Well, I think that makes sense," Owen said.

"Wait a minute. We can't evacuate CV in ten minutes."

"Why would we want to? If there's going to be minor damage—"

"May I ask it a question?" Mattison said, nodding toward the computer.

"Certainly."

"Mitzi, compare damage to human beings aboard Sea Venture under the two assumptions."

"First assumption. Severe damage to human beings. Second assumption. Moderate damage to human beings."

"Define moderate damage."

"I'm loading more data. Estimate three percent fatalities. Seventeen percent injuries requiring hospitalization. Forty-four percent minor injuries."

"Three percent of forty-five hundred people is a hundred thirty-five deaths," Mattison said.

"Let's try to be calm," said Owen. "How long would it take to evacuate Sea Venture? Where would you put the people?"

"I'm loading—"

"Not you, Mitzi, I'm talking to Colonel Mattison."

Mattison sighed. "Forty-five hundred people, two exits, say you could get them started ten minutes from now, then four abreast at each location, say eight a second, that's about ten minutes more, but we'd never do it. We'd have to drill them every day for a month. Where you'd put them is another question. Mitzi, can you estimate damage to buildings on Treasure Island?"

"I'm loading data. Estimate severe damage to buildings."

"Well, I think that's right. The transportation isn't available to get that many people to high ground. I'd say cast off, and the sooner the better."

"Do it, then, please, Colonel Mattison."

The problem of government, as Lord Acton pointed out long ago, is the corruption of power: great offices are sought by men who need power over other men, and who, when they get it, will stop at nothing to hold it. Those who would govern best seldom rise to the seats of the mighty. Perhaps it follows that only those who are unwilling should be chosen. We ought to find them where they are hiding, as the Romans sought and found Cincinnatus, who served as dictator, defeated the Aequians in a single day, and then went back to his plow.

Or, perhaps, we should find one such person, create an expert system based on his decisions, and then let a passionless computer govern the nation.
—JAMES MORTON SELBY

38 President Draffy spent the morning of November second with Elsie, Larry, and Buz in the Lincoln Sitting Room, watching early returns. They had GBC in one holo, and CBS in the other with the sound turned down; every now and then Buz would switch to NBC. The computers projected a substantial majority, not as big as his first win, but not bad for a second term. Draffy was thinking that his worries were over for a while, and that all things considered he might just as well have a Bloody Mary or something, a nutritious drink of that kind. He could say, "Well, I'm not a morning drinker myself, but in honor of the occasion I think we all ought to have a Bloody Mary." Or a Screwdriver?

The phone window in the other holo was blinking. Buz leaned over and spoke to it. Draffy could see the face in the holo; it was Admiral Benedict, the chairman of the Joint Chiefs. "Lower sound," he said irritably, but then both holos lowered their sound, he couldn't hear either one, and by the time Buz got that straightened out, Benedict was saying, ". . . ordered all units in port or close offshore to put out to sea, and I think the President should declare a state of national . . ."

Draffy said, "What the hell is this?" Buz made room for him to sit down at the holo.

"Mr. President," Benedict said, "there is a tsunami out in the Pacific, ETA San Diego in about an hour and a half, two hours to San Francisco, and so on up the coast. We're in for a big one."

"Holy Christ," said Draffy. "Excuse me, dearest. Admiral, are you in the Situation Room?"

"Yes, sir, and I've got General Tinker here with me."

"All right, I'm going down to the conference hall. Buz, get me a few more people, Metcalfe, science adviser, whoever you think, and I want you and Larry to watch on passive from up here. Good God, what a thing to happen."

* * *

The private elevator sighed open, sighed shut. Draffy's footsteps echoed. He opened the door and closed it behind him, relishing the silence. The conference hall, in the hardened sub-basement of the White House, contained one chair and a long oval table. Three or four of the holos around the table lit up after Draffy sat down, and more images appeared until the table was almost full—Benedict and Tinker and their aides, Secretary of State George Metcalfe, Russ Domenici, the national peace adviser, and so forth.

Draffy said, "All right, gentlemen, first order of business is the declaration of national emergency, and I want some input on that. First question, what are the chances this is a sneak attack by the Commies?"

Admiral Benedict looked grave. "Mr. President, we can't rule that out. The detonation of a large device on the ocean floor near the coastline could generate—"

"I know that. How do we tell if they did it, or if it's just an earthquake?"

"Analysis of the sea water would—"

"How long?"

Benedict and one of his aides put their heads together, murmured for a moment, straightened up again. "About a week, to get the necessary samples."

Draffy glowered. "Jesus, can't you give me a simple yes or no? What about opportunity—any Soviet ships around there?"

Benedict said, "There were three Soviet trawlers in that general area, but they left two weeks ago. That doesn't really mean anything, because they could easily have dropped a device with a timer."

Draffy could feel the pressure growing in his temples. "In fact, it could have been anytime, is that right? Two months, three?"

"That's not impossible."

"God dammit, why else would it happen on election day in *California,* for Christ's sake?"

There were sympathetic murmurs. "All right," Draffy said. "We'll keep this on ice until we find out something. Meantime I'll just say there's been an apparent earthquake in the Pacific, et cetera. Larry, rough me out a declaration and put it on the flatscreen, and get me airtime, say 'bout half an hour from now. But in the *meantime,* I think we ought to go on yellow alert. No public announcement, but get all your key people into hardened shelters. Larry, of course that means you and Buz, et cetera. And Elsie."

Stevens was undergoing a series of electric shocks from electrodes applied to his ankles and wrists. The shocks came in a series of graduated intensity; number six was the strongest. This was number six.

When it was over, he relaxed, sweating. Dr. Schultz, in the holoscreen, seemed to be looking down at his notes. Then he glanced up with a listening expression, and Stevens heard a faint voice, something about a warning.

"Well, what do you want me to do?" Schultz said. The voice said something Stevens could not catch.

"All right." As an afterthought, Schultz said, "What about the subjects?"

This time Stevens heard: "Back to the cages."

The door opened and the two MPs came in. "May I ask what is happening?" Stevens said politely.

"There's a tsunami warning," said Schultz's voice. "Excuse me." He disappeared from the holo.

Stevens stood up and removed the leads from his head and body. As he straightened, the nearer MP came at him with a pole. Stevens turned slightly, grasped the pole as it went by, and pulled. Off balance, the MP staggered forward. Stevens kicked him in the knee, then in the chin. He took up the pole in time to push it at the face of the second MP, who dodged away and tripped over the chair. Stevens kicked him in the head as he went by.

Out in the corridor, two or three people hurried past, paying no attention to him. Somewhere a holo was blaring, ". . . severe damage to coastal cities . . ."

Dr. Schultz came out of a doorway carrying a clipboard. "Oh, hello," he said automatically; then his eyes widened. Stevens took him by the jaw and banged his head against the doorframe. Dr. Schultz's glasses fell off and his eyes turned up.

A woman in a lab coat came out of another doorway as Stevens was lowering the body to the floor. "What's the matter?"

"It's Dr. Schultz—he's had some kind of seizure. I'm going for the medics. Loosen his collar, will you?"

When he was halfway down the corridor, he heard the loudspeakers begin to blare. "Your attention, please. Your attention, please. Sometime during the next few hours we may be experiencing unusually high wave activity. All detainees, please secure all movable objects immediately. When movable objects have been secured, lie down on your bunks and strap yourselves in using the webbing provided. Instructions for using the webbing are on the wall over your bunks. You will have at least one hour to complete these preparations. There is no reason for alarm if you comply with these instructions. Remember to secure all movable objects first, before strapping yourselves into your bunks."

The speaker cleared her throat. "Staff members and employees who do not have sleeping accommodations aboard, first secure all movable objects in your work area, then contact your supervisors or Marine guard units for further instructions. That is all." Voices were echoing in dismay.

At the first intersection he turned left into a dim corridor; he followed it to another and moved sternward. This was a place where he had never been before; the MPs had brought him down by the most direct route. Now he was in a maze of machine shops, deserted bakeries and kitchens, storerooms, carpenter shops. Scattered lights glowed dimly in the ceiling.

Deep in perm country he found a service elevator that would take him where he wanted to go; the door was secured by a hasp and padlock. He went back to one of the dusty storerooms and overturned piles of tools until he found a two-foot pry bar. Armed with this he returned to the door and forced it.

The elevator took him up into the residential area. He went straight to Julie's apartment and knocked. Her voice came faintly. He knocked again. This time he could make out, "Who is it?"

He knocked five times with the pry bar in measured strokes, their old signal. After a long time she came to the door. "Oh, it's you. Thank heaven, come in."

In the conference-hall holos people came and went. Shortly after two, they were watching the GBC broadcast from Los Angeles. In the big flatscreen, a sunlit shoreline was tilted upright. The remote voice was saying, "There is still no sign, although we are told— Oh-oh, I think I see it down there." The camera zoomed toward the water, and with a thrill of horror Draffy saw a kind of ripple gleaming in the sunlight. The voice rose in excitement. "Yes, I think that's it. It's not very big yet, it's coming toward shore, they tell me, about eighty miles an hour but it will slow down now—" The ripple looked more pronounced. Then it was not a ripple anymore but a curved ridge in the water growing higher and brighter, and as it met the shore it rose into a monstrous gleaming wall.

Draffy winced as the viewpoint suddenly changed and he was looking out apparently from the top of a building at a line of water higher than the buildings that gleamed in the sun and then turned gray, shot up plumes. In the background there was a confused rumble, then a roar.

A voice was shouting, ". . . is incredible. I'm watching the water sweep up into Redondo Beach—it's just gone, there's nothing there but white water. The oil fields are gone. The Palos Verdes Estates are gone. It's like a great beast washing over the land, tearing everything under."

Another voice interrupted, "We switch you now to Merv Walker in San Diego. Merv, come in."

Another helicopter view, high above the ocean and the shore. They watched as the wave struck the point at Cabrillo, fell beyond it, and raced across the inlet to North Island. Then the same monstrous wave rose and broke over Silver Strand Boulevard, fell into the bay. Draffy watched in helpless fascination until the wave reached the mainland and swept up over National City and Chula Vista.

"I believe this is the worst naval disaster in American history," said the anchor. "Wouldn't you say so, Brad?"

"And very likely one of the worst civilian disasters."

"You're right, but I was thinking that the blow to our Navy is unbelievable. Every one of the naval installations on the peninsula, North Island and the mainland have been completely wiped out, and not only that, but the Marine Recruit Depot, Ream Field and the International Airport, they are all gone."

A telephone window was blinking red in the holo beside him. "What is it?"

"Mr. President, a hotline message," said the computer.

"All right, put it on."

The message came up on the flatscreen to his left. "The General Secretary of the Communist Party of the Union of Soviet Socialist Republics extends his heartfelt sympathy to the President of the United States of America in this hour of national tragedy." Draffy wished he could see Cherbotarev's face when he said that. There had been some talk about upgrading the hotline to a holo link, with translators standing by at both ends, but nothing had come of it; the hotline was still what it had always been, a glorified teletype, and just as well, probably; if it was live, God knew what he might say right now.

"Related information," said the computer.

"All right, what is it?"

"The Soviet ambassador has requested an audience with the President."

"Okay, give that to Larry and tell him to take his time." Draffy returned his attention to the big screen and watched while the giant wave slowly receded, leaving miles of dark rubble that steamed in the sun.

"Now, gentlemen, we've heard what the Soviet Union has to say, and we also know the value of any statement they might make. What about it—is this a sneak attack or not? If it is, can we do the same thing to them?"

Admiral Benedict cleared his throat. "First of all, Mr. President, I have to say that this scenario is very unlikely. The Soviets would know we would trace the damage to a nuclear device and that we would certainly retaliate."

"Admiral, thank you very much, but that's not what I asked you."

"We have the capability of dropping a large device to the ocean bottom," Benedict said.

"Where would you drop it? Let's see a map of the Soviet Union." After a moment the map appeared on the big flatscreen.

"The Soviets are not as vulnerable as we are to this type of attack," said Benedict. "Only a few of their important cities are on the coast. Computer, flag cities of more than one million, located within fifty miles of the ocean."

After a moment he continued, "You see here, there's Leningrad and Arkangel and that's about it on the northern coast. Then—"

"Leningrad!" said Draffy. "What's wrong with that?"

"One problem is that it's pretty close to Helsinki, which is the capital of a friendly nation. A tsunami there would be devastating. Then another problem, the northern part of Europe is not in the earthquake zone. So any attack there would probably be seen as such immediately. Now on the southern coast we have Riga. That is in the earthquake zone, and it's a large population center."

"I don't care about the earthquake zone. How long would it take to do it?"

"In Leningrad, sir?"

"Yes."

Benedict and one of his aides conferred briefly. "Mr. President, at present there are some technical problems. We'd have to modify a ship, probably a supply ship. Say six to ten weeks for the modifications and then another six weeks to deliver the device."

"That's too long."

"Mr. President, if I may," said General Tinker. "I understand the desire to retaliate in kind, tit for tat, and I share that desire. But from a broader point of view, it would be better to retaliate in a more conventional way, using an IBM or a laser from orbit. Not only would delivery be quicker, but we would gain valuable information about our weapons systems and the enemy's defenses. In fact, I would go so far as to call that vital information. Mr. President, we have never fired an IBM over that range, and until we do we'll never know whether we can hit the target within acceptable limits or not."

George Metcalfe said, "Let's put this in a bigger context, shall we? Tit for tat is not the only way to go. We have a lot of other options. Now, the Soviet Union is less vulnerable to a deep-sea explosion than we are, as Admiral Benedict just reminded us, but they're much *more* vulnerable to a conventional nuclear strike. You hit Washington, or you hit New York, and this country is still in business, but you hit Moscow and it's all over. They run *everything* from Moscow. The Soviet Union would fall apart in a week, and they know it. So I say if we're going to hit them, let's not fool around. Let's hit them where it hurts and get it over with."

"Are you talking about a saturation attack?"

"No, I'm not, because that would leave us without a plausible second-strike deterrent. I'm talking about just enough missiles targeted on Moscow to make sure that at least one hits the Kremlin. Current doctrine says that's about one hundred. I'd say make it a hundred and fifty."

"Russ?"

"I agree about the numbers and the doctrine, but

before we come to any hard decision I think we ought to look at the alternatives. What if this isn't a Communist attack, what if it's just an offshore earthquake?"

"I'd say do it anyway," Metcalfe said, "and the quicker the better. Because you know and I know there's somebody in the Kremlin right now saying we didn't do this but there's no way the Americans are going to believe that, so we'd better hit them first before they hit us."

Benedict said, "I think there's a contradiction here. George, if they did this, why haven't they hit us *already* with everything they've got? If they really are more vulnerable than we are, and I don't dispute that, wouldn't they be crazy to start anything?"

"I've heard that argument before," said Metcalfe, "and in my opinion it comes straight from the Kremlin. They are crazy. Crazy for world domination. They'll do anything, and let me tell you, Al, the reason they did this to us is they believe we're too wimpy to strike back. They think they can wash out every naval installation on the Pacific Coast and we won't do a thing. They'll say, 'Oh, we didn't do it,' and even if we pin it on them, they'll say, 'Oh, it was an accident, too bad,' and that'll be the end of that. Where does it stop? I say it stops here."

"Admiral, why did you say a week to get water samples?"

"Because there's very little mixing between the surface and deep water. We'd have to take samples from the bottom layer, and, the reason I said a week, the closest oceanographic vessel we have is in the South Pacific. It would take about five days to get here, and then figure a couple of days for the tests, call it a week."

"Wait a minute," said Tinker. "Haven't we got a research vessel right in San Francisco Bay? What about Sea Venture?"

Benedict looked surprised. "Why, that's true. Of course, that would be ideal, but on the other hand, what kind of shape is it in?"

"See if you can find out, Admiral," said Draffy.

Benedict turned and spoke to someone invisible outside the holo.

"General," said Metcalfe, "what is your current estimate of damage to this country in a full nuclear exchange?"

"Survivable," said Tinker firmly. "We have to accept a risk of losing Washington, five or six other places, but we'll be in shape to rebuild and they won't."

"Mr. President," said Benedict, looking up, "my information is that Sea Venture is adrift in the Bay. I don't have any current information about the state of her depth-sounding equipment, but I would expect some deterioration."

"All right," Draffy said. "Hell with it, then. Gentlemen, I know you will all agree with me when I say there is only one thing to do now—pray for guidance."

He bowed his head silently. When he raised it again, his jaw was firm. "Gentlemen, I've heard you all and I thank you from the bottom of my heart for your advice. My decision is, we go ahead, and may God give us victory."

He saw their faces change; there was shock on some, excitement on others; a few had turned pale. But nobody moved or spoke.

"General Tinker, please send me the football."

"Yes, Mr. President." The General spoke into his phone.

Presently a young Army major opened the door. Under his arm, with a chain to his wrist, was a black attaché case—"the football." He advanced and saluted, then laid the case on the table, unlocked it with a key and stood back. In the open case was a computer keyboard and a red button. "What do I do now, son?" Draffy asked. "You enter your identification number, Mr. President," said the young officer.

"Oh, yes." He knew all that, of course; he had been drilled in it often enough, but at a moment like this you had to say something. Draffy found the little folder in his wallet, peeled back the plastic seal, and read the number written underneath. He punched in the seven digits and saw the message CODE ACCEPTED appear on the screen.

Draffy was sweating a little. "General," he said to the holo across the table, "I'm accepting the proposal for a hundred fifty missiles targeted on Moscow. What is the code for that?"

General Tinker was ready with a pocket computer in his hand. He held it up so that Draffy could read the numbers. As he did so, the young major folded like a rag doll and dropped out of sight beyond the edge of the table.

Draffy stood up and stared at the limp body on the carpet. "Jesus Christ!" he said. "Get some medics in here! Get Grummond!"

He sat in his chair again, trembling. The *major* had been carrying the infection, for God's sake. Now he was in for it. If he pressed that button, he might drop dead the next minute like Tom Yount in Texas and that guy in Afghanistan, and the one in Nigeria.

Aware of the eyes on him, Draffy stared at the red button with loathing. The right thing to do would be to go ahead and press it, regardless of his own safety. History would say so. But what if it wasn't the right thing? There were arguments for delay, good arguments. What good would it do him to die? The veep would be sworn in, that poindexter, and he might not have the nerve—if he *did,* maybe he would drop dead too. The Commies had won. He knew it, and there was nothing he could do.

The door opened and two medics came in. One of them knelt beside the young major.

"McNulty's?" Draffy asked hoarsely.

"Looks like it, sir." The medics unfolded their litter, got the patient onto it, and wheeled him out.

Warm tears were leaking from under Draffy's eyelids. He tried to hold them back, tried to control his voice, but it broke like a child's. "Gentlemen—" He tried again. "Let's wait. Let's wait until—" To his horror, he heard himself sob. He bent his face into his hand, pawed at the table for the holo controls. When he looked up again, he was alone.

There was something indefinably unpleasant about being in Draffy's mind, even when he was not as frightened as he was now. Under the slick confident surface, it was a roiling colonic mass of doubts and uncertainties held down by a voice that thundered over and over: *I won't think about that, I won't think about that!* And there were other, darker things down there: his hatred for his parents, his brothers and sisters, and all his schoolmates; his dislike of his wife and daughters; his distrust of all his political associates except for the inner circle, and occasionally of them too; his doubt of his own masculinity; the shameful knowledge that he would betray any principle, tell any lie, to save his own skin. How had such a person become the leader of one of the greatest nations on Earth?

They probed deeper, found the buried resentments

and horrors that had driven the man out of boyhood, made him determine to succeed in spite of "them." He had worked hard; he had learned to assume any mask, because he could not bear to be kept down.

Grummond came in, then a nurse with a hypodermic on a tray, a safe conduit, a woman who had already served as a host. With relief, as she poised the needle over Draffy's arm, the observers slipped away into a mind as calm and clear as water.

39 Julie had put nearly everything breakable in the closet. Stevens added his pry bar, shut the door and moved a bureau against it. From the bed, Kim watched him solemnly. On a bracket in the corner, the holo was showing scenes of disaster from Los Angeles and San Diego. Stevens tested the bracket; probably it would do.

He got into bed with Julie, one on either side of Kim, who buried her head against her mother's side. Stevens pulled the webbing over and secured it. Then they held each other and waited.

"The revised ETA for San Francisco is now two twenty-three," said the anchor's voice, "and that is approximately one minute from now. At the moment everything looks peaceful, and that's what's so eerie, isn't it, Brad, because there is nothing out there to tell you anything is going to happen."

"That's right, and it does seem strange. You expect

howling winds or storm clouds, or something, but this is just like a picture postcard. And there's a kind of helpless feeling . . ."

"Can you turn the sound off from here?" Stevens asked.

"No, I lost the remote. Listen."

". . . as if we are all at the mercy of— Wait a minute. There it is, I see it!"

In the holo a bright line was moving through the mouth of the Bay. Sunlight sparkling on the water obscured details, but there were two or three dark blobs down there, one of which might have been Sea Venture.

They held each other and waited.

The room tilted violently and swooped upward. The world was sideways. The bureau fell over, the closet door sprang open and a rattle of objects ran across the floor; Stevens had a glimpse in the porthole of an insane horizon. There were distant screams all around them, and a sound like that of crockery falling into a garbage can.

The room tilted again, the opposite way, hung level for a heart-freezing instant, and fell. The child screamed, "Daddy! Daddy!"

The room hit bottom at some immeasurable depth and turned upright again. Stevens felt wrung out by fear, shaken and half destroyed. Julie was sobbing and crying; he had to pry her fingers away from his arm. The first time he tried to sit up, he was too dizzy. Finally he rose, unfastened the webbing and got out of bed. It took an effort of will to put his feet on the floor; at every instant he had an irrational feeling that the vessel was about to leap again.

Julie, still holding the child, looked at him with a blind demented stare.

"Is she all right?" Stevens asked. His lips were thick; it was hard to speak.

After a moment she said, "I don't know. My neck hurts. I think I'm going to throw up."

"Do it, then. Get it over." Stevens tried to think. Under the screams and moans in other staterooms, there were groaning sounds in the carbon and metal of CV.

He staggered and sat down on the bed again. In the holo now there were scenes of desolation. The gray water was sweeping across the Presidio and Golden Gate Park; the whole peninsula looked like a rock awash in the ocean. Stevens could see a few buildings standing, apparently intact.

"The second wave is expected in approximately three-quarters of an hour," the anchor was saying.

"Going to be *another?*" Julie cried, and began to weep.

"May be four or five," Stevens said bitterly. "Come on." He found the pry bar in the clutter on the floor.

"Where you going?"

"All of us. Come on." When she hesitated, he went to her and dragged her out of bed. The child screamed.

They went out the door, Julie carrying the child. In the corridor, moaning people were lurching, crawling on the floor, some trying to cling to the walls. Stevens led Julie to the elevator and punched for the Boat Deck. He had to get out.

Owen and Mattison had strapped themselves into the command chairs in the Control Center, where they had flatscreen views all around CV. When the first wave passed, Mattison looked faint. "Think I broke something," he mumbled.

"Want me to call a medic?" It was hard to think, hard to talk.

"No." Mattison unstrapped and staggered up. His eyes were wide and bleary. "Can't take another one." He opened a panel on the board; Owen could see the red readout, LIFEBOATS.

Mattison stared at the panel awhile, then pulled down a microphone and thumbed it on. His voice was blurred. "'Tention, please, attention. Going to evacuate everybody by lifeboat. Go to the Boat Deck. If a boat is full, go to the next one. You understand? Room for everybody. Go directly to Boat Deck. Good-bye." He pressed a control; a transparency lit up: DOORS OPEN.

"No!" said Owen, and moved toward the console. Mattison caught her wrists. "I'm in command," he said. Owen kneed him in the testicles, brought her elbow up into his throat as he bent over. She stepped across him, knowing she had only a moment to act. She touched the CLOSE DOORS button, and then LAUNCH ALL.

Stevens stopped at the first lifeboat bay and tried to open the door; it was locked. He put the edge of the pry bar into the crack, leaned all his weight against it. Suddenly it gave, and the door slid open. Inside, the doors of the two lifeboats were also opening.

"What did you do?"

"Don't know. Come on." Stevens ran into the lifeboat. It was as he remembered it. He looked for the launch button. "Strap yourselves in," he said. Then a horn was blaring, and the boat slid down.

Owen thumbed the microphone on. "This is Harriet Cleaver Owen," she said. "There has been a change in plan. The vessel will not be evacuated by lifeboat. Go to your rooms and lie down on your beds. Those of you who do not have beds on board, share with others who do."

Mattison was getting up. "Have me arrested if you want to," Owen said, "but it won't do any good now, and we've got to work together. I'm sorry I had to do that."

Mattison, who was looking very green, said nothing.

40 At the end of the month Owen called the staff together for a final conference. Some of them were bandaged; one or two, including poor Donald Strang, had had concussions and were still in the hospital, but all things considered they had come through very well.

"I want to compliment you all on what you've accomplished," she told them. "We've learned how to drive the parasite out of its host with electroshock, and we can detect and kill it in transit between hosts. Reinfection will still be possible, of course, but we can at least keep certain essential areas free of parasites and gradually expand those areas, and that is the recommendation I have made to the President. I talked to him on the holo this morning, by the way, and he was *very* complimentary. He is pleased with us because we held the vessel's population together, and of course the country is very pleased with him about his wisdom and restraint over the tsunami crisis, when it was thought that a Soviet attack might be involved.

"Now about the future of the project. After what has

happened, it would be difficult for us to continue with the statistical part of our work, but luckily the results we have already obtained are firm enough to make that unnecessary. We'll release almost all of the present detainee population, including those who were the source of certain complaints, and Senator Gottlieb has told me that he will be satisfied with that. R and D of our devices is going to be turned over to law enforcement laboratories and private companies—" There were a few groans. Owen raised her hand. "No, that's sensible. They have the facilities and manpower to develop our devices quickly and get them into production. That's not what we're for. We will *certainly* continue to work on other devices, things that no one has thought of yet. We'll continue certain parts of our experimental work, and we'll undertake a study of birth-infected children. I told the President, and he agrees, that this is a long-term project of the greatest importance.

"Now there's one thing more. I have a tentative agreement from Peace and from the President that Sea Venture will be recommissioned and set adrift on the Pacific again." Murmurs of surprise. "The reason for this is security. There was a moment when the whole population could have been dispersed; three detainees actually did get away in a lifeboat that was found later at a dock in Richmond. We can't allow such a thing to happen again. Colonel Mattison, before he was transferred, told me that he fully agrees about this. And the President likes the idea of getting the children all the way off the continent."

"You're going to keep the children incarcerated on CV—how long?" Melanie Kurtz wanted to know.

"We're setting this up as a twenty-year study. The details haven't been worked out yet. Another advantage of using Sea Venture is that we'll be able to keep the children and their families humanely, in ample quarters, with plenty of recreation and so on, and still be able to control their contacts with the outside world. We'll also be able to educate the children right up through high school and perhaps beyond."

"But you're going to keep them confined in this place for twenty *years*?"

"No. No. That isn't the idea at all. There will be supervised field trips to Honolulu, Manila, Tokyo, and so on. Another advantage is that we will be able to collect experimental subjects from various places around the circuit, and that will be an important test of the validity of our work. Now I know that for some of you it will be out of the question to commit yourselves even for a year to this kind of life; many of you have families, children in school, and so on. There will be jobs for about half of you, and we're hoping that about that many will choose to stay with us. Talk it over with your spouses and families. If you have any questions, I'll be here."

Something distressing happened to Tom Singer on Monday morning while he was driving across Oakland on his way to work. Traffic was as sluggish as Singer's digestion; he was creeping along in his ancient Toyota, half listening to the radio and not paying much attention.

Suddenly a man on the sidewalk only a few feet away toppled and fell. In that moment of unexpected intimacy, Singer had time to glimpse the man's pale bearded face and red necktie, the black hat falling, a rolled umbrella.

He looked back, but there was no way he could stop without being rear-ended. He saw people gathering around the place where the man had fallen; then the traffic moved on and they were out of sight.

The incident had shaken Singer for some reason he

could not define. Just the suddenness of it, maybe, or the fact that he had been looking into the man's face when it happened. Or the feeling, *what if it had been me?*

He parked in the lot behind the Irvington Animal Laboratory twenty minutes later and got out. The air was cool and there were fat blue-grey clouds over the hilltops; he thought about the umbrella. He went into the building, hung up his outer clothing and put on the lab coat, said hello to Sandy Hong. The rats were looking at him when he went in. One of the females put its paws up on the wire; its whiskers were trembling.

Singer reached in and scratched it on the top of the head: its ears began to quiver, an infallible sign that it was in estrus.

He picked it up, noted its number on his chart, then deposited it in the breeding cage; as he did so he slipped down across the grey space, and as she slipped in again, a chorus of scents broke against her nostrils. She was looking up through her own whiskers at a world that was not black and white, knowing now that it was safe because her sisters had told her, but shades of brown like an antique photograph. The smells were much more important to her—sex smells, food, feces, the scent of the giant's paw overlaid with tobacco and soap, chemical reeks that she associated with fear.

She watched the giant alertly, nevertheless, and saw it coming back with another person in its paw, a male who was watching her and struggling a little. The giant put the male down and closed the top of the cage.

The male sniffed his way around the cage, sniffed the air in her direction. Presently he darted toward her and put his cold nose under her tail. Strange feelings were awash in her. She circled away, then ran to the male. She whiffed up his rich scent, danced away and sat down; her ears were quivering. The male had not moved; his great brown eyes were staring at her, his nose and whiskers busy. She ran at him again, danced away; this time he followed and mounted. Her head and hindquarters went up, her back hollowed; her ears trembled violently, then lay flat. The male went away and licked his penis.

The sensations and the smells were tantalizing, and she wondered if persons experienced the same pleasure that giants felt in copulation. The male came back and mounted again, got off as before and licked his penis: she speculated for a moment about what that felt like. It would be interesting to find out, but now the male was mounting her again, and this time she felt his penis sliding in: but he got off again and licked himself.

He repeated these movements several times, always licking his penis afterward. Finally he mounted, entered her, and began to move quickly. She could feel his teeth gripping her and hear his squeals; her pleasure was so slight that she barely noticed it, but as the tiny swimmers in her birth canal fought their way to the eggs, she englobed them and felt herself divide. In those tiny spheres inside her body there were four new sparks of life that were supremely herself.

Now the giant was approaching. She slipped out and in again, and now he was looking down at the red-eyed animals in the cage. Poor little breeding machines. For some reason, a couple of lines from "The Walrus and the Carpenter" were running through his head:

And thick and fast they came at last,
And more, and more, and more . . .

F   Knight, Damon
KNI   Francis, 1922–

           The observers

$16.95

DATE			